A CAT
IN THE ACT

Brian Arsenault

Copyright © 2024 Brian Arsenault

All rights reserved.

No part of this publication may be reproduced, distributed, or transmitted in any form or by any means, including photocopying, recording, or other electronic or mechanical methods, without the prior written permission of the publisher, except in the case of brief quotations embodied in critical reviews and certain other noncommercial uses permitted by copyright law. For permission requests, write to the publisher, addressed "Attention: Permissions Coordinator," at the address below.

This is a work of fiction. Names, characters, businesses, places, events, locales, and incidents are either the products of the author's imagination or used in a fictitious manner. Any resemblance to actual persons, living or dead, or actual events is purely coincidental.

Rattling Good Yarns Press
33490 Date Palm Drive 3065
Cathedral City CA 92235
USA
www.rattlinggoodyarns.com

Cover Design: Rattling Good Yarns Press

Library of Congress Control Number: 2023952334
ISBN: 978-1-955826-59-4

First Edition

For my Soul-Matey, Skip

"Once we believe in ourselves, we can risk
curiosity, wonder, spontaneous delight, or any
experience that reveals the human spirit."

~E.E. Cummings

One

There's nothing worse than walking out of the vet's office with an empty cat carrier. A vague, vacant feeling seeps into me, coupled with a reluctance to face this all too familiar gaping hole in my life. All I can do is surrender, as the emptiness settles inside me once again. I'm afraid to look at this mislaid piece of my heart that I know I'll never recover. Add to the mix this nasty, abrasive New York City winter wind off the river biting into me, and yes, I'd call it a pretty shitty day.

Hobo. Our feisty feral female cat we'd rescued from the shelter has crossed over unexpectedly. Witnessing her last moments was so heart-wrenching, that I completely lost it in my final kiss on her sweet head. She was a fighter from beginning to end.

I've been struggling to heal from an even deeper, unresolved ache in my life, and now this. It's hard to believe that just over a year and a half has passed since the love of my life was lost to this unbelievable plague that's taken so many in our community. Beautiful, free-spirited Timothy caught my eye back in 1982 on the first day of rehearsal for what was to be the most fun-filled and fabulous summer stock tour of my somewhat uneven musical theater career.

How can you go wrong with *Hello, Dolly!*? What a great show to celebrate the bountiful joys life has to offer, not to mention that the entire male ensemble was gay, except for one poor guy who would take cover in the dressing room whenever the backstage shenanigans began.

"What was that silly name of your character?" says a voice off to my right.

"Cornelius Hackl," I reply without thinking. "Wait...what? Who said that?"

"Really Matthew, I can't even fathom how you could share the stage with your fellow thespians and answer to a name like that."

"Okay, as if this day hasn't been weird enough, now I'm hearing things."

"Not things, just *me*. Check out the garbage can tucked into the lower landing of this decrepit brownstone."

I guess I really am losing it. Despite her demise just an hour ago, I see my dead black and white cat daintily perched on a trash can lid. And if that isn't crazy enough, she's talking!

"Hobo!" I cry. "Is it really you?"

"Of course it's me, you silly boy. You can't get rid of me that quickly."

Gathering my courage, I ask, "What are you doing here? You know we made you an indoor cat and you're not allowed outside."

"Matthew, darling, all bets are off when it comes to being cooped up in that little box of an apartment you call home. I get to go back to my feral roots now, and come and go as I please."

"But you're supposed to be at the Rainbow Bridge, not down here in all this concrete. You're supposed to be in kitty heaven with open vistas and expansive light-filled landscapes."

"I guess that just wasn't in the cards for me Daddy Boy. Catch you around town."

And just like that, she's gone again. She even called me Daddy Boy, the name Timothy gave me when we first brought Hobo home. It feels like so long ago now.

We had been warned Hobo was pretty rough around the edges. Feral cats are notorious for not trusting humans. But we decided we were up for the ultimate challenge of being the best cat dads ever.

In the beginning, you couldn't go near her without getting a swipe and maybe a nip. Thus began the slow process of winning her over with time and plenty of patience. We had tiny breakthroughs, initially using food combined with just the slightest touch. Each new behavior was like a revelation. One day, after months of hunkering down under the table, she jumped up on the couch next to Timothy. In a few more weeks, she actually let him ease his leg over to make a connection. We began to gain her trust more and more as she came to understand we were offering her safety and love, something she had never before experienced with humans.

I really don't know what to make of this feline apparition. It must just be the stress of letting go of the last reminders of love and comfort in my life, not to mention the fact that it's fucking freezing out here.

I head down Amsterdam Avenue, maneuvering my way through the nameless bodies moving swiftly past me, and take a left on 69th Street. For New York City, it's not a bad block. But it gives me the same confined feeling these barren trees do, lining the street but trapped in little squares of dirt on the sidewalk. I avoid this perfect breeding ground for dog shit and whatever else that's been abandoned by the people trudging by.

Rows of brownstones occupy both sides of the street, standing shoulder to shoulder like aging sentinels providing refuge from the constant hammering of the city. Each one is slightly different in its upkeep and decoration, giving it that "character" so many New Yorkers hunger for in their quest for shelter with a style that identifies them. I'm an Upper West Sider. Evidently, that's a thing.

Finally, I've made it back home. Hobo is right. It *is* a little box of an apartment. And now the space is so empty, leaving nothing but the memory of loved ones that have drained away. I feel like the walls are closing in on me even more as I look around at what was once a haven of happiness.

We kept the furnishings simple and clean, considering the small scale of the place—very "gay-tasteful" in shades of gray and white, but still with that casual, lived-in feeling. The contemporary sofa along one wall faces two armless side chairs, with a clear glass coffee table to anchor it. A vintage wood fireplace mantel, distressed and painted white for an antique look is on the other wall with bookshelves on each side. Too bad the fireplace was covered over, but it still gives the impression of the comforts of home. I zero in on the pictures of Timothy and me scattered about the bookshelves, a testament to our three years together, with Hobo completing our little family.

"You're going to need to lighten up a bit, Daddy Boy," Hobo says.

Oh my God, she's back. "What the hell is going on, Hobo? Where are you?"

"In this lame excuse for a bedroom that barely fits the queen size bed."

I race into the bedroom to find her on the coverlet, kneading the fabric. "I remember Timothy was so proud of finding this bed in one of those used furniture stores up the street," she says without missing a push-paw beat. "And I do think I'll miss lounging on it for those fourteen hours of nap time a day. But I have bigger fish to fry now, and not the kind that comes out of the can, thank you very much."

"But why are you here? And what is this all about?"

She gives me that all-knowing smirk I've come to recognize over the years. "Oh, my handsome and headstrong Matt. You are *such* a drama queen. I'm here to remind you that this town is yours for the taking. You just need to get off your ass and move on with your life."

I can't help but roll my eyes on that one. "I've heard it all before Hobo, from all my friends."

"Take a good look at yourself. That sandy blonde hair and Irish good looks of yours makes you a shoo-in for all those juvenile roles. You don't look anywhere near that milestone number of three zero you just hit."

"Did you really have to bring that up?"

"As for me, I'm not ready to leave the city yet. Can you blame me? You're going to have to get used my visitations from time to time."

"I'm not sure I can deal with this, Hobo. You're probably just some kind of coping mechanism."

"Get over it, boyfriend. I'm as real as every other spirit that roams this town. Haven't you ever wondered who lurks about in the shadows of all those old historic theaters on Broadway? There are ghosts of every persuasion floating about. Maybe if you're lucky, I'll even introduce you. Oh, right—you've never been in a Broadway show. How can you call yourself a professional if you haven't even made it on Broadway?"

"*Ever* made it on Broadway? Do you know how hard it is to achieve that? It's the top, the pinnacle. Not many actors even get there. You know as well as anyone I haven't worked for close to two years. Taking care of Timothy, and then dealing with life without him has really done a number on me. I've lost my purpose. I'm stuck, and I can't dig my way out."

"Get a grip. Your unemployment is long gone, so you'd better hop to it, Daddy Boy, and get your sorry ass back in the game. Being a cater waiter isn't going to cut it."

"Speaking of which, I have a gig with Fabulous Foods tonight at the Armory on Park Avenue. So I'm going to need a nap. I've got to present myself to a bunch of A-list blue bloods."

"Oh yes. The very fashionable FabFoo. The catering company that requires every out of work actor/dancer/model to inhabit their servile fantasy role with the utmost style and grace. And you'd better not crack a smile the whole night. It's all about attitude, my dear one. And let me tell you, I've scratched out an entire book on that."

"Yeah, yeah, will you let me get some rest?"

"Just because I got to sleep all day doesn't mean you get to."

"Stop already. I can't take—" Where'd she go?

"Hobo? Hobo?"

And once again, she just vanished. I'm not going to even think about this now. I've got to get some rest. Maybe I'll wake up and realize it was just a dream. Why do I get the feeling I haven't seen the last of this persnickety puss.

What would Timothy think of all this? He'd probably feed me the same line Hobo just did: Get out there. Audition. What do you have to lose?

What do I have to lose? Just another layer of the last vestiges of self-confidence I've been trying to drum up. Another nail in the coffin of what I thought was my true calling. All the years of classes and dedication to my craft, just to end up with another rejection.

Of course, it's great when you're working. All your dreams about being a performer are coming true just by being employed, even if it's only a summer stock tour. You're still doing it. You're a professional getting paid to do what you were born to do.

That *Hello, Dolly!* summer tour was flawless. First of all, getting out of the smelly, grimy, hot summer in the city felt like a gift. I got to escape the oppressive urban landscape for New England's fresh green hills and pristine shores. We hopped on the tour bus for Yankee land, where the lobsters are plentiful, and there's just this special feeling of a culture steeped in centuries of east coast traditions. I loved it.

The absolute high point of the tour was in the quaint little town of Ogunquit, Maine. Such a New England storybook village. Ogunquit means "beautiful place by the sea," and was it ever. Strolling with Timothy along the dramatic rocky cliff walk, with the waves crashing below, the ocean and sky seemed like they were having their own love affair. That path, called the Marginal Way, still evokes the magic of our tour romance.

But the crown jewel of the town was the Ogunquit Playhouse. Built in the Colonial Revival style, its crisp white exterior with forest green trim was a testament to the fussy queen who owned and ran the venue with an iron fist. Add to that the lobby filled with headshots of glamorous stars from the 30s and 40s who'd played there in the olden days on what was called the Straw Hat Circuit, and what do you have? A fairy tale come true.

Oh, to fall in love surrounded by the sparkling light reflected off the heady salt air of the sea, creating the perfect radiant playground. The beautiful breezy days would then segue into the bright hot lights of the stage. How could I resist Timothy's blazing persona? My new romantic boy wonder. I'd see him appear on stage every night in his lemon drop bright colored suit, belting out, "Put on your Sunday clothes." He was quite a sight, but seeing those clothes come off was even better. Love was definitely in the air...and boy, did we make quite a pair.

Two

I arrive at Park Avenue and 66th Street with plenty of time to spare before the elegant guests arrive. That list would not include me. I take the back entrance and maneuver through the hectic activity going on in the large kitchen, taking in the mouth-watering, savory smells they're producing. But I can't let that distract me as I steer past the chefs and head down the hallway to find the tables and chairs already set up in the grand hall, decorated to the nines and anchored with extravagant centerpieces.

But it's up to us, the hired help, to position the plates, the cutlery, and the collection of crystal glasses with perfection, not to mention mastering the art of napkin folding to add just that special flair to the presentation.

When our privileged guests arrive, they will look at their place settings and be awestruck, knowing it's a true reflection of their wealth, power, beauty, or celebrity. It's the ultimate definition of how they have earned a place at the table of A-list New Yorkers.

I scan the cavernous room, filled at the moment with only my fellow cater waiters. Why do I feel like I just walked into a black-and-white dreamscape of the most attractive men this town has to offer? Every tuxedo-attired guy in this hall looks like they're doing the holiday cover of *Gentleman's Quarterly*. They come from cities and small hamlets you've never heard of. They are drawn like honeybees to the sweet nectar of celebrity in all its abundant guises, hoping to get their chance to take a bite out of what I've lately been calling *The Big Crapple*.

Fabulous Foods Catering Company is notorious for hiring only the cream of the wanna-be crop. Who knows who the next rising star will be? And what do you do while you're waiting for your big break? How about making some extra cash in professional purgatory as a cater waiter? If you fit the mold, you can survive by slinging hash for the uber-rich until you hit paydirt. But you not only have to look the part in your formal attire, you need to act it too. Just before the guests enter the party, they will line us all up on opposite sides of the room and instruct us on the stoic and staunch attitude that is the hallmark of this regime. Like Hobo said, you'd better not crack a smile, or you won't be asked back.

"Damn, there are so many hotties here tonight."

Oh shit, she's back. Holding court on my table top. "This isn't a good time, Hobo. I have work to do."

"Okay, but get a load of that dreamboat at table number twenty-seven. I bet you could make a four-course meal out of him."

"Will you shut up? Anyway, I know that guy. His name is Christopher. He's a dancer."

"Why am I not surprised. Do I know your type or what?"

"Charlie introduced me to him at the last Gala gig. I haven't had time to say hello yet. And yeah, he's pretty damned cute, but right now I need to put the final touches on my table. So, scram!"

Luckily, she's gone by the time the head man inspects my complex positioning of each polished piece. I get the all-clear now, so we have some downtime before the proverbial curtain goes up. I spot Charlie taking a break out in the hallway and head over to him. Charlie was the dance captain for *Hello, Dolly!,* so we have a shared history. All those years of touring have worn him down, but how many times can you get excited about being on the road and pulling into another week in Cleveland? He somehow manages to slide along from one show to the next, whether he cares anything about the production or not. Yeah, he's jaded, but still fun to hang around with.

He still looks the part—barely. He has an urban edge, most likely from growing up in Queens. And like a lot of natives from any one of New York's boroughs, he doesn't mince words. But at thirty-eight years old, the façade is beginning to crack. I'm wondering if his closely cropped jet-black hair is now holding its inky sheen with the help of a new men's hair dye product I just discovered at the Duane Reade Pharmacy. Just For Men is the name of it, which describes Charlie to a tee.

He's always on the prowl, zeroing in on his prey with the most intense gray-blue eyes I've ever seen. They remind me of a Siberian Husky. So striking. They seem to deflect any effort to go deeper into what's really happening inside of him. I've known him long enough to understand he prefers it that way. His medium height and muscular frame exude a masculine persona that serves him well at leather bars like The Spike, one of his usual haunts. You can't stay young and hot in the chorus forever, but his connections always seem to land him something.

"Hey man, don't you ever get enough'a these glitzy shindigs?" he says as he adjusts his bowtie.

"Hey Charlie. It's all about the paycheck for me. That's all I've got coming in now. But what are you doing here? You always seem to have another show lined up."

"I know. And I gotta keep up my reputation as the ultimate tour whore. But I can always use the extra cash in between gigs. Speaking of which, the guy who was rentin' my second bedroom just blew me off for the bus-and-truck company of *Cats*. Do you know anyone who's lookin' for a place?"

"You mean like me for instance?"

"Yeah, you'd be a great roommate."

"Money's tight, but I'm going to stick it out on my own for now on 69th Street. Anyway, I bet you have another show lined up."

"You know it's bad luck to talk about that kinda stuff." He smiles with just the slightest hint that I could tease it out of him if I tried. "I'll use the line every other Broadway baby uses—I'm just waitin' to hear back."

"Yeah, I have that one etched on my forehead. But lately I can't even use that as an excuse. I got nothin'."

"Come outside with me for a minute, so I can get my cancer fix before it's showtime."

"Still smoking? Really?"

"I know, I know. I gotta quit it. But an aging chorus *papi* has to have some vices. Besides, a lot of my tricks think it's hot."

We hit the outer courtyard and get blasted by a strong gust of the elements. You'd think we were right off the East River, but the park can whip up some nasty gales too. "Jeez, I'm not going to able to feel my hands if I stay out here," I say.

"Oh, get over it, man. Think about what this breeze will do for them high cheekbones of yours. You gotta look your best for all those Romeos inside."

"I still don't think I'm ready for any dating yet. But some of those guys are hard to ignore."

"The reality is the majority of those bitches ain't worth a second look. They're too busy lookin' at themselves."

"Yeah, you're probably right."

"But you can't be too choosy, or you'll end up like me. One wild and wonderful night per specimen is about all I can handle. Then it's don't let the door hit'cha where I just bit'cha."

"You're too much Charlie. Can we go back in now?"

"Before we do, I'll let you in on somethin' I heard is coming up. Do you remember *The Normal Heart*?"

"How could I not? Timothy was still alive when it opened in the spring of '85.

Charlie takes a last drag on his cigarette. "I was thankfully on the road for that entire year so I missed it. Course I heard all about it, but I can't really stomach that kinda stuff."

"We were barely hanging on to any semblance of a regular life at that point. But Timothy insisted we go down to the Public Theater to see it. So, what's the deal?"

"I heard tell of a sequel in the works with songs. Right now, the working title is *Our New Normal*."

"Is it supposed to be a big show?"

"No, it's not a full-scale musical, but singers will be needed. And the calls are goin' out to agencies for casting."

"That could be amazing. I haven't talked to my agent in I don't know how many months, with everything that's happened. I just haven't felt up to it."

"Well, make sure you get seen for this one, man. You'd be perfect for the character of Felix. I'm sure you remember he was the boyfriend of Ned Weeks, who got flattened by the virus."

"It really tore my heart out sitting next to Timothy and watching that."

"Yeah, well, I hear his spirit comes back in this production, and he'll be leading some kinda Greek chorus, is all I know."

"So you think I could play Felix?"

"With your looks and that soaring tenor voice, you need to be seen."

"Yeah right, tell that to the casting director as he sifts through five hundred other headshots and resumes."

"Someone has to get the job. And it might as well be you."

"Thanks for the tip. We'd better get inside. They're starting to line us up."

The evening follows all the usual protocols with cocktails and passed hors d'oeuvres, as the glittering crowd jockeys for a position of prominence. I've done enough of these that I'm beginning to see repeat performances of many of the couples. But, of course, the women's gowns and jewels could never be seen twice. High society sometimes reminds me of high school. But the stakes are as high as the skyscrapers they've come to worship.

Eventually, everyone makes it to their table for the first course. After the small plates are whisked away, yours truly goes into high gear, balancing a gigantic silver platter of food on one hand. With the other, I proceed to show off my expert technique at French service—a talent that requires maneuvering a large, ornate sterling silver fork and spoon to dole out the main course and sides. Ladies first, *bien sur*. I've gotten pretty good at it. Maybe that's why they keep booking me for these scintillating soirées. The rest of the evening glides by, and with the guests out of the way, all that's left is the cleanup.

"Now's your chance to schmooze it up with that Christopher guy."

"Hobo! Get off of my table. I'm still working here."

"You can't fool me. I had a bird's eye view of the whole night from that crystal chandelier down front and center."

"Oh, did you now."

"There were quite a few lingering looks in the direction of table twenty-seven. And it wasn't because you were comparing table manners, either."

"Yeah, he's adorable, and you know I have a thing for dancers."

"Dancer butts is more like it."

"Stop that. My stomach goes into a spin cycle if I start talking about this too much."

"So just go over and say hi to him. You've already met, so the worst is behind you. Did I say 'behind'?"

"You're too much. Okay I'll go if you promise to disappear."

"Done. I'm outta here."

Why am I so drawn to dancers? This guy looks so sweet and reserved, with those deer-in-the-headlight eyes of his beaming back at me with a sense of curiosity. He wears his chestnut brown hair carelessly, so compatible with his dark and mysterious look. Even in that tux, I can tell he's lean and muscular. From the way he carries himself, he could've been a gazelle in another life. As long as he's not a Giselle. Nothing against them, but I'm just not into girlie boys. But Hobo's right. *Le buttox d'un danseur* is a whole other story. Boy, this night has really gotten under my skin.

But what makes someone want to be a dancer? What makes them sacrifice so much of their lives to the daily discipline of fine-tuning their bodies? What drives them to express and embody their emotions on stage? They somehow allow you into their skin, letting you feel their movements in your own body when you're observing their performance. That's part of their brilliance. And they sacrifice the security of an average life to give everything to that moment. Then it's over. The next day they're back in class.

That's it—that's my opening line to him. I amble over and flash him my best laid-back grin. "Hey Christopher. I bet that first plie tomorrow is going to feel like hell after tonight."

"Matt, how are you? Don't answer that. You must be as exhausted as I am." He puts down the napkins he's been collecting and runs his fingers through that beautiful mane of his. "It's been quite a night."

"It certainly has." I'm guessing he missed the cat hanging from the chandelier...

"A warm bed sounds pretty good to me right now."

Did he just mention going to bed? Relax Matt. Take a breath. "Yeah, I'd really like to get out of this uniform and off my feet." Shit, now I'm doing it, talking about taking my clothes off!

"You're right. Dance class is tough after a late night like this. But you just get your gear together and go.

"I guess it's all about the discipline huh?"

"Yep, like brushing your teeth. You don't question it."

I need to keep this conversation going. "Where are you taking class?"

"I'm on scholarship at the Merce Cunningham Studio down in the West Village. That's pretty much where I live these days."

"I don't know much about modern dance, but someone told me old Uncle Merce is a bit of a tyrant."

"I'll just say that he's a very distinctive choreographer with a singular focus."

"That's a pretty smooth way of putting it." He gets a chuckle out of that remark, and I'm even more struck by his appealing smile.

"But the actual technique is really strong, and I'm hoping to use it as a springboard for concert dance work."

"That's great! Are you working on anything right now?"

"As a matter of fact, I'm in rehearsal with one of Merce's company members who's putting on their own concert at The Kitchen next month."

"The Kitchen? Is that like a dinner theater?"

"Ah, no." he replies with the patience of a monk. "It's an avant-garde performance space on West 19th."

"Oh, sorry for the confusion." Now he must think I'm a typical musical theater type, only interested in show biz. I've got to rectify this. "When is your concert? I'd love to come."

"You don't really mind a lot of body lines set to environmental sounds?"

"Um... okay. Full disclosure. I'm not actually sure I know what you're talking about, but I'm game, regardless."

"Body lines are just the different angles your body makes when you move into different positions," Christopher says with a chuckle. "And the different sounds are supposed to make you rethink what you're hearing, which has an impact on what you see."

"Okay, this is all new to me." My imagination immediately goes to his body lines. Maybe I *am* getting better. "But I'd like to see something different. When you're in show business, it pretty much takes over your life, but I've had some downtime lately so I'd love to come."

We both pause for a moment.

"How about I give you my number and you can call me with the info," I finally say.

"Sure. That would be great."

More silence as we look at one another, wondering if this is the right move. "Okay. I'll be right back." I rush back to the kitchen area, looking for a scrap of paper, finally finding what I need on a counter behind the door. As I bolt back out to the dining room, I can't help but think that Hobo would be proud of me. I'm finally making a move to get out there.

Three

Will this winter never end? It's only the end of February, still way too soon to begin my annual ritual of coaxing all these trees in Central Park to let their little buds peak out. They must be feeling like my frozen fingertips right now. Popping out today would be suicidal for the poor little newborns, considering this glacial sting I'm feeling. But I figured getting some air in the park and then heading over to the Y for a swim was the next best thing before I take the subway down to Christopher's concert.

I spot Hobo stretching out on a tree limb above me. "You just need to grow a better fur coat."

"Oh, hiya Pussyface." I have to admit I'm really glad she showed... "You know, I'm getting used to you popping into my life, but I guess that doesn't include any lap time."

"No physical contact allowed for us spirits. What I do miss is those thrupple cuddle sessions with you and Timmy together."

"Tell me about it. I could definitely use a hug right now. Lately, I've been thinking that maybe I should figure out something else to do with my life."

"Come now, it can't be that bad."

"After the fifth try, I finally got through to my agent, only to find out she's no longer my agent."

"What's that supposed to mean?"

"Before, when I was working more, she would just send me out and get a piece of it if I got the job. We never actually signed a contract or anything."

"So why can't you keep doing that?"

"Well, as we know, these last couple of years have been a big zero. So she's cut ties with me."

"Daddy Boy definitely has a dilemma."

"All I can do now is wait for the open call. God, those are such a pain to deal with. I might get a chorus job out of it, but that's a step back for me. The open call is in March so I have some time to decide."

"Decide? Damn it, if nothing else, you owe it to Timothy to go."

"Okay, now you're just trying to guilt trip me."

"Hardly. This is an opportunity to be in a show that really means something to the struggle that your community is facing right now."

"But what about my struggles?"

"You need to rise up and take on this challenge. Let go of your self-doubt and fear. Make a move forward, take some action. Just like in the original play, *The Normal Heart*."

"It really was a groundbreaking show."

"I can only imagine this next show will drive that message home even stronger. It's unconscionable what's happening these days with the epidemic, and people are tired of sitting on the sidelines. You need to stand up and be one of them, in any way you can."

"But Hobo..."

"Don't you 'But Hobo' me. I'm out of here."

"You don't have to..." and she does the disappearing act.

So much for my excuse for having a tendency to want to process stuff. Procrastination is more like it. Maybe it *is* finally time to get on with things. Move forward with my life. And I do owe it to Timothy to do whatever I can to fight back against this virus. This new show could be part of the answer to that. All I know is, something about this malaise I've been struggling with has to change.

At least going out tonight is a start. I need to open myself up to new possibilities. Could Christopher be a part of that? I look around and just try to be open to what's in front of me. Even in my decidedly uneven mood, I'm still struck by the day, dissolving into the dusky beginnings of the night.

I head out of the park through the 69th Street exit and continue south on Central Park West. It's only a few blocks to the 63rd Street entrance of the West Side Y, the one rock I can count on to help me feel grounded.

I'm always delighted to come upon this sprawling fourteen-story gem of a building. Timothy, being somewhat of an architectural nerd, loved it too, and had informed me that the construction began in 1928. The Young Men's Christian Association sought to "improve the spiritual condition of young men." Of course, my mind goes to The Village People! A certain condition of a young man is the name of the game for them. Cruising the Y is not exactly my scene, but I have to chuckle when I think about how things have changed. Being "out" the way we are now would have been unimaginable back in 1928.

I stop for a moment on the sidewalk, taking it all in. Timothy had lectured me on the blending of the Italian Renaissance and Romanesque styles on the lower stories of the building. The accent lighting makes it look like an air castle that just floated down to earth. There's this sense of whimsy about it. Who knew it would attract impressionable young men to such fanciful decoration?

The interior has definitely seen better days, but it's the indoor pool that's my daily bread. Once I change and move through the large, open shower room, ignoring a few lingering glances, I gain entry to what has become my sanctuary. I inhale the moist, chlorine-saturated air. The peeling walls and cracked plaster ceiling only add to the appeal for me, along with the corroded Pompeian tile work.

I find an empty lane and go into my aquatic zone for a good hour. This soothing body of water is breathing new life into me. Now that my renewed sense of being is sufficiently oxygenated, I'm ready to head downtown to Christopher's concert.

As I shower off the chlorine residue, the usual suspects, who always seem to be dawdling under the drizzling spray, begin to make their move, slowly lathering up areas that start to show signs of coming to attention.

It's been a long time since I've seen any action. This is definitely not the way I want to begin again. What is it with these people? Rent one of the rooms upstairs! I hear the availability for a certain kind of male acrobatics is non-stop. I'm still not even sure if I'm ready to date, but I'm definitely not ready for anything like this, so I make a quick exit.

New York City has a way of showing off her jewels at night. The lights shining through the windows of the high-rise buildings sparkle like sequins on her beaded urban landscape. People are everywhere, heading out into their evening adventures, even on this brisk night. The energy is tangible. That's part of the enticement. Humanity is out in search of fulfilling an endless wish list that this fashionable lady of the night provides in abundance.

I enter the subway at Columbus Circle and make my way below to the downtown C train platform. Immediately, the strong and smokey smell of creosote from the railroad ties permeates the air. It reminds me of a combination of tar and kerosene; not a pleasant smell, but at least it's slightly warmer down here. Waiting for the train, I'm intrigued by a lone drummer pounding out a sensuous rhythm with his collection of cans. No one else seems to be paying him any attention. They're all looking toward the northern darkness of the tunnel, awaiting the coming light of the train.

The pulsating sounds of his beating are captivating me, so much so that I make my way over to him. We now share a palpable energy with each other. I stand directly in front of him and allow his pounding rhythms to take me in. Immediately, he cranks his drum beats up a few notches. Other people notice and are drawn over to him as well. His heightened performance connects with the gathering crowd's energy. We're all absorbing these dynamic tempos and rhythmic sounds, having a quintessential New York moment.

The beating of the drums now begins to combine with the distant sound of the coming train. The energy changes again, and some of us pull out some dollars and change. We drop them in his hat and head to our train, leaving the lone drummer on the platform, continuing to rap out his existence.

After the quick train ride drops me at 23rd and 8th Avenue, I head up the steps. And just like that, I'm in the oh-so-current and hip gay neighborhood known as Chelsea. What was once like a bedroom community for gays who couldn't afford Greenwich Village in the 70s has now arrived as Manhattan's latest gay mecca. Boy-land abounds all around me as I continue down to 19th Street and then two more long blocks west to get me past 10th Avenue. One of the hardships of my life on a strict budget is lots of walking, no matter the weather.

It's still early when I arrive, but the crowd is beginning to gather. Does anyone wear anything but black these days? I know this is a more artsy crowd, but come on. I think meeting Charlie here for the concert was a good call. Oh, and there he is, making his way in. I don't like the way he looks. He's a lot thinner than the last time I saw him a month ago. He definitely has that frail look about him, like he's lost a part of himself. I see it so often now as I walk these New York streets. Young men wasting away as they try to hang on to their fragile lives. Hopefully, Charlie isn't going to join the ranks. I can see him trying to rev up his energy when he catches my eye.

"I don't know how you talked me into comin' to this, Matt. These aren't exactly my people."

"What do you mean, Charlie? Avant-garde isn't your thing?"

"If it gets you between a dance belt and a certain downtown ballerino's derriere, I'm happy to hold your hand."

"Thanks. You're a good friend."

"But just don't expect to see me at the finish line. You can finish him off yourself."

I have to chuckle at that one. "So, are you okay? You don't really look yourself."

"I had the worst flu that I can remember in years. It just knocked me out, man. But I'm definitely on the mend now."

"Glad to hear it." I say with as much conviction as I can muster.

Then I spot the epitome of a straight guy's fantasy, a tall and radiant young blonde woman walks in with a gentle sway of her hips, the perfect showgirl. Though she's all wrapped up in a coat, I, for one, know she's got the essential qualification required of a chorine: a pair of long, shapely legs that practically go up to her tits—which are the other obligatory prerequisite. And I recall they were in perfect proportion to the rest of this golden-haired Venus.

This young enchantress may not do it for me in the dream date department, but she's Timothy's friend and former dance partner. Helen. Beautiful and kind-hearted Helen. She and Timothy were known as the "Royal Couple" in the *Hello, Dolly!* tour. You couldn't even watch any other ensemble duos when they took over the stage. The choreographer knew it too, because he always placed them front and center.

Suddenly I feel a pang of sorrow as I think back on that time. Why was Timmy taken from us in the prime of his life? He was so talented and had so much to offer the world. Damn it... I feel the paralysis set in again.

I've got to hold it together. "Helen!" I practically shout, "What a wonderful surprise! It's so nice to see you."

"Well, if it isn't two of my favorite guys. This place is usually out of bounds for you show biz types. What brings you downtown?"

"You may not realize it, hot stuff," says Charlie, "but my address is below 14th street in the East Village. Ever heard of it?"

"Stop it! Then I guess you're allowed a pass. What about you, Matt? I never took you for a modern dance lover."

"A lover of some cute buns in tights is more like it." Charlie chimes in. "He's here to see a guy we know from catering gigs. Christopher somethin'."

"Oh my gosh. It must be the Christopher I know. That's why I'm here. I take class with him at the Cunningham studio."

"Really?" I finally get a word in. "What are you doing taking modern classes when you're such a Broadway baby?"

"I like to say I have the soul of a modern dancer," Helen says, "but the right equipment for show biz. Musicals are great fun and pay the bills, but a part of me will always have one bare foot in this scene."

"Speakin' of shows," Charlie says, "me and Helen are gonna be working together again in a production of *Annie Get Your Gun*. We start next month for a short run at the Paper Mill Playhouse."

"Congratulations both of you!" my happy face is saying. "Oh, the lights are flickering. We'd better find our seats."

I can't take my mind off their news for the entire concert. I really am happy for them. But once again, I feel like I'm no longer a member of the club. When you're not working in this business, you're nothing. It's my own fault for not being able to face those auditions. Should I just resign myself to the ranks of the thousands of unemployed actors in this town?

I guess my own preoccupations should give me a clue that I'm not really that into this performance. The dancers are doing their best to amaze us with their precision and grace, but what's the point? There's no story, crazy sounds for what I guess they could call music, and just this dry, academic movement. I feel like I'm watching Jackson Pollack throw paint around, and he's having a lot more fun than I am.

Christopher is beautiful, of course. And a wonderful dancer. Why else would I be here? There's something about him I'd like to discover, but I'm still not sure I'm ready, and I certainly haven't a clue as to whether he'd like to get to know me too. I still need to take things really slow.

Four

Yet another multi-block urban oasis, surrounded by never-ending construction, comes into view. When will they finally finish with this town anyway? I have arrived at Madison Square Park, compliments of the R Train. It appears before me like a Manhattan mirage as I get used to being above ground again after coming out of the damp subway, my eyes now adjusting to the open, yet confined park space.

The station exit drops me at the southern perimeter of the park, so I head into it. The best part about this designated patch of dirt is the view it offers of the Flatiron building. The twenty-story structure just south of the park is a must-see for the hordes of tourists that descend upon this town daily. But I think we locals get the same satisfaction when it enters our cityscape vision.

Once again, I think of Timothy and how he loved to point out its Beaux Arts architectural style with some French and Italian Renaissance thrown in. He would go on and on about the details, but the triangular shape of the structure is what really gets me. Viewing it from the north, my vision takes in the peak of this geometric wonder. The iconic thoroughfares of 5th Avenue and Broadway split off to the right and left of the building. These two busy streets define its symmetrical shape, almost as if the city planners took a bold pen made of asphalt and taxi cabs to outline the perimeter.

The oddest history lesson I got from him was that there were originally no women's bathrooms. Talk about suffrage! The opening in 1902 wasn't exactly a stellar year for women's rights. But eventually, they changed that and designated a ladies' restroom on alternating floors to give them a little relief. Nice of them.

First, a coffee date with Christopher that we had set up after his show, then on to the open call at 890 Broadway. Also known as the epicenter for theatrical rehearsal spaces. Back in 1978, Michael Bennett bought the eight story building with his *A Chorus Line* winnings. He transformed a former belt and shirt factory into a series of spaces to be used for professional shows in every phase of development, from holding auditions to presenting workshops to rehearsing for a show going into production. And there's the glaring rub—you fall into one of two groups when you walk into that lobby and push the elevator button for the floor you need. Either you're working, or you're not.

You're very likely to bump into someone you know, and you can tell immediately from the expression on their face which category they belong in. Of course, they're scoping you out too. And ideally, you're a part of the working elite and have a sense of belonging to something. You're in.

Or maybe you're a part of the other mass of long shots just there to put your asses on the line for whatever you're auditioning for. The stressful process is written on every striving face, and now my face joins the ranks of this wishful crowd of ambition.

Can I really go through with this audition after all this time has passed? I hear Hobo's voice in my head: You're going to nail this audition Daddy Boy. Even if it's a tad early to be nailing Christopher. That puts a smile on my face.

I take a deep breath and head into the building. Blessedly, the theater gods have granted me a reprieve as the elevator door opens onto my floor. Some of the faces look familiar, but I don't see a soul that I know. Maybe it's because I've been out of commission for so long, or it's due to the fact that I'm two hours early for this call. My game plan is to be one of the first to sign up so I can get a low number, then get out of here until I come back to sing.

Even coming in this early, I still score number eighty-nine. This is going to be one long afternoon. I can't imagine how the casting directors are going to be navigating the waters of these hundreds of headshots they'll be sailing through today.

Stay focused, Matt. At least you showed up. Stop thinking about anybody else and tap into your inner guide for strength. Maybe I've found my own voice for a change.

Mission accomplished. I make it back out of the lobby, winding my way through the hopefuls going up to my floor to sign up. Outside, I spot Christopher in the window of the diner across the street and head over.

Is it my imagination, or does he seem to glow from within? I haven't felt this kind of attraction in a long time. His smile is already calming me down as I go in and hustle over to his table.

"Hi Matt. How's it going?"

"Not bad." I say as I sit down, "How about you?" Can he tell I'm nervous? I guess that's to be expected since we have no excuse to be here, but for each other.

"Oh, I'm getting through my day with a minimum of bruising."

"Yeah, I know how it is. I was very close to someone who rarely missed a day of dance class."

"Oh really? Where did they take class? Are they still dancing in the city?"

"No, unfortunately, that was in the past tense. He died over a year and a half ago."

"Oh, I'm sorry."

"Thanks. It hasn't been easy for me..." We both pause, but I'm not about to bare my soul right out of the gate. "Anyway, have you ordered anything?"

"Yes, I just ordered a hot tea."

I get the attention of the waitress and place my order while I'm wondering where all this is going. That was a pretty rough start to a conversation. But his demeanor is so calm and low- key, unlike the usual extroverted chorus boys I'm used to. "Sorry there wasn't much time to talk after your show, but I thought you did a really great job."

"Thanks. Did you really like the concert?"

"Well actually, if I'm being honest, it was cool to see everyone moving like that. And I know it takes incredible skill, but I just didn't get the piece as a whole."

"I like your honesty," he laughs. "Modern dance can be challenging if you're not used to it. And sometimes the choreography just isn't that good."

I lean back in my chair a little more, starting to feel more comfortable. "Well, that's a relief. Then maybe I'm not a total idiot after all!"

"I've only been dancing in New York for two years, so I take what I can get for now."

Man, I know what I'd like to take. Calm down, Matt. You're getting way ahead of yourself. "What's your long-term game plan?"

"Well, I'd love to get into a major company like Cunningham, but the spots for that are few and far between. For me right now, it's just about absorbing every bit of experience I can. It's all a work in progress, but that's why it's interesting to me."

"That sounds wonderful. Doing musicals sometimes feels more like a business. You just want to keep working."

"But what about creativity?"

"You may get lucky enough to work with a creative bunch of people, but if the show's a hit, you could be doing it for a year or more."

"I never thought of that. It's different in concert dance. You work on a piece for a few months then you perform it for a few weekends."

"That's hardly any time at all. Definitely not long enough to get bored with it."

"Some companies are lucky enough to go out on tour for a couple of months at a time. Nothing like years, though."

"How do you make a living on that?"

"For the most part, you really don't unless you're in a big company. That's why you see me catering. It's always a challenge. But like old Uncle Merce, I'm pretty focused."

"I really do respect that." I can't help but zero in on the fullness of his lower lip... Get a grip Matt. Stick with the conversation!

"There's something about being in Manhattan that seems to create that focus," he says.

"What do you mean?"

"Have you ever noticed when you're walking down one of these streets, how narrow your vision is? The buildings on either side force it forward. There's no wide view. It becomes a mindset."

"Wow, I've never really thought of it that way." Man, this guy's deep.

"You'll probably think I'm a little bit nuts, but I feel my surroundings are a part of me. I don't separate them. Whatever my senses take in, I am that. I guess it's all the meditating I do."

"I'm not sure I'm following you." Maybe a better word to describe him would be mystical. He's really out there.

"You can watch dance that way too. The movement with the lights and sound all blend together to become one. That's what makes it abstract."

"So do you mean everything combined can be looked at as one thing?"

"That's right. It works in everyday life too. Think about how you feel connected to people. Maybe you feel compassion or empathy?"

"Or how about being pissed off at someone?"

"Absolutely. Emotions play a big part in all this. Everything affects everything else."

"Yeah, but can you really live your life that way, Chris?"

"Actually, I prefer Christopher. Calling me Chris reminds me of my past when I was called Sissy Chrissy."

"Sorry about that."

"See what I mean? I have issues too. We're all a work in progress."

"But what about emotions? Isn't it just as valid to feel things that come from just you?"

"But do they?"

"Well, you got me there. I guess the emotions are always part of a reaction to something."

"That's how I would look at it."

"And that's why I love doing theater. If I'm lucky, I sometimes I get to work out some of this angst in a character."

"How do you mean?"

"Well, just as an example, let's take this longing I might feel. I can't describe what it's about. But if I sing it, and I dig down deep in my guts, my character acts as a catalyst to bring it out on stage. Then I'm somehow transformed by it."

"I can relate to transformation."

"That's why I'm still battling it out, trying to get another show. Sure, it's work. But it's also a lifeline."

"Life is often full of contradictions."

He runs his hand through that beautiful mane of his. I can't help wishing it was my hand. "Tell me about it," I say. "I also just like entertaining people. Making them laugh and having fun with my character."

"It sounds like a good balance to me. Sharing your talent is good karma. In eastern religions, it's called right livelihood."

"I just wish I wasn't dealing with so many of those contradictions you were referring to right now."

"And what would be the nature of this conflict?" Christopher responds gently, "If I might ask."

I pause to consider whether I want to lay all my queer cards on the table. What do I have to lose? I fill Christopher in on my beautiful Timothy, and our three-year relationship ending with his untimely death. I even share the story of Hobo's long journey from not trusting us, to eventually understanding that she didn't have to act as prey. Once she finally allowed herself to be touched with affection, it turned her life around.

I eventually get back to the fact that I haven't worked in the business in two years. And now, I'm taking my first step back into this very crowded pool of thespians with this audition.

He takes it all in with an ease that makes me feel like all my troubles are flowing out of me. But instead of absorbing them, they seem to go right through him. Something he calls Buddha nature. Regardless, by the end of our date, I feel lighter somehow. And I'm sure hoping I'll get to see him again. I even tell him that!

Neither of us feels comfortable with making a move toward a physical expression of goodbye. I guess we're both in the slow lane when it comes to real dating. But the lingering glances aren't a bad substitute.

So, after we part ways, it's back across the street to the 890 building. As soon as I step into the lobby, I'm hit with a couple of former comrades from the chorus of my past, Charlie and Helen. At least I consider them good friends. They must be rehearsing here for *Annie Get Your Gun*.

"Matt! How wonderful to see you!" says Helen.

"Hey you two," I say, "how's life with 'Buffalo Bill's Wild West Show'?"

"Right now, I feel like I been roped and branded all over my entire achin' body," Charlie quips. "All I can think about is a hot bath and shot of whiskey to ease the pain."

"Whatever gets you through," I say. He looks even thinner than the last time I saw him. I hope he's okay.

"The second week of rehearsal is always the hardest," Helen says. "Charlie's our swing, so he has to learn the whole show. And I'm the dance captain."

"I can just imagine you cracking the whip," I say. "Charlie's lucky to have you."

"I couldn't be happier," he says. "I had a relapse of the flu, so Helen's been dragging me though it."

"Speaking of shows. Are you here for *Our New Normal*?" Helen asks.

"Yeah, I'm number eighty-nine, heading up to the call right now."

"I know you don't usually go to open calls," Helen says, "but I think this one's worth it."

"Don't forget man," Charlie says, "that chorus is Greek. I know you can relate to that."

"Very funny. So can most of these guys."

"Just stay focused on what you can bring to it, and your gorgeous voice will carry you through," Helen says.

"Thanks, I'd better head up." I join the gaggle of guys going into the elevator, and we all ascend to the challenge ahead of us.

Five

The elevator door opens to a mass of male humanity, everyone wanting the same thing. It feels like an army of aspirants. The entire lot of them, ready and eager to do whatever it takes to be one of the chosen. I can't remember the last time I saw so many guys in one space. They're crowded into every inch of this long wide hallway. Talk about blending together—the energy and ambition of this group is unmistakable.

I'm afraid this is going to be like a who's who of every guy I've known from my now fading musical past. Then I spot a familiar face I'm actually happy to see, the incomparable Gabriel LeBlanc. If anyone can get me through this afternoon, he can. This fireball of Creole energy is such a live wire, you can't get too close, or his sparks will singe any sense of normalcy you thought you had a handle on.

"Well, Matthew McKinney, as I do live and breathe! What a pleasure to see your fine figure of manliness."

He's always so over the top. It's hard to believe this male version of Diana Ross crossed with Eartha Kitt comes from a successful set of highly respected academic parents. "Hi Gabriel, how's it going?"

"Well, putting up with this zoo of rejects just got a whole lot better now that I'm takin' in that handsome face of yours."

He makes a move to pinch my cheek, but I playfully swat his hand down. "I'm just so glad to see you," I say, trying to calm this queen down. Let me clarify that. *Quuween* is more like it. But ya gotta love her. "How long has it been?"

"Oh, I shudder to think. It's a good thing black don't crack honey, because I just hit thirty.

"We'll let that be our little secret now that we've both joined that club."

"Stop! With your All-American Boy looks? You could probably play a teenage Opie in a *Mayberry* movie of the week!"

"Thanks for the compliment, but I just want to stay employable for a little longer. I couldn't get an agent submission, so I thought I'd take a chance and show up for this."

"You know, this could be a really cool gig," he says. "And I don't need to tell you how few and far between parts are for some of us of a darker coloration."

"I think you have a decent shot at this Gabriel. I'm sure you know this Greek chorus is made up of guys who have died from AIDS. That includes a lot of ethnicities."

"In all seriousness, Matt, they're also the group that gets the worst care, because there isn't any funding for them. The way this administration is ignoring us is immoral."

"After Timothy died, I pretty much lost hope of the whole mess," I confess.

"I can't even begin to imagine what you've been through. But I think it's time to get up and fight for our community now."

"Wow. You sound pretty resolved about this."

"I am. I went to a meeting a little over a week ago. We officially formed an organization called: AIDS Coalition to Unleash Power: ACT UP. We're going to have our first demonstration of civil disobedience in just a few days."

"That sounds pretty serious."

"It's going to be on Wall Street. We'll be protesting against the profiteering of the manufacturer of AZT. We're going to demand that they make it more affordable. And we're going to demand the release of drugs that could save our lives that the FDA hasn't approved yet."

"I didn't know there were any other drugs."

"There's a lot going on they don't tell us about. They're doing these double-blind studies where some AIDS patients aren't getting any drug at all."

"That is incredible, Gabriel. I had no idea anything like this was happening. It's just so easy to get caught up in your own pathetic little life."

"Your life is not pathetic, Matt. It means something. Timothy's life and death mean something. And it's time we fight for that."

"You sound like someone else I know..." I'm surprised Hobo hasn't shown up here too.

"I wouldn't wonder. We're all facing this, and we need to face it together. That's what ACT UP is about, and I'm thinking that's what *Our New Normal* is very likely gonna be about too."

I've never heard Gabriel speak this way. "It really is unusual to audition for a show like this," I say. "I'm so used to the revivals, which are fine. They have their place and help make life a little more tolerable."

"Yes, they do," he agrees. "But now we have an opportunity to really make a difference."

We continue to delve into all the ramifications of what we're dealing with non-stop, until my group of ten is called. Numbers eighty through eighty-nine line up and prepare for our individual swan dives. That's what it feels like. You have to open your arms wide, expose your heart, and dive off the high board for your sixteen bars. One by one, we go in. I continue to move up, getting more nervous as each guy finishes. Number eighty-seven, number eighty-eight, and finally, number eighty-nine.

I walk into the room and hand my picture and resume to the assistant. She hands it over to one of the four people sitting at the long table. I recognize the casting director from other auditions, and he seems to know me.

He scans my resume while I try to calm myself, and hands it off to the woman next to him. I get a "Hi Matthew, what are you going to sing for us today?"

"'Corner of the Sky' from *Pippin*." Of course, everybody knows what it's from. I didn't need to say that. I try to brush that thought off and hand the music to the guy at the piano.

"Wonderful." he says, already looking every bit like the zombie I'm sure he's becoming, listening to this never-ending train of singers, hitting their high note as their picture and resume flashes by.

The piano begins and I give it my best shot. I actually feel good about my sixteen bars when I'm through. Yes! I didn't suck!

"Thank you, Matthew. What was that high note you hit at the end of the song in falsetto?"

"It's a C."

More scribbling on my resume. "Well, thank you again Matthew."

"Thank you." I say, and I'm out of there.

The room feels like it's beginning to spin as I step out into the hallway. Of course, all eyes are on me since they could all hear me through the door. It's the old sizing-me-up routine. This floor show doesn't hold the slightest resemblance to showing up at Uncle Charlie's Bar in the Village. Not that I've seen the inside of a gay bar in years, but instead of scanning a potential beau, these looks are all about: Is he better than me? Am I the same type as him? Did the production team like him? Would they choose him over me?

I've been down this road too many times before. You can so easily psych yourself out of a decent audition if you let it get to you like that. Complete focus is necessary for what you present to the people judging you inside that room. Because sixteen bars flash by like lightning, and if you don't make an impression, they're already thinking about the next guy.

I give Gabriel a thrill as I simultaneously bestow a friendly smack on his behind and wish him well on the audition. Then it's all about me getting the hell out of here so I can take a breath.

Christ, just being outside feels like a gift. I've got to clear my head of all this. There's no way of knowing what will happen, but at least I can manage to be a little upbeat now. I've finally taken the first step toward getting back in the game.

That just gives me a crazy idea. I really need to get a blast of fresh air after this cattle call. And the best way to shake this off and get some space is by heading as far south to the edge of this rock of land mass as I can get. I'm already imagining what escaping this island and getting beyond its perimeter will feel like.

You can flee Manhattan and head out into the New York Harbor for the bargain price of twenty-five cents. It's actually a reasonably bright day, and there should still be plenty of sunshine left when I get down to the South Ferry exit from the R train.

So back underground I go. I take a seat in a mostly empty car and allow the rumbling of the train tracks to lull me into a state of hypnosis as my subterranean chariot charges through the dingy black tunnel.

Looking across the car at my reflection in the inky darkness of the opposite train window, I'm not sure what my image reveals. I've seen this face so often. Is it the "me" I thought I was or some new version? I somehow see a little deeper into myself. How do I reconcile all that's happened up to now? Does this new person have the courage and determination to embrace this new reality? I'm still not sure. The jury is still out.

My portrait disappears as the lights of the station invade the window, and we come to a stop. Okay, I need to leave all this deep soul-searching behind. And in just a short walk from the subway exit, I arrive at the turnstiles for the entrance to my version of the Love Boat—Manhattan style. That bright orange wonder known as the Staten Island Ferry.

I can't complain about the fare, but it has gone up a bit from when the city of New York assumed control of the ferry in 1905. Back then, it was five cents. Not bad for the five-mile, twenty-five-minute ride that it is today. There's just something romantic and almost cinematic about this commuter craft as we take off into open water. For me, this is the New York I love.

We voyage out into the expansive harbor that seems to have no bounds. Looking back at Manhattan Island, it gradually diminishes from my sight and mind in equal measure. Now the majestic views of ocean and sky take center stage. With a renewed sense of freedom, I head to the food counter and get a beer and a pretzel to treat myself for what I've decided was a job well done.

"I guess there's no point in ordering me one," Hobo says. "Do they have any over-the-counter catnip?"

It's pretty crowded in here, so I don't take the bait with an answer, but I look around and spot Hobo on a shelf above the doors that lead outside.

"Let's catch some of this sea breeze and get out into the elements, Daddy Boy."

"That was my plan all along," I say, now that I'm sure no one is around. I go through to the second-level deck at the back of the boat. It's chilly, but you're not as blasted by the wind in the back, and there's nothing more inspiring than being out in the open sea.

"So, you did it," she begins, as we find an out-of-the-way spot where no one will be paying attention to me talking to the salty air.

"Yes, and I feel pretty good about it."

"Well, you should. You didn't see me in the room, but I had a ringside seat of your somewhat abbreviated performance. You were pitch perfect, and I should know. We cats have incredible hearing."

"Thanks, Pussyface. I felt like my high note practically floated out of me. They at least got some sense of what I can do."

"Yes, they certainly did. Will you take a look at our Lady Liberty! Why didn't you ever take me with you when you used to come out here with Timothy?"

"Oh right. What was I supposed to do? Throw you in a backpack and hope you didn't escape over the railing to a watery grave?"

"Perhaps you're right. We kitties aren't particularly fond of water. But now I blend well with everything. Can't you tell how unruffled I've become?"

"Sure. Unflappable," I sarcastically reply.

"My dear Matthew, you'd better get used to my directives. How else am I supposed to light a fire under that cute butt of yours?"

"I think I can take responsibility for warming my own rear end."

"Everyone can use some guidance now and then."

"Whatever. Right now all this fresh sea air is just making me want to sing out."

"But that's what I've been chattering about. What is it with this love/hate relationship you have with the city? One minute you're marveling at some building and the next you're complaining about urban oppression."

"I'm allowed to have mood swings you know."

"But your attitude about the city, and especially show business, is what's holding you back."

"Since when did you all of a sudden become an expert in mind control?"

"Oh, I'm all about control, Daddy Boy. Remember: Dogs have owners, cats have staff."

"Tell me about it."

"Now, where was I? Oh yes. Why do you love it? Why do you hate it? Are these highs and lows to make your life feel like it means something, now that Timothy is gone?"

"Just the opposite. Timothy was like the anchor of my ship. We were really there for each other."

"All right, Mister Matt. Then I think it's time to take a hard look at yourself and understand that you are the one responsible for how you view everything. Take showbiz for instance. When you look at it as just a trade-off, it becomes one. Change how you view things and your view changes."

I take a big gulp of my frothy beer and let her advice sink in for a moment. Looking out into this wide open bay, Manhattan suddenly feels so small and far away. "You're probably right Hobo, but sometimes it all just feels out of my control."

"You need to understand that you, Matthew McKinney, can navigate your life just fine. You can find more of a balance with how you choose to live from day to day."

"Wow, Hobo. I really don't have a comeback for that."

"None needed. I'll take my leave now and let all this wash over you, so to speak."

And she evaporates in the sea breeze. Man, that cat can really do a number on me. I take the rest of my beer and pretzel inside now and sit with the Staten Island residents that board this ship as a vehicle to get them home.

I need to settle into everything that's transpired today. Timothy was constantly telling me what a control freak I was. I guess that's still true. Now Christopher is telling me that my emotions are a reflection of how I interpret everything around me. I guess that means it's really all on me. If I can start believing in myself more, maybe that will be a reflection of everything I do, like this audition today. I can start believing more in the people that come into my life too. I can have more trust in some inner part of me.

I stay glued to my seat for the rest of the journey over and go back on the same boat and seat as well. Returning toward Manhattan, I head outside again and brave the salty blast so I can witness the surreal experience of watching the cityscape grow larger and larger as the ship moves closer to the island's edge. The reality of my life expands as my view of the city does the same. I'm ready for it now. I'm prepared to take it all in.

This boat ride and everything that's happened today has given me the perspective I need. I should give Hobo some credit for that too. My sweet and sassy Pussyface has become a lifesaver for me. Now I just need to embrace it.

Six

Something feels very wrong... I can't get my breath... It's the middle of the night, and I've been awakened by my own coughing...I can't get a good breath...I feel my...body is dripping in sweat...the sheets are soaked...I'm trying to understand what's going on...I... can't breathe... what's happening?... I'm so hot... my body feels like it's on fire... I can't get... my face is tingling...I can't catch my breath... my heart is pounding in my ears... I'm not right... I need help... what do I do?

Do I call 911?... my breathing is so shallow... I'm getting dizzy now when I try to stand...no, I can't get up... the bed is spinning...I've got to get... I can't breathe... I've got to phone 911... why does the damn phone have to be in the other room? I've got to get up... it's so hard to breathe... I've got to try... my legs feel like rubber... I'm alone... no one is here to help me... I just want to cry out... I can't breathe! ... someone help me!

I hear the ambulance on the street. It's such a common noise, it could be for anyone... but it has to be for me... I've got to get outside somehow and flag it down... I don't think I'm strong enough... my breathing is so fast... I'm starting to shiver in this cold sweat... I've got to wrap the sheets around me and go find the ambulance... the sirens are roaring... I've got to get there... I grab the sopping sheet, and now I can see lesions on my hands and arms. How did they get there? No! I don't have it! I can't have it! I can't have AIDS!

"Wake up! Wake up! Matthew, you're having a nightmare honey. Get up! Open your eyes! It's me, Hobo. Wake up! It's just a dream."

"What? Oh My God, Hobo! That was terrible." I take a deep breath. My eyes are now open to a much calmer scenario. The early morning light of dawn is filtering in from the window as the sound of another siren screams by. I guess my conscious mind can handle the noise better than my subconscious. The sheets are actually wet, and my heart is still pounding, but I'm okay.

"Mathew, my dear, when I've called you out for being a drama queen, I didn't quite know the lengths to which you'd take it."

She looks a bit like the reclining Buddha on my dresser, but I'm so glad she showed up again. "I owe you another one, Pussyface. You've rescued your Daddy Boy once again from his self-torment."

"Mama's always there when you need her, my sweet. Now it's time to shake this off and hop in the shower. You've got a date with a demonstration downtown."

"I know, I know. I already called Gabriel and told him I'm going."

"So, what are you waiting for? Get your rear in gear!"

"Well, for one thing, it's a very vulnerable position to put myself in."

"What position? You just stand your ground and be part of a chorus of voices that demand to be heard."

"I've never even marched in a Gay Pride Parade before, much less participated in a protest."

"Well it's about time."

"Good Catholic boys are trained never to rock the boat."

"Forget about your boat rocking. You need to jump ship. You're a strong swimmer, remember? You can do this."

"You're right, damn it."

"That's the spirit."

"I'm doing this for everyone suffering right now. I'm also doing it for Timothy."

"And I'm sure he'd be right beside you in this fight if he could be."

"He was always so brave. I still get nauseated when I think about how I watched him waste away to a sort of living death."

"His spirit is still very much alive in both our hearts."

"You know he took after you with his saucy streak, but he was so much fun too."

"You're right, he was a lot like me—a real fighter. He didn't let anybody give him shit and insisted on living his life exactly the way he pleased."

"Yeah and he was quite a party boy, too. But not long after we met the night life began to lose its luster for him. I think it surprised him even more than me."

"Timothy really settled in when I entered the picture. So give me some credit."

"Yes, he found real contentment in our little domestic nest. Once he became really ill, this apartment became a sort of refuge."

"Don't forget all the snuggles I provided, too."

"Never. You were a godsend. His body was in such agony, he really didn't want to be touched, but he could nestle in with you just fine."

"So, you're heading down to the first ACT UP protest. Do you have any idea of what you're getting into?"

"Not a clue. I'm meeting up with Gabriel and we'll just see what happens."

"Where's your 'Reagan is a shithead' sign?"

"That's just not me, Hobo. Gabriel filled me in with the specifics, but I have no idea what's going to happen."

"Well, you give 'em hell from Hobo!"

And once again, she dissolves into the particles of light from which she came. I'm surprised at how used to it I've gotten.

I hustle into the shower, grab some breakfast, and I'm out the door before I even think about what I'm walking into. I've got to get to Wall Street and Broadway by Trinity Church. It's essential to be there for rush hour. Obstructing the snarled-up traffic will have a big impact.

As the subway car hurtles down to my destination, I again think about Timothy and all the other friends I've lost to this epidemic. A whole generation of vital and talented human beings cut down in their prime. So full of life and promise. It's just devastating, and it makes me so angry. I'm furious at the pharmaceutical companies for their outrageous pricing of AZT. It's the only drug we've got, however imperfect. It should be affordable. The FDA should make that happen along with releasing other experimental drugs. It's a disgrace.

Damn. Riding the train at rush hour really sucks. I'm hardly ever on it at this time. I'm so glad I'm not on the nine-to-five gravy train, even if I am just barely making it with these catering gigs. So many people. All loading on for this typical Tuesday morning on March 24th, 1987. I should remember this date as the first time I stood up for anything like this. I just didn't think it was in my DNA before today. I've witnessed so many groups of people have their human rights trampled in my past, but I was never brave enough to stand with them and let my voice be heard—until now.

The number two train catapults me back down toward the bottom of the island. All these stops. All these people coming and going. The business of the day is starting for them. Don't they understand people are suffering and dying from this disease? I just get more and more worked up with every stop. Finally, we make it to Wall Street. I bound up the steps, only to be confronted by more throngs of pedestrians and noisy traffic rushing to get to work. It's as if they're bowing to the almighty dollar that will buy some kind of lucrative life they think makes it worth living.

Wall Street is in gridlock, and the horns are blaring. Good. I don't see any movement in this congestion of idling motors, so I guess that means the protest is already in full swing holding everything up.

I walk up Wall Street towards Broadway and pass a Tiffany & Co. store on my left. More rewards for corporate greed if you know how to play the game. And now the next block houses the New York Stock Exchange. This really is the ideal spot to point out how financial gain takes precedence over human life.

Finally, I make it to Broadway and Wall Street. The repetitive sounds of chanting add to the chaos of the day, with the full orchestration of honking horns to back them up.

People are everywhere with signs and chanting: *WE ARE ANGRY! WE WANT ACTION! WE ARE ANGRY! WE WANT ACTION!* There's got to be at least two hundred and fifty people, many out in the middle of the street. Some are lying down. The buildings on either side of Wall Street feel like matching mountains of the status quo. They create a sort of canyon for the opposition down below. I look up above this trough of humanity to the Trinity church. Its gothic revival spire gives me the impression of a needle piercing the heart of the sky. It's like what's happening in our community; we've been impaled by this plague. But we won't go down without a fight. I see an effigy of the FDA

Commissioner, Frank Young, hanging on the façade of the church. The message is loud and clear.

WE ARE ANGRY! WE WANT ACTION! WE ARE ANGRY! WE WANT ACTION!

I see posters of Reagan everywhere with his idiotic matinee idol smile. One reads: REAGAN GUILTY OF CRIMINAL NEGLECT. And the writing above another one of his poster boy portraits simply reads: KILLER VIRUS. The chanting is like a song that keeps skipping back to the same refrain.

WE ARE ANGRY! WE WANT ACTION! WE ARE ANGRY! WE WANT ACTION!

"Matthew! Over here!"

"Gabriel! This is incredible! I can barely hear you over all this shouting."

"I know, isn't this fucking amazing? Shout with me! *WE ARE ANGRY! WE WANT ACTION! WE ARE ANGRY! WE WANT ACTION!*"

"That's a great sign Gabriel! How did you come up with it?"

"Oh, isn't it just flawless? FDA YOU SLAY ME! I'm just speaking the truth."

We hear a new chant begin: *RELEASE THE DRUGS! RELEASE THE DRUGS! RELEASE THE DRUGS! RELEASE THE DRUGS!*

"Come out into the street, Matt! Feel this power! Join our circle and hold my hand! *RELEASE THE DRUGS! RELEASE THE DRUGS!*"

"You know Timothy died in the summer of '85 just when AZT went into its first drug trial in July. There was nothing for him."

"I know, and these jerks have been fucking around with these trials ever since, with people who are dying, still just getting the placebo. Now we finally just got it approved last week by the fucking FDA, and it's so expensive, not everyone will get it! They should be giving that shit away! And what about all the other drugs they're holding back for testing! *RELEASE THE DRUGS! RELEASE THE DRUGS! RELEASE THE DRUGS!*"

"Baby, we need some better shit than just this AZT," Gabriel says, as he tries to draw me deeper into the crowd. *RELEASE THE DRUGS! RELEASE THE DRUGS! RELEASE THE DRUGS!"*

"Jesus there are cops everywhere!" I say, beginning to get a little on edge. I can't imagine where this is all going.

The chanting takes up a new lyric: *BUSINESS AS USUAL, NO MORE! BUSINESS AS USUAL, NO MORE! BUSINESS AS USUAL, NO MORE!*

"I feel like I was born for this!" Gabriel shouts, pulling me even closer toward the center of the action. "We've got to stand strong. Time to put our asses on the line. I'm gonna join this sitting circle in the street. Come down here with me!"

I hear the police over the megaphone: "If you refuse to move, you'll be placed under arrest for disorderly conduct. I'm ordering you to leave at this time."

AIDS KILLS WOMEN! STOP THE PROFITEERING! AIDS KILLS WOMEN! STOP THE PROFITEERING!

"I can't do it Gabriel." I say, releasing myself from his grip. "I can't get arrested."

"What do you mean? Where's your commitment to this cause? Sit the fuck down and join us!"

"I'm sorry, Gabriel. I just can't take it that far. I'm not getting arrested. My life is complicated enough!"

I find a way to the edge of the crowd and out of the middle of the street, just as I hear the megaphone again. "All right. You are all under arrest for disorderly conduct. If you resist arrest, an additional charge of resisting arrest will be lodged against you."

I can't believe I'm seeing this. The cops are dragging these people on the ground, some of them still holding on to each other as they take them to the police cars.

AIDS KILLS WOMEN! STOP THE PROFITEERING! AIDS KILLS WOMEN! STOP THE PROFITEERING!

I see Gabriel being dragged out with all the others. Damn, that is one fierce queen. I'm just so torn up about all this, but I know my limits, and getting arrested simply exceeds them.

I count seventeen people being dragged into police cars. Their commitment to this civil disobedience is truly humbling. This fucking virus has wreaked such havoc on my life for years now. I feel like I'm barely treading water to stay afloat. But damn it, I haven't sunk down below the surface yet. Maybe I'm not ready to get arrested, but I'm still standing. At least, I can say that.

The street has been cleared now, so the gridlocked traffic is slowly starting to untangle and continue on its daily grind. The climax of the show is over. Time to go. But not in retreat. A battle was waged today and hopefully, all the media coverage will be part of our victory.

"You should feel a sense of victory too, Daddy Boy."

"Yeah well, it doesn't feel so sweet, Hobo. Where are you anyway?"

"I'm up here. On top of this phone booth on the corner."

"You were always trying to jump up on any high surface at home. I guess I shouldn't be surprised."

"Being high up is the best strategy. Try to grab me from below, and you'd get a swipe, as I'm sure you remember."

"How can I forget? You never got used to being picked up and carried anywhere. It always had to be on your terms."

"Of course. Is there any other way?"

"I guess I did this protest today on my terms too, didn't I?"

"Yes, you did. What a clever Matt Cat you can be sometimes. You've embraced my teachings once again."

"Glad to oblige."

"You are counted today as one of the courageous who showed up. Don't feel guilty about not getting arrested. Give yourself a pat on the back for just being here."

"But Gabriel is so pissed at me now for not joining in the circle."

"That queen bee is on her own trip. You're not one of her drones, you know. You don't just do her bidding."

"I still feel a bit guilty. And I really have so much respect for what he's done today."

"As well you should."

"So now what?"

"I'll give you a subtle hint. You're looking right at your next move."

"This phone booth? What are you cooking up now, you crazy cat?"

"I think you might want to give a certain someone a call and see what he's up to."

"You mean Christopher? I guess he'd be finished with his morning classes by now. And I do have his number in my wallet."

"What are you waiting for? You just slayed the corporate dragon, or at least got the process started. Time to proclaim your victory and bend the knee to his 'heinie-ness.'"

"Very funny, Hobo." As I search for Christopher's number in my wallet, she once again makes her departure, dissolving into space...

Actually, Christopher is the first person who comes to mind as someone who will understand what I've just been through. It's amazing how he takes it all in when I open up to him. I hardly even know him, and yet on some deeper level, I do. Not only is he a good listener, but I feel like when I bear the searchings of my soul, he reflects it all back to me in a way that's accepting and not the least bit judgemental. I've got to go with my gut on this one. I'm making that phone call.

Seven

I follow Hobo's marching orders, deciding to walk up to Greenwich Village instead of taking the subway. I can take direction well, especially from a certain conniving cat. So far, she hasn't steered me wrong.

First off, I can't believe Christopher actually answered his phone. Nobody answers their phone anymore. And he's free for lunch! I know it's only been four days since our last coffee date, but I really want to see him. He just has a certain way about him. There's a kind of sweetness in how he tosses his head around, and his wide-spread soft eyes remind me of a young colt. He always seems so present, like it's all-new, again and again.

This day is going to be a win-win. I still feel guilty about Gabriel, but I'm sure ACT UP has a posse of lawyers working on whatever process is required for his release. I'm going to focus on the positive. Christopher sounded very encouraging about the whole thing over the phone. So, I'll take that as a good sign too.

It's such a lovely crisp and breezy spring morning, might as well take a walking tour of downtown Manhattan. That gives me plenty of time to be at his restaurant pick for lunch. Whole Wheat 'n Wild Berry's, at 57 West 10th Street. I've never heard of it, and I'm thinking it's probably vegetarian, but what do I know? I usually just devour the ultimate in NYC nourishment, pizza by the slice. It's cheap, it's fast, and it fills you up.

I figure about an hour and I should be there, heading northeast on Broadway and taking a left toward Trinity Place. It's like another world down here, like being an alien in a strange land. There are so many office buildings. The biggest, of course, is the twin towers. The only reason I ever come down here is because you can get half-price tickets for Broadway shows at the TKTS booth in the World Trade Center, and don't have to wait in those long tourist lines at the one in Times Square.

These twin babies may be the tallest buildings in the world. Still, I've never been that impressed by their '70s elongated blocky look, like a couple of toothpaste boxes on end. I guess nobody can accuse me of being a size queen, at least when it comes to skyscrapers.

Touring the multitude of neighborhoods between Wall Street and The Village is always a fun adventure, especially with the anticipation I'm feeling right now of seeing Christopher again. Each designated area is so varied and has its own character and neighborhood history. And they keep changing. I guess that's one of life's lessons I'm learning to adjust to—change.

The complexity of the sights and sounds of this city is never-ending. I get more and more excited as I pass through one locale after the next, leading up to West 10th Street. I've finally arrived. A right turn takes me toward the restaurant, even though I haven't thought this lunch through. I do really like this guy. Besides the fact that he's so cute, it just feels good to be in his company. But there's so much I don't know about him. Maybe he's a vegetarian. I don't even know that. Why else would he want to meet me here?

I guess I'm about to find out. I enter the restaurant and the comforting smells of what is likely to be delicious food overwhelm me. Wow, this place is so crunchy granola; it's like I've stepped back into the '60s. The vibe feels so laid back and friendly. I spot him in the back and head over to his table.

"Hi Matthew. Good timing. I just got here," he says.

"Great. I walked all the way up from Wall Street, so I've worked up an appetite."

"Have you ever been here before?"

"No, never."

"This place is like my Earth Mother. The organic vegetarian food reminds me of home."

"Where are you from?"

"Eugene, Oregon. Talk about a world away."

"I've never been that far west."

"Now you see how committed I am to dancing, coming all this way."

"Yeah that's quite a leap." That gets a laugh out of him.

"Well, it's the epicenter for dance here."

"This town is the epicenter of just about everything. I came from the Chicago area. It's still quite a change."

"At least Chicago is a major city. Eugene is really a college town, lots of hippies and liberals." He does one of my favorite moves of his, running his hand through his hair as he tilts his head slightly back.

"Moving here must have been quite a shock for you," I say. I can't get over his beautiful brown eyes. I've "decided" he must have been born with an extra set of lashes—and those lips...okay I need to change my focus.

"Yes, it really was." He shyly looks down at the menu, then seems to get brave again. "Let's order. I recommend the Everything Salad with tahini dressing."

"I've never had tahini dressing, but I'm game." How sweet that he took control of the situation. He can tell how clueless I am about this kind of food. Now that the ordering is done. What's next?

We put down our menus and have no excuse but to look straight into each other. I can see him blush a little as he asks, "So, how did your audition go?"

"It actually went very well, for what it's worth. It's such a long shot, though."

"You never know."

"True. I haven't given up hope. It usually takes a couple of weeks for them to get back to you. If I don't hear anything after a few weeks, it's back to square one."

"You mean they don't let you know either way?"

"Nope. Not until after the callback. If you don't get cut from that."

"Sounds pretty brutal."

"That's show biz." There's another pause again as we both look around the room. I wonder where this is all going. Our last coffee date was so cool, getting into all that Eastern philosophy stuff. But what about his personal life? I still don't know much about him. "So tell me about life back in Eugene."

"It's actually just me and my mom and dad. Maybe that's why I'm so close to them. They pretty much fit into the Eugene paradigm."

"What's that?"

"Oh they've always been very open to my interest in dance and my personal life too."

"That must be nice."

"Is your family back in Chicago supportive?"

"Not particularly." Should I get into this? Why not? "I come from a very traditional Irish Catholic family with four older brothers. My interest in theater wasn't really encouraged."

"That's too bad."

"I'm just so different from all of them. You know that feeling of otherness? It was subtle, but always there."

"Yes, it's kind of like the artist's point of view, being on the outside."

"Right! Sometimes I think my need to perform comes from not being accepted. Maybe that's why I love the audience connection so much. I know they get me."

"That makes sense. Oh, here's our food. Hold that thought while we dig in."

"Delicious! I think I could get used to this organic vegetarian stuff." It's just nice to share a meal with this sweet guy. I feel like I could tell him anything. I'd love to hear more about him too. "What was it like growing up gay in Eugene?"

"Kind of a mixed bag. You know how kids are. But my parents were always accepting."

"You're really lucky to have that. It wasn't like I got thrown out of the house when I came out, but I don't fit in with their lives now."

"Yeah, it's all so different here. You don't see many families."

"I've made my friends my family. It's important to feel that."

"I know what you mean. Eugene feels so far away."

"Do you have any people you've met here that are like family?"

"I've gotten to know Helen in the last year. She's such a sweetheart and feels like a big sister to me. Always ready to listen."

"I couldn't agree more. I think it's pretty amazing we both know her. Maybe we'll all have to get together sometime." I've got to keep coming up with ways to keep seeing this guy. I wish he would make a move, but that doesn't seem like his style. I get it. I even find it very attractive. Oh, be still my heart. Oh, be still my crotch! Does this mean I'm finally letting go of Timothy a bit more?

"That sounds like it would be fun," he says. "Maybe we should go out to New Jersey to the Paper Mill Playhouse and see her show."

"What a great idea!" He actually made a suggestion to see me again. "My friend Charlie is in it, too, but we probably won't see him perform because he's the swing."

"He's a funny guy, always making wisecracks at those catering jobs. Helen says he's feeling a lot better and putting his weight back on."

"That's a relief. I was getting worried about him." The silence takes center stage for a moment. We both know the dark cloud which has been cast over our community. Anybody who looks even remotely sick becomes the next possible victim of this plague.

I'm not sure I even want to get into all the turmoil of my nightmare again. I need to get off this topic. "Speaking of shows, have your parents come out to see you dance?"

"Not yet. I'm waiting to be in something really good. I'm determined to show them how great dance is out here. How about you? Have your parents made a trip out?"

"No, they haven't made it out either. My dad keeps asking when I'm going to get on Broadway. That's his idea of making it in the theater."

"But it sounds like you were doing pretty well until Timothy got sick."

"I was, but there's quite a history with my dad. He's a bit of a ham himself. When I was still living at home, he would tell me to enjoy the spotlight, but don't try to make a living at it. I have some issues with him. It didn't help that I was under his roof for so long."

"What about college? Did you get a break from all that then?"

"I lived at home while I went to college. That's when I came out. Just coming to terms with that was a big deal. It seemed to impact everything. No one in my family understood it."

"Sounds like a learning curve was needed."

"That would be an understatement. They couldn't understand how much things had changed for me."

"That must have been frustrating."

"It sure was. Not only did they not get how I could be gay, but having a career in theater was just so foreign to them."

"I guess it was like speaking a different language."

"Right! So, we all got together for a dinner to celebrate my twenty first birthday. I'm sure you'd agree that's a big one."

"Yes, you're officially an adult."

"I was in my final year as a theater major in college. I told them I was moving to New York after I graduated. That's when Dad told me he thought I wasn't good enough to make it in the theater. Can you fucking believe that? *Happy Birthday, Matthew. You don't measure up to your dreams* was what I heard inside."

"I'm so sorry."

"I was in shock. What a fucking asshole. Of all the disagreements we had, I certainly didn't have a comeback for that one."

"What could you say?"

"I think everyone at the table was pretty embarrassed so we just ate my birthday cake in silence. I should have walked out right then. I did eventually scrape together enough money to move out for the rest of my senior year."

"And then you moved to New York after that?"

"Yeah, I moved here after graduation. I've worked hard to make it here, but his words still clutch at me."

"I guess you probably agree that some things make you stronger."

"Yeah, and every time I'd hit a wall in this business, I'd remember his words. Then in my mind I'd say back to him: Fuck you, Dad. Just watch me. Watch me make a living in show business. Watch me get in a Broadway show. Watch me fulfill my dreams in spite of you, and in a weird way, because of you."

"So it's a motivation to keep going. I applaud you for that."

"Thanks. No matter how much I love them, dealing with family will always be a work in progress. How about some dessert?"

"The Apple Mountain Cake is amazing here."

"Works for me. Do you want to share a piece? I'm pretty stuffed already."

"That sounds great."

We get our waiter's attention, and he takes our order while clearing the table. "You know, Christopher, it's been so nice sharing this meal with you. I feel like I need to tell you that."

"I've really enjoyed it too."

"Since Timothy passed, I've had to get used to a lot of solo meals."

"I eat alone a lot too, but I've never actually had a long-term relationship. I'm guessing you're still missing Timothy quite a bit."

"Yes, today was particularly emotional with the ACT UP protest. Maybe if we were fighting this hard back when people first started getting sick, Timothy might have had a better chance at getting some drug. It was just bad timing."

"I'm sure he was very much with you in spirit today and would have been really proud of you for showing up."

Then Christopher does something that really blows me away. He calls the waiter over and asks for three forks to accompany the dessert, which has just arrived. I almost feel like I'm watching a ceremonial dance as he places each fork elegantly down on the table, surrounding the plate on three sides. I'm speechless as the tears begin to form in my eyes, looking from the plate to him.

"I thought Timothy might want to join us, Matt, for this victory dessert."

Without even thinking, I reach across the table and grab his hand. "Thank you. This is so sweet." More silence as the tears drip down my face. I break it and let go of his hand as I try to laugh a little and wipe my eyes. "Timothy did really love his desserts."

"Well, I'm glad we can accommodate him. Isn't this cake great?"

"Yes, it's so hearty and rustic, just like this place."

I can't remember having a nicer lunch in a very long time. But of course, the goodbyes are always awkward at this stage in the game. We stand outside the restaurant and realize our paths are now going in different directions.

"I'll check in with Charlie about when the best time to see the show would be," I say.

"Yes, and I'll do the same with Helen in class tomorrow."

"This place is awesome. Maybe you'll convert me to vegetarianism!"

"It's one of the Buddhist precepts, but let's take it one meal at a time."

I'm thinking that means a yes for another date. "I'd like that." What now? Do I make a move? Oh, fuck it. I grab his hand again and take a step closer.

"How about a hug?" He says. "Californians think they have some kind of proprietary rights on hugging, but we Oregonians like them too."

"That sounds perfect." I close in around him. We can feel each other's hesitancy. But I take a couple of breaths and just let it be what it is. Another starting point to a heart connection. I sense the side of his face so close to mine, feeling his gentle warm breath on my cheek.

Does he feel sparks like I do? There's a chemistry here that I can't ignore, nor do I want to. We pull apart and lock eyes again. I feel my heart pounding, and all of my senses are heightened but I don't give in to them. "We'll talk soon then."

"Yes, enjoy the rest of your day," he says. With one more parting glance, he turns and heads east down 10th Street.

Eight

I'm beginning to rethink this brunch. Why do I put myself in these situations? I don't think I've ever hosted anything like this by myself. Here's hoping I can pull it off. Timothy was so great about the pretty factor when it came to entertaining. I seem to have missed that part of the gay gene. I just want it to be really nice.

A quick trip up to 80th Street and Broadway secured me a vegetarian quiche from Zabar's. You can't go wrong with their bagels and cream cheese either. I made a little side salad with fresh produce from The Fairway, another Broadway shopping staple at 74th Street. I do love picking up groceries in my neighborhood. There's just this special character to the Upper West Side. Lots of different cultural backgrounds. I particularly enjoy seeing all the Jewish families. It's like I'm seeing the history of a New York culture unfold before my eyes. It also means lots of great Jewish delis that I've happily come to depend on.

Lots of show people live in this neighborhood too, including plenty of dancers heading up to various studios along Broadway—Steps Dance being the premier studio for jazz dance, and right next to the Fairway. Timothy was often there for class and one-stop shopping afterward.

Hopefully, this brunch will be a fun way to see Christopher again with some of our mutual friends. He doesn't know Charlie that well, but he and Helen see each other all the time. I think this Sunday's matinee will make the perfect date. It's only been five days since our lunch last Tuesday, but I'm trying to keep the momentum going. We can have an early brunch and then hop in the van that takes all the actors out to Milburn for the show. Helen has some pull with the transportation, being the dance captain. She made sure there were a couple of seats available for us. We just have to get down to Manhattan Plaza. Then we'll all go out together.

I buzz the front door for my first arrival and double-check to make sure everything is in place. From the sounds on the stairs, it's at least two of them. "Charlie! Helen! Did you come together as a date?"

"Absolutely," Charlie says. "We're pretty much joined at the hip these days anyway. Ain't that right, lovely lady?"

"Charlie's right. We're constantly working on steps and spacing, in case someone has to miss a show."

"Lucky for me that hasn't happened," Charlie says, "so I just sit around the dressing room watchin' all the hot chorus boys playing Indians in skimpy loin cloths. And I'm even gettin' paid for it."

"Sounds like it's right up your alley." It's a relief to see him looking so much better. He really has put some weight back on in the past couple of weeks.

"Thanks so much for having us over," Helen says as she heads over to the shelves with all the photos. "Would you look at these pictures of Timothy and me from *Hello, Dolly!*? He was the best dance partner I've ever had."

"He used to say the same thing about you. Can you believe it's been almost five years since we did that show?"

"How about a drink?" Charlie asks.

"Charlie, you shouldn't!" Helen is the voice of reason. And she's right, even if he's not going on.

"Oh, all right. Will you get her? No one else gets away with telling me what to do."

"Maybe it's because she's so sweet, but at the same time doesn't pull any punches."

"Which reminds me," Helen says, "I just told my latest squeeze to take a hike. Can you believe he refused to show up here today because he thought he might catch AIDS from one of you? I told him to never speak to me again."

"That's what I'm tellin' you, Matt. This lady is one tough chorine."

"It's a shame there's so much fear and prejudice about this disease," she says. "I'm ashamed I even went out with him."

"Oh, there's the buzzer. It must be Christopher."

Charlie and Helen each grab a glass of orange juice as I go to the door. This is the first time Christopher will be coming into my home, the home I shared with Timothy. A million moments of my life with Tim flash before my eyes as I hear Christopher coming up the stairs. I guess this is part of the process of letting go.

"Hi, Christopher. Come on in." I step aside and usher him through the doorway. How bad am I that I can't help but notice how his pants cling to his backside? Get a grip Matt, you have guests.

"Hello everyone. Am I late? I seem to be the last one to arrive."

He couldn't look more adorable. "No, not at all," I say. "I guess no introductions are needed."

"Hey you two," Christopher says, with a relaxed sincerity that feels like his signature energy.

"Hi, sweetie. Don't you look cute!" Helen seems to be everyone's doting mother today.

"I figured you guys were worth dressing up for."

"How about a glass of juice?" I ask. "Helen and Charlie are going virgin, but I have some vodka."

"No thanks. I don't drink much. I don't want to fall asleep on the ride out to New Jersey."

"Oh the ride's not too long. This theater is just slightly out-of-town," Helen says.

Everyone settles down on the sofa and chairs, and a conversation gets going about the origins of the Paper Mill Playhouse. It actually was a papermaking factory way back in the day. Now it's a thriving Regional Theater. I'm busy making sure all the food is in place, and at the same time, I feel a sense of gratitude for having such wonderful friends. I can't remember the last time this apartment had such warmth and laughter. It's so incredible how everyone is connecting. Kind of like a new family is forming. Am I starting to get my life back? This apartment still has so much of Timothy in it. I need to be okay with that and just include it in what's happening now.

"All this chatter is making me hungry," I say. "Let's eat, everyone. Grab a plate and serve yourself. Casual dining is a must in this house."

"It all looks wonderful, Matt. Thanks for making it all vegetarian," says Christopher.

"Not at all. After that delicious lunch, I got inspired."

"As long as you don't give up your taste for a certain kinda sausage," says Charlie, "I'll give you a pass."

"Oh stop it, Charlie," says Helen, "and concentrate on what's on your plate."

"Yes mama. See, there she goes again!"

"Well, somebody needs to teach you some manners."

"Watch it, or I'll start callin' you Miss Manners," he says.

"As long as you listen to mama and be a good boy, you can call me whatever you like."

"That reminds me of a funny story about Timothy," Charlie says. "Matt, you weren't in our dressing room so you missed a lot of it. But the chorus boys' dressing room was a riot. Timothy was always cuttin' up. He'd pretend to be Rose Louise from *Gypsy* and start cakin' on more makeup than a Kabuki. Then start talking to his mama about being pretty."

"*Gypsy* was one of his favorite shows," I say. "It kind of parallels how gay people are so misunderstood when we're young. And then we come out and we find ourselves."

"Yeah," Charlie says, as he piles food on his plate. "Then he'd switch gears and go into a song and dance of 'I Feel Pretty!'. The boys would all flock around him and join in."

"You guys always had all the fun. We girls couldn't begin to compete with all that campiness."

"It's just part of our DNA," says Charlie with an authority that speaks of the many miles on the show biz road.

"I do beg to differ here," Christopher chimes in, speaking in more moderate tones. "I know a lot of modern dancers who are gay and are actually pretty introverted."

"I can vouch for that," Helen says. "I step into the elevator at 890 Broadway, and all the show people are talking a mile a minute. At the Westbeth elevator for the Cunningham studio it's completely silent."

"Well, I stand corrected," says Charlie. "But I do maintain that a tight ass in a dance belt has a universal appeal, no matter what art form it takes."

"I'll drink to that!" I say without considering how Christopher might react. I don't want him to think I'm some lecherous queen. I'm relieved to look over at him and just find his beatific smile with those luscious full lips of his. He so often seems in a blissful state. Maybe the vodka's kicking in. Oh, right, he didn't have any. I could get used to having his energy around more often. I shoot a glance up, thinking Hobo might be hovering about. I'm sure she'd approve, but she's nowhere to be seen.

"That reminds me," Charlie says, "be sure to keep an eye out during the Wild Horse Ceremonial Dance today. The Indian Braves have really skimpy loin cloths, so every time our hunky warriors start dancing, the flaps fly straight up, showin' their bare asses and their dance belt in front."

"Shocking!" I say. "I'll have to cover Christopher's eyes. He's just not used to our wicked ways. I don't want to tarnish him at his tender age."

"I'll have you know I've crossed over the threshold of twenty-five years, and I do know my way around a dance belt or two," Christopher replies.

I love that Christopher is such a good sport at playing along with our teasing games. Score another one for him. Maybe it's part of his blending theory. Whatever it is, I appreciate it.

"Helen," Christopher continues, "I thought you were inviting your new beau here today. What happened to him?"

"It's more about what's not happening to him. Like having anything to do with me for instance. That jerk thinks he can get AIDS off of these plates and glasses so he was afraid to show up here today."

"Oh, that's really a shame," Christopher says. "There's so much fear surrounding this disease. I get it. All we can do is try to educate people."

"Yeah, you're right," I say. "That's why ACT UP has come up with a new slogan, and they're plastering the posters all over town. It's a striking image. A black background with a pink triangle. Inside the triangle are the words: 'Silence' and 'Death' with an equal sign in between. 'Silence equals Death' pretty much says it all when you think about what's happening right now."

"I saw some of those posters just the other day," says Helen. "They really do make you stop and think."

"Well, we're not going to be silent anymore," I say, "because it's killing us. We're just people, like everyone else, and somehow everyone needs to understand and respect that."

"Can we change the subject guys?" Charlie asks. "I don't want to spoil this feast with all this depressing talk. Outta sight, outta mind is my motto. If I start thinkin' about it too much, I'll lose my mind."

"Okay Scarlett, we'll let you off the hook and you can think about it tomorrow," I say.

"Good. Tomorrow's my day off so you can forget about it happenin' then either."

I don't think I'll ever convince Charlie to face this epidemic. Christopher, of course, seems to take it all in stride and continues stressing how we have to have compassion and empathy for how people are dealing with this. But there's something missing in these speeches. I'm not feeling like it's really all coming from him. More from the teachings he's into. I'm sure he believes it all, but there's a vulnerability about him that makes me wonder how comfortable he is with these stressful times. He's still a bit of an enigma to me. I want to learn more about what's really going on inside of him.

Regardless, the rest of the meal goes well, and he insists on helping me with the dishes while Charlie and Helen relax with all my old photo albums of past shows before we leave for our musical afternoon. They've obviously grown even closer doing this show together. I'm happy to see it.

Nine

Our little troupe has now made it to 43rd Street and 9th Avenue with plenty of time to catch the van to New Jersey. This spot is home to so many actors and performing artists; no wonder it's the pick-up point today. With this many people filing in and out of the revolving door of the corner tower, you'd think we were back in the business district downtown.

Two high-rises that were established as government-subsidized rentals in the '70s bookend this block. That's when the Times Square area was dominated by a seedy collection of peep shows and triple-X-rated movie houses, both gay and straight, right alongside the Broadway theaters, talent agencies, and restaurants. The idea was that giving this community affordable housing would help boost the vitality of the neighborhood, and it worked. Many more businesses were established to support everyone, and slowly the area got cleaned up.

I look up with envy at one of the two forty-six-story red-brick buildings that dominate this entire block. Now seventy percent of these apartments are designated for performing arts workers. Not just actors but writers, directors, costume and lighting designers, dancers, and people in the film industry. There are like sixteen hundred of them.

"Where are we? This place is like Grand Central Station," Christopher says as we come to the street corner.

"This is Manhattan Plaza," I say, pointing out the second building at the other end of the block as well. "It's a subsidized complex for artists."

"Wow, they have a true performing arts community here. How much do you have to pay to live here?" Christopher asks.

"Well it ain't free," Charlie adds, "But they give you a pretty good deal. You have to pay a quarter of your monthly income for rent, no matter what you make."

"It's a great aid in this feast or famine business," Helen chimes in.

"So, you pay a decent amount for rent when you're on Broadway and next to nothin' if you're on unemployment," Charlie continues. "Or nothin' at all if you're not makin' a dime."

"Where do I sign up?" Christopher asks.

"The waiting list is so long. Getting an apartment will take years at this point," I answer. "I've always made do with my little apartment in the brownstone. At least it's rent controlled."

"Yeah, I like having my own place too," Charlie says. "I don't want the government nosin' in on how I live."

I love my street and neighborhood," I say. "But talk about the sense of security living here. I certainly wouldn't turn it down these days."

"I can't imagine anyone would," Helen says. "It's also become a godsend for anyone who lives here and has become sick. You don't have to leave because you can't afford your rent."

"That hadn't even occurred to me," I say. "There are so many that have become ill now in our business."

"I hear they've even created an organization called 'Neighbors Helping Neighbors'," Helen says. "That's what I call true community."

The van arrives, and we start to see the other actors gathering to get in. It feels a bit strange to get on board the vehicle with all these people in the show, but Helen takes charge and introduces us to everyone. I'm surprised I don't know anyone. Maybe this is a whole new crop of kids, snatching up the jobs that I used to get. Talk about feeling out of it. Once again, I'm not a member of the club. The "gainfully-employed" club, that is.

I take Christopher's cue and keep quiet. It's the first time I've sat so close to him. We're pretty crammed in our seat, with Helen and me on the ends and Christopher in the middle. I feel his shoulders connecting to mine and inch my knee over to touch his. Suddenly Hobo comes to mind, and I have to chuckle to myself. Timothy should be here giving me a lesson in inching closer and closer like he did with Hobo.

The traffic is a nightmare as usual, but it's slowly inching along towards the Lincoln Tunnel. There are only so many ways on and off this island, and the Lincoln Tunnel is one of the main arteries. Anyone not living on Manhattan Island is designated as the "bridge and tunnel" crowd. We New Yorkers, of course, avoid them at all costs. No wonder we're all so caught up in ourselves.

After what seems like an eternity, we finally make it down to the two lanes the tunnel offers. This underground pathway was completed in 1934, and it certainly looks its age. Luckily, Charlie is distracting us by entertaining everyone with his usual bantering, and a few of the others are joining in.

Slowly we continue down into the underpass tunnel. It's hard for me to believe the Hudson River is actually above us, but somebody obviously figured out how to make it work.

Okay, now we're down to just a crawl, as we inch along toward the mid-way point of the tunnel. I'm always fascinated with the lights on the walls and the raised path along it for emergencies. Then we come to a complete stop.

"What do you think is going on?" Helen asks as she looks at her watch.

"Relax Missy, we still have plenty of time to make it to the theater before the half-hour call before the curtain rises," says Charlie.

"I need a lot more time than that to set my hair and make-up," Helen says, "not to mention warming up. We've never been stuck here before."

"I'm sure we'll start moving in a minute or two," I say as the horns start to sporadically blast.

"At least we're warm in here," adds another cast member.

"It actually feels very warm to me," says Christopher. "Would you mind turning down the heat a bit?"

"Please don't change the heat," another chorine pipes up. "I'm going to have a hard enough time warming up for this show."

We're still at a dead stop after a long ten minutes, with the horns now honking nonstop. I can sense that Christopher is growing anxious. He's unzipped his jacket.

"Are you okay?" I'm beginning to be a little concerned that his breathing is quickening.

"Christopher, what's wrong?" Helen asks with a look of worry coming over her, too.

"I'm just not good in tight spaces," he pants out. "Why aren't we moving? I'm actually having a hard time with my breathing. Can we open a window?"

"Absolutely not," says the disgruntled driver. "The fumes in this tunnel are terrible."

Christopher is getting more and more agitated. "Can't we do anything?" He pleads. "We need to get out of here. I can't get my breath."

"Okay," Helen says. "Matt, make room so Christopher can put his head down on my lap. Christopher, you're fine. Just lie down and close your eyes. Good. Now start taking some deep breaths through your nose. Good. Nice and slow. Matt, look in my dance bag. I have a towel in there, he's sweating bullets. Good, Christopher, just like in yoga class. Nice, long, slow, deep breaths."

I don't even realize it, but I look down and find I'm holding his hand as he lies below me with his legs over my lap. Despite his discomfort, he looks like an angel to me. I want to hold him close to comfort him more, but that's probably the last thing he needs if he's feeling claustrophobic. After a few minutes, he seems to be relaxing, and suddenly, we're moving again. Thank God.

"You're feeling better now, right?" Helen asks as she continues to dab his face.

"Yes, much better. I can breathe again."

"Maybe you should lie down for a bit longer," she says.

"No, I really feel fine now," he says as he sits upright again. "I'm so sorry everyone. I just have a thing with tight spaces sometimes. This horrible feeling of being trapped comes over me."

"No problem!" Charlie says. "I'll take that over feelin' trapped with a lousy lover anytime." Everybody gets a good laugh with that one. Leave it to Charlie to bring a little levity to the situation.

The van continues moving, and everyone is pretty quiet for the rest of the ride. They all have a show to think about, but I'm wondering about Christopher. What happened to that calm he always emanates? I can't imagine it was all an act. He usually seems so sincere and easygoing, even self-confident in the choices he's making with his dance career. What about all this meditation and Eastern philosophy he keeps referring to? I never feel it's anything but genuine and heartfelt when he's talking about it. And I'm sure he believes what he's saying. There's this sense that he has a profound connection to his spirituality. And he tries very hard to make that a part of his daily life. Maybe that's it. Maybe he's trying too hard.

Thankfully, there are no more delays as we pull into the parking lot of the playhouse. The original paper mill from 1795 is obviously long gone, including the windmill. Now the building's traditional red brick façade is complimented by plenty of white trim, including shutters and doors. The A-frame entrance kind of reminds me of a big barn. This twelve-hundred-seat playhouse seems a world away from Broadway but has a real inviting, rural Northeastern feel to it. No wonder it's so popular in this area.

Not being in the show makes me feel like a "civilian." It highlights that I'm no longer in the service of "The Theater." I can't help feeling sad and left out about it. I'll be going in the front door with all the other civilians instead of the stage door. I miss being one of the gang, being in a company of players. Everyone comes together in a show. The show and the people in it give you an identity, which you share with the entire cast and crew. It really is a special feeling.

"Well it looks like we have plenty of time before the half-hour call," says Helen, with a renewed focus on preparing for the show.

We all have our preshow rituals, but I have a feeling Missy has a set of exercises that are pretty extensive. You don't have a body like that unless you keep working at it. "Helen, any ideas of where Christopher and I can go until the lobby opens?"

"Oh, I hadn't thought about that. Why don't you two go hang out in the Green Room for a while. Nobody ever uses it until after the performance. Come with me, I'll show you where it is."

I guess I get to go through the stage door after all. Even though I've never worked here at the Paper Mill Playhouse, it still feels like home in a strange way. All theaters do. *Annie Get Your Gun* is a big splashy musical with plenty of cast members, so everyone is running around in warm-ups, the girls with their hair in curlers and with more make-up on than most ladies of the oldest profession in the world would wear. The stage manager is checking lighting cues, and the set and props are getting organized. Dancers are warming up on stage with their Walkmans, and I can hear vocal warm-up exercises going on in the stairwells. I miss it.

Helen ushers us into the Green Room, which is just a bunch of empty sofas and chairs waiting to be filled with admirers after the curtain comes down.

"This sofa looks pretty comfy. We should be fine here until it gets closer to show time," I say, wondering how this is going to go with nothing else to distract us. I'm still unsure of what to expect when I'm with him.

"Well, here we are," Christopher says. "Alone at last again. Just kidding, but it is nice to have some time for just us."

"I couldn't agree more." Just us—that feels like he's talking about our new relationship. That's new behavior... and no, I'm not going there with more Hobo stories. "There's so much going on backstage, this feels like a quiet oasis."

"I'm a big advocate of silence. It's amazing how noisy the city can be. It took me quite a while to get used to it when I first moved here."

"I didn't have that big of an adjustment, being from Chicagoland."

"I did. There's so much more stimulation here, it's been a work in progress trying to get used to it."

Christopher's sensitivity to everything was pretty obvious when I met him. I find it endearing, but I never thought it would be an issue for him. "Even after two years?" I ask.

"Yes. And I'm still a bit embarrassed about what happened in the tunnel today. That felt like a panic attack on steroids."

"It sure surprised me."

"I never had them until I moved here, and they're not usually that severe. Mostly they feel like an energy rush."

"Like when you get that first rush after taking more hits on a joint than you should?"

"It's actually a very similar feeling. Sometimes, I don't know if it's just anxiety or more like a heightened consciousness. It's frightening but exhilarating."

"Kind of like a rollercoaster?"

"Exactly, and it can come over me at any time. Everything just becomes more immediate and my senses go on alert. I usually feel flushed and my heart begins to flutter."

I think about how my heart has been fluttering more when I'm around him, but it's clearly not the same at all. I feel an urge to draw him close to me again, to bring him down to earth a bit. "But you're okay now, right?"

"Oh absolutely. You know, yoga and meditation help quite a bit. For me, it's like a spiritual energy. When I resist it, that's when I get into trouble, like today."

"How can you fight against something like that?"

"You have to relax into it more and just accept it. I've actually gone through periods in the last couple of years where I've felt slightly stoned continually for weeks at a time."

"It sounds like fun, but I guess that would feel weird after a while."

"I've been even wondering if vegetarianism might have something to do with it. You feel lighter when you don't eat meat."

"I didn't know vegetarianism could do that."

"It's just a theory. Your body doesn't have to use as much energy to digest simple foods, so it shows up in a different way."

"That makes sense."

"So, I try to work with the heightened feelings by doing yoga. I can focus and move the energy to different parts of my body with breath awareness."

"I'll confess this sounds a bit over my head," I say, "I'm not sure how to even talk about it."

"That's just it. It's like a new kind of language happens when the body and mind become one. I learned that from all the years of dance training too."

"You mean like focusing feelings in your body?"

"That's right. But there's a flip side to it. Sometimes I just start to feel spacey and I completely lose my focus."

"Sounds a little freaky."

"I have to confess, that's part of why I've enjoyed spending time with a more solid guy like you. Being around you feels like it balances me out in some ways."

"Is that a compliment or a backhanded way of telling me I'm pretty clueless about all this spirituality stuff?"

"See what I mean? You just did it. You broke the spell and made me smile with your sense of humor. Sometimes I just carry all this way too far out in space."

I can't resist taking his hand again. "Well, if it's my earthbound energy you like, I'm happy to provide it."

"In all seriousness, Matt," he says, squeezing my hand a little harder, "I don't know where this is going. It's been a long time since I've shared so much about myself with anyone. I'm pretty sure the same is true for you."

"Yes, it is."

"I know this goes against the gay manifesto of jumping into bed and finding out who you wake up with after the fact, but I'm just not wired that way."

I never expected this Green Room conversation to go anywhere near this direction. He is so sweet and sincere. "I get that. Not to worry, I obviously have my own struggles with moving forward. But I am enjoying getting to know you as a friend, and that's a good start for both of us," I say, wondering if I even believe myself. I want more of him now, damn it. Talk about casting a spell, it's happening. He looks more beautiful than I've ever seen him.

"Being your friend would mean a lot to me," Christopher says, taking my other hand now.

"Well I think we should consider that done," I say, pulling him up as we both stand together. "How about another one of those Oregonian hugs?"

"Works for me." As we embrace, I just know those sparks are igniting for both of us now. Maybe our next step to a romance is coming sooner than I thought...

"I'm sure we can take our seats for the show now," I say as we separate. "Let's head out to the lobby."

I feel the urge to hold his hand again on our way out. Too soon for that, but listening to him open up makes me want to get even closer to him. I want him to know that he can feel safe with me. Just like I was a part of Hobo's safety net, I want to be there for Christopher too. Another lesson learned from that cat and she didn't even have to show up for it.

We almost bump into Charlie as we leave the room. "Hey, you guys. I don't know what you two have been doin', but the show's startin' soon so you better take your seats."

"Yes sir," I jokingly say. We're heading back out to the lobby right now."

Helen has managed some house seats for us, which will be a real treat. There's nothing like watching a show when your seats are right in the center and the perfect distance from the front.

It's been too long since I've taken in a show, and my stomach starts to flutter as the lights go down. It's so exciting to feel the anticipation. Everyone in the audience is focused on this moment. The overture begins, and we're transported into the magic of live theater.

It's almost as if the orchestra is teasing us with all these great tunes as we listen to the overture. We know the musical numbers will soon come to life with all the actors on the grand stage. First, the audience gets this little taste, stirring in us a desire for more and often jogging nostalgic memories of songs we know and love. And then our wish is granted. The curtain rises, and the sassy and splashy Wild West Show kicks into high gear.

The show ends up being lots of fun, and fully realized in so many of the ways I was hoping to see and hear. I'm not even feeling like I'm missing out by not being in it. There's really no major part in it for me.

This musical is a prime example of why I don't want to just be a singer in the chorus. I watch the supporting cast playing cowboys and then later switching to Indians. But they just get placed around the stage like they're part of the scenery. They're only backdrops for the leads, regardless of whether they're singing at the time or not. At least the dancers have something to do. They get to showcase their skill, and yes, in this case, their bottoms as well. It was a bit distracting, but I'm not complaining.

I even catch some of the members of the chorus not focusing on the scene and doing things to distract each other. That's a classic case of what we call in the business: "phoning it in." Because they're not the main focus, some of these chorus people get bored and don't give one hundred percent, doing a lackluster job of singing and dancing. Matinees are notorious for this happening if you know what you're looking for. Believe me, I plan to be a tattletale and make sure Helen knows about it. Iron Lady is likely to trample that behavior before the next curtain rises.

We're all pretty quiet on the ride back to the city, having already spent plenty of time backstage congratulating everyone and joking around some more. I'm pretty wiped out, and I wasn't even in the show. The van lets us all out and, once again, we all go our separate ways with hugs all around.

Christopher is the last person I hug, but there's too much going on with everyone surrounding us for it to be more than just a quickie. It's strange how it leaves me feeling like I'm wanting more. I haven't gotten used to that yet.

Ten

I find myself staring at the phone a lot. It's been over two weeks, and I still haven't heard anything about the audition at 890. It's now Monday and still nothing. I've been checking my machine all morning and...oh my God, there's the phone. The number's not on my caller ID, but I'm just not capable of answering it. I feel paralyzed. I'm going to sit here until it stops ringing. I hold my breath for the message.

"This message is for Matthew McKinney. We're calling to let you know you've been called back for the production of *Our New Normal*. The callback will be on April 24th at nine a.m. at the Belasco Theater at 111 West 44th Street. Please call Casting Inc. at 212-555-7181 to confirm you got this message, and to get more specific information about what we'd like to see from you for the audition."

"Holy shit, I got the callback! I can't fucking believe it! Out of all those guys they're considering me!"

I don't care if it is just chorus. I really want this show! I wonder what they're talking about with specifics. Usually, if it's for the chorus, you just go and sing again. I simply can't contain myself with this news. "This is amazing!" I shout. "I just want to dance around the room and shout it from the rooftops. I got a callback! I got a callback for a Broadway show!"

"I hate to disappoint you, but I don't make much of a dance partner these days." I hear Hobo say.

I spot her crowning the top of the fridge. "There's nothing that could even begin to disappoint me right now," I say.

"Glad to hear it, Daddy Boy."

"I'm actually filled with gratitude Pussyface. You've been a lifeline these past months."

"You're quite welcome."

"I don't know how I would have gotten through all this without you... even if you don't really exist! I'm still glad you're here."

"How could I leave my Matt Cat in his time of need? And what do you mean I don't really exist? Speaking of which, I think I'll dematerialize my dear. I'm sure you have a few people you'd like to call with the news."

"You're right. I've got to tell someone!" I barely finish my exclamation before she disappears again. What an unreal world I'm living in these days. This news seems unreal too. I can hardly believe it.

I hope telling a few people I got called back doesn't jinx it. A part of me just wants to keep it to myself so I don't have anyone else anticipating the final decision of whether I get in or not. I have no idea how many guys they called back or how many they even need for this. Maybe they'll give me a better idea when I get back to the casting office.

Okay, I'm going to try Charlie first. "Hey it's Matt. Pick up, Charlie. Are you there? Pick up."

"Hey man. You know, I can count on one hand the amount of people I actually answer this phone for."

"Well, I'm honored. This is your day off right? How's it going?"

"I'm actually pretty bored... Man, if only the St Mark's Baths was still open. Christ, was that ever convenient. Right around the corner. Know any backrooms that are open during the day?"

"Sorry, can't help you there. Hey, I have some news. I got the callback for *Our New Normal*."

"Way to go man! When is it?"

"April 24th at the Belasco Theater."

"Ah, the classic Belasco Theater. That's where the original Broadway production of *Oh! Calcutta!* started."

"And that's relevant because..."

"So, will your show be done in the nude? I'll reserve my tickets right now if that's the case."

"I seriously doubt it, Charlie."

"Any fishnet stockings and stiletto heels?"

"What is with you today?"

"You know another show that opened there which pretty much bombed, was *The Rocky Horror Show*."

"I had no idea."

"Yeah, and if your show opens at the Belasco, I hope it does a whole lot better than the measly forty-five performances that one lasted."

"I loved the movie. Wonder why it didn't work on Broadway?"

"They obviously didn't cast that blonde hunk that played Rocky in the movie."

"Yeah, that must have been it."

"Enough talk about blonde boy toys. I'll get plenty of that in my *Pizza Boy, He Delivers* video."

"Boy, you really are on a tear today."

"On second thought, maybe I'll actually call in an order. Gay for pay, delivery guaranteed."

"Sounds like you have an interesting afternoon planned."

"Man, how did you ever get me so distracted? I'm really stoked for you. I know it's been forever since you got back into the game. Getting a callback for somethin' like this is a big deal."

"Thanks, Charlie. I'm not sure it's really sunk in yet. I just got the news."

"Have you told Helen?"

"She's my next call."

"Well, give the Divine Diva my love. I'll be seein' her all too soon at work."

"Enjoy the rest of your day off. Bye."

"Cheers man."

Boy, that guy certainly has a one-track mind. But I'm hoping it's mostly just an act. I have no idea how careful he's being in that department. Some guys think they're invincible, which is suicide these days. I hope he's being safe if he's fooling around that much.

For me, it's just been easier to be celibate. There are so many unknowns, and I'm in no hurry considering what I've been through. Luckily, Christopher doesn't seem to be either. Maybe he's been talking about me with Helen this past week. Let's see if she answers when I call. I wonder what info I can get out of her. "Hi Helen, it's Matt."

"Hello? Oh, hi Matt."

"Wow, you actually answered! I'm two for two today."

"What?"

"Charlie picked up when I called him, too."

"Oh, I always pick up. What if a handsome suitor is calling me? You know, Mama can't ignore a pretty face any more than you can. It's just a shame most of them are of your persuasion."

"I can't help you there. But I can assure you, your prince is bound to come soon. And I'm not going to be vulgar and be any more literal than that."

"Of course you're not. A good Irish Catholic boy like you?"

"Yeah, I got paper stuck in my mouth more than once from those stern sisters. It seems I was a talker."

"Why am I not surprised."

"I don't know why the Catholic church thought that nuns would make good teachers. They were clueless about how to handle children."

"Luckily for me, I went to public school. I actually enjoyed it. But it was the dance classes that really got me through. That was my true religion."

"Should we start singing some celebratory hymns? I just found out I got called back for *Our New Normal*. Can you believe it?"

"That is so fantastic, Matt! Congratulations!"

"Thanks, I'm going to be a nervous wreck, but I'm pretty thrilled about it too."

"You're a very talented guy. And I don't see any reason why the part shouldn't be yours."

"Well it's just chorus, so I'm not thinking it's a particular part. They did say there are some specifics about the callback."

"What are they?"

"I actually don't know. I haven't called them back yet."

"Well, don't wait too long. They're going to want to make sure you're still available."

"We both know I've been more than available, for just about any reason to get my life jump started again."

"Think about it, Matt. It's only recently you've opened yourself up to all this. You put yourself out there, and look what's happening. Your professional life is back on track, even if there are no guarantees on getting this job. And a certain dancer I know seems to think the world of you, too."

"Really? Okay, spill it. I know he's been talking to you about me. Is he just gushing with praise?"

"Christopher isn't exactly a live wire when it comes to expressing himself."

"Yeah, he's sort of understated in his demeanor."

"In some ways he's a lot like you though, like a caterpillar insulating himself in his self contained chrysalis."

"I guess that's one way of describing it."

"I will tell you that since he met you, he seems to be climbing out of it. I wouldn't say he's completely free and, frankly, I don't think you are either."

"I feel like I'm at least at the breaking out of my cocoon stage, especially after today's news."

"Matt, I can't remember the last time I've heard you so excited about anything. It just warms my heart. Why don't you give Christopher a call and tell him your news? I saw him in class this morning, and he said he was going back to his apartment afterward, so he's very likely to be there."

"You know, I think I will do just that. Maybe we can meet up for lunch. It's time to spread our wings."

"You do that. And congrats! Bye now."

"Bye sweetie, you're a treasure."

Christopher is my next call, and I'm three for three. Connection achieved. Engage. Blast off! I'm so thrilled by this callback, I'll just hop on a cloud to take me down to West 10th Street back to our favorite lunch spot. I wonder what organic creation we'll have this time.

It's so nice of him to offer to take me out to lunch to celebrate. The more he lets me into his inner world, the more it intrigues me to get to know him even better. I've never met anyone like him, so I'm never quite sure where I'm stepping. He's like a field of fresh clover. If I tread lightly enough, go slowly, and pay attention, maybe I'll have the luck of the Irish and find that rare sprout with a four-leaf configuration.

It seems the luck of the Irish isn't holding well as far as the weather goes. A chilly rain is falling, but a little April shower isn't going to dampen my day. That's the thing about this city. Not too many people in Manhattan can get in the car, which is conveniently parked in their garage, and just drive somewhere. You have to get out in these elements. No matter how hard they blast at you.

So, with a decent raincoat, sturdy boots, and an umbrella, I brave the shower. It's actually refreshing to smell the rain-soaked air. Everything seems to glisten as the droplets bounce off the pavement. And it's really not that far a walk to 72nd and Central Park West. Yes, the C train pulls right up after my descent down into the bowels of the subway. With raindrops thoroughly shaken from my umbrella, I get on board. My luck is still with me. I snag an express A train at 59th and avoid a few extra stops on my way down.

After the train drops me back in Greenwich Village, I realize that I've developed quite an appetite… I get off at West 4th Street. Now I just need to avoid all these puddles and walk up several more blocks. The rain seems to have gotten worse. My pants are getting soaked, and the rest of me feels like a wet mess as I head back up 6th Avenue and take a left on 10th. Deluge be damned. I've made it. Whole Wheat 'n Wild Berrys feels so warm and inviting as I step inside. I can't wait to peel off my drenched coat, but there's nothing I can do about my pants. Maybe the heat I've been feeling for my sweet and sexy boy crush will do the trick. And there he is. Even at the same table. I'm warming up already.

"We've got to stop meeting like this," I say when I make it back to where he's sitting. "People will talk."

"Yes, maybe we'll end up on Page 6 of *The Post*."

"Christopher, I wouldn't peg you for a *Post* reader," I counter, as I throw off my raincoat and take a seat, ditching my umbrella. "You seem more the *Village Voice* type."

"You're right there. I can't get enough of Debra Jowitt. She writes really perceptive dance reviews for the downtown scene."

"Maybe I'll check her out next time I get it."

"Anna Kisselgoff at *The New York Times* is worth a look too. She dissects the intricacies of the late Balanchine and the like."

"Remember our conversation about speaking another language?"

"Am I doing it again? I'm sorry, I can get very carried away sometimes. Did Timothy discuss dance and reviews with you much?"

"Not really. He was more into just being a performer. Dancing in shows was his passion, but he did love the choreography of Bob Fosse. He never got to work with him, but he got cast in some of the old revivals of his shows."

"I guess that doesn't include *Singin' in the Rain*. Are you really soaked?"

"Nothing a warm meal won't fix." It's nice to just bask in the glow of whatever this is. I've stopped trying to figure it out. Maybe this is a lesson in going with the flow, so to speak. "How about some soup?"

"Sure, they make a great homemade veggie minestrone here. Their avocado and melted cheese sandwich would go perfectly with that."

"Let's order," I say, taking command of signaling the waiter. I'm still just so energized by what's happened today. "I know it's pouring outside, but for me, a huge raincloud has lifted away from these last couple of years. I actually have something to look forward to."

"I'm really happy for you, Matt. Have you found out about the specifics?"

"No, I haven't called them back yet. I'll do it this afternoon."

With our food ordered, we settle into some easy chatting as we wait for it to arrive. I seem to lose track of time with him. It just flies by. He's even more distracting than Hobo. In a good way. He must have gotten caught in the rain, too. His hair looks a little damp, doing its own casual dance, tossing about his head. With those flushed cheekbones balancing out his wideset Bambi eyes, I'm having a hard time not leaning in for a first kiss. I'm sure it will happen, and I can just imagine it as he rattles on about the new dance piece he's been asked to be a part of.

Bambi Eyes, maybe that will be my new nickname for him. It might be fun to make up affectionate names for each other. Probably not at that stage yet, but I'm sensing a new dynamic we share now. I look at him and get this strong sense of *us*. Like we have a bond that's ours alone. How did that happen? I'm so elated, it's time to try it on for size now. "You know, just looking at you is bringing up some strong emotions for me. I've come to realize that the time we've been spending together has created something new for both of us."

"Yes, I've been feeling that too. It's nice to hear it from you. Oh, here's our meal. Wow, it all smells and looks so delicious."

We both get distracted by the food and dig in like we haven't eaten in days. And just like that, the conversation takes on the same comfort level as all this comfort food we're consuming.

"There's enough food here to feed an army," I say between mouthfuls. "That reminds me of some happy memories of Sunday dinners at home with my grandparents included."

"It must have been nice having such a big family."

My mom was the Midwestern queen of casseroles. She and my grandmother would make this family favorite dish together called Hamburger Heaven. All that beef with noodles was perfect for all us hungry growing boys."

"By the time I was a teenager, my Mom's cooking bible had become *The Vegetarian Epicure*."

"Why am I not surprised?"

"I think she cooked just about every menu in it. Her favorite was a baked bean casserole with hot scallion cornbread."

"That actually sounds so good I'd forget it was vegetarian."

"I guess we have quite a clash of family cultures. Our backgrounds couldn't be more different, but the love of getting together for meals is universal."

We both share more stories of our families but leave out the drama this time. Eating together has been a basic part of our social fabric of family bonding all our lives, and now we're establishing a pattern of doing it together.

The afternoon lingers on, as does our conversation long after we've finished eating. It's been the perfect way to celebrate my news. I'm so content to be here. I've shared another meal with what I'm beginning to realize is an endearing and supersensitive guy. What a dreamboat he's turned out to be. We even have a favorite hang-out now.

Am I getting too far ahead of myself? I need to take a hard look at how lonely I've been. Am I trying to make up for lost time? What would Hobo say? Probably something about being okay with exploring my options. Just staying in the moment. It doesn't have to be anything more than it is right now.

"Matt, you seem so far away all of sudden," Christopher says.

"Oh, I just zoned out for a minute. I'm really stuffed now. That was so good."

"You sure you don't want some dessert? They have a pretty sinful peanut butter ice cream pie."

"You know, I'm really full. Maybe we can try that next time."

"Sure, this has been really nice," he says as he gestures to the waiter for our check.

"That soup was the ticket. I can't think of a better way to have spent a rainy afternoon."

"Me neither," he says as he pays the bill. "Do I sense a song coming on?"

And we both launch into "Soup and sandwich, soup and sandwich…"

With a laugh, I can't resist saying, "Keep your day job. Just kidding! You have a nice voice."

"Thanks, but I'm no professional like you. I'll stick with the dancing."

"And I'll just keep singing your praises. But seriously, back to what I said earlier, something is happening with us."

"Yes, we've become an 'us' now. It's wonderful. And it's very new for me. I haven't had a serious relationship like you have."

"It's not like being in a relationship is something you get good at because you've had a few of them."

"No, that's not what I mean. I just don't have a frame of reference for it. With me, there is a real mixture of emotions happening, really more like a twister."

I feel like telling him that it's okay, Dorothy, the house will drop back down, and you'll be in full technicolor if you're ready for it. "What did you say was your mantra? 'No resistance,' right?"

"Yes, and I've been resisting telling you something for a while now, but I think this is the right time."

"Sure, what is it?" The universe seems to pause.

"I've tested positive for HIV. I just thought you should know that."

I take a breath. I can't believe I'm hearing this. It's like some kind of surreal deja-vu. How am I supposed to react to this? All the pain of dealing with Timothy's long, drawn-out sickness and death comes crashing back to me. What the fuck am I supposed to say? I've got to pull it together and not give away the despair that's devouring me right now. That all-too-familiar feeling of emptiness is back. I begin to form words in response, but are they real?

I hear myself saying: "Thank you for telling me Christopher. I'm really glad you did." I can't imagine what he's reading on my face, as I experience all the blood drain away. "I'm touched you'd share something so personal."

"I just felt it was time."

"I honestly think it's a step toward making our bond even stronger."

"Thank you. That's very sweet of you to say that."

"Of course."

"I try not to look too far into the future, but hearing your words allows me to still see you there in some way. Believe me, I'm well aware of your personal journey down this road. Now you see why I've been so hesitant and slow to move forward."

"Yes, it all makes sense now. It was pretty obvious that my past was holding me back, but I wasn't sure what was going on with you."

"I guess all this discipline with how I live a healthy life makes a lot more sense to you now too."

"Yes, and I really do respect you for it."

"Thanks. Strangely enough, there's a flip side to it too. I'm cautious about my health, but I also have to come to terms with the fact that I may not live a very long life. It makes the time I do have that much more precious."

"I understand completely."

"I've come to realize, this is it. Do exactly what feeds your soul with this life you have now, because it could be gone in an instant. I can be safe with my health, but I can't afford to make safe choices about my career. I have to give it everything I've got now, because now is all I have."

"Now is all any of us really have," I say. "Hey, I think I learned that from you."

"I'm glad to have had some influence. You've made a difference in my life these days too. I can honestly say it's gotten better knowing you."

"Thanks, and thank you for lunch. I know we got together to celebrate my callback, but let's also celebrate a kind of deepening of us today. What do you say?"

"I say that's a beautiful way of expressing it. I'm filled with gratitude."

"Me too..." We both handled this with care. I did *believe* everything I was telling him as I responded to his news, but I was separated from my words as well, like I was witnessing them being spoken. It was almost as if it was someone else talking. I'm not sure which person is really here right now. I have some processing to do. "Are you ready to brave the elements?"

"Yes, it looks like we've been given a little break from the rain anyway."

We stand in front of the restaurant, again face to face. The rest of the drizzling world disappears again as I look into his eyes. We search into each other. Then we both surrender into the unknown as I open my arms wide and step in for another hug. Neither one of us lets go for another timeless moment. I feel my eyes tearing up with emotion. More of my armor is dropping away from me, and I don't want to totally lose it, so I pull away and inch back. Once again, our faces meet. We both share in this new vulnerability, and hold our gaze in a reflection of our deeper selves. We kiss. It's gentle and so softly sweet. Our eyes meet again as we release, only to let go of the moment as we separate.

"Is that an Oregonian tradition too?" I say with all the lightness I can muster.

"No, I think that one has a more universal following."

"There you go again with that universe stuff. I thought I was supposed to be pulling you back down to earth."

"You have no idea, Matthew. You have no idea."

"Stay dry, Christopher. Take care."

"I always do. Goodbye, Matt."

"Bye." He goes east. I go west. Another New York story as we head in opposite directions down West 10th Street.

Eleven

"Matthew, my dear, are you taking some kind of feline inspired hermitic hiatus? I'm the one who's supposed to be sleeping all day."

"What? Oh... you again. Really? So now you've decided to be my alarm clock?" My drowsy eyes slowly crack open and adjust to horizontal rays of sunlight, streaming through the blinds of my bedroom window. Looking across the room, I see Hobo lounging on the dresser. The sunlight is shining on her with parallel lines of shadow and light, framing her in a graphic illumination. She's provocatively posed, lying on her side with one leg straight up in the air. It's a quintessential feline position in which cats clean their nether regions, and she's doing a very thorough job.

"It's Sunday," I say. "Do I really need to see that right now? I haven't even had my first cup of coffee."

"Get over it Daddy Boy. I had to come up with something shameless to wake you up."

"Well, you succeeded. Besides, I should be allowed to sleep all day if I want. Not like it feels much different than most days lately."

"What do you mean? You got your callback call last Monday, and you've been working on your song all week. Don't you feel ready?"

"I guess. I still have two more weeks to go, but with nothing going on, one day drags into the next."

"Yes, I've definitely observed a bit of malaise in your demeanor this past week. We can't have a Daddy Boy in the doldrums going into this audition."

"I'm sure I'll snap out of it," I say, climbing out of bed and heading to the kitchen. "Maybe a jolt of Café Bustelo will perk me up."

"I have a notion there's something else you haven't come to terms with."

I give her the silent treatment for a change as I pop a sesame seed bagel in the toaster oven. I have to admit this whole week has been about doing some real soul-searching. Maybe a schmear on my bagel with some much-needed caffeine will snap me out of it.

"If you let it fester too long, you'll just end up retching it up like a big old fur ball," she says, magically reappearing on the mantel.

"Will you stop already?" I land back on the couch in the living room and throw my feet up, determined to get some comfort out of this breakfast. "I'm trying to eat in peace, okay?"

"No, it's not okay. Your world has been turned upside down with the news that Christopher is positive and you haven't been able to recover any balance since."

I just glare at her while I eat my bagel. Fuck! Can't I just have a normal life? Can't I just enjoy my breakfast and coffee like a normal person who isn't facing this fucking plague head-on again? Do I have to go through the hell of sickness and death all over again?

"Matthew, sweetheart," Hobo says, with a purring tone. "Even if you won't talk to me, remember I can still hear your thoughts. You're allowed to have them, but I also think you're allowing fear to get the better of you."

"You're right," I say. "I want to be so supportive for him, but all this has really thrown me."

"That's not the least bit surprising."

"What I went through with Timothy keeps coming back to me. I think about what may lie ahead for Christopher, and I have all these flashbacks of the suffering I had to witness. I just don't know if I have it in me to go through that again."

"This internal struggle is very valid. Ultimately, you're going to need to look deep inside yourself so you can follow your gut."

"What if my gut feels like it's in knots?"

"Just breathe more deeply into it. Your emotional center won't steer you wrong."

"It's pretty obvious that I like the guy. Besides being so beautiful and deeply sensitive, I feel like he needs my protection. I just want to wrap my arms around him and take care of him."

"Carrie Fisher says every successful relationship should have a gardener and a flower. It's pretty obvious which one you both are."

"Fine, but what about me? Am I honoring my own boundaries and taking care of me if I start getting involved with him?"

"Sometimes the simple act of taking care of someone else becomes the expression of taking care of yourself. It can affirm where your heart lies."

Damn, this cat comes up with some good ones. "I just can't decide what my next move should be in all this."

"There's no right or wrong decision. If it's too much to invest more of your life right now, you have to be okay with that."

"I guess you're right."

"If your feelings are strong enough, then you have to be willing to move forward. You're not on a schedule. You're not committed to anything. You obviously have grown to care about this person. You can honor that, but also honor yourself and your own boundaries."

"That makes sense," I say, her purring starting to make me feel calmer.

If I think about it, I need to understand that Christopher hasn't been through anything remotely like I have. The pain of losing a lover is life-changing. It's as if we both dwell in different landscapes. If this bond is right, the boundaries on both sides will slowly continue to expand outward toward one another. We're nowhere near touching yet. It feels like a long way to go before we become one land.

"Thanks for helping me put it into perspective, Hobo. I kissed him, you know."

"Goodness gracious, what a daring Daddy Boy you've turned into! Of course I know you two shared your first kiss. Mama Puss knows all. Haven't you figured that out yet?"

"Yeah, I had a feeling a little drizzle wasn't going to dampen your presence in our parting. Don't you have any other spectral duties to perform?"

"Oh, I've become quite the cool cat about town, hanging out with all manner of spirits...one in particular is quite theatrical, but more on that later."

"Now what are you cooking up?"

"All in good time my dear. In the meanwhile, I wouldn't miss my Matthew movie-time for anything. You're so good at melodrama, how can I resist?"

Why does she always have the final say? She's checked out again, leaving no trace. Good. I'm wondering now, about this theatrical spirit she referred to. I don't have time to think about all this because right now, I need to get moving. I actually have something fun to do today. Gabriel has elected to forgive my decision not to join him for the sit-in at our ACT UP protest and left a message that he wants to meet for an afternoon drink at The Townhouse.

We did the usual phone tag routine, so I finally just left a message saying I'd be there. I've never been to The Townhouse, but it's in his neighborhood on the East Side in the upper 50s. It's another beautiful crisp spring day, so I can walk across the park.

I'm relieved Christopher has been too busy to meet again because of rehearsals for a new concert he's in. Plus, he's picked up some shifts as a waiter at our favorite eatery. It always helps to get free meals where you work, especially for him, since the place is vegetarian.

Hobo's right. I'm not on a schedule. I don't have to jump into something I may not be ready for. I've got to trust my gut and realize that what is happening with Christopher will grow into whatever it should be. I can't be tripping over my past and letting it screw with my present. We'll find some way to work through this. I'm just not sure where I'm going with this idea of *us*.

I give myself time for a nice long swim at the Y. There are no new revelations as my arms and legs carve through the water. None needed. Just gliding on the surface gives me the feeling that I am moving forward with my life. Maybe going at a swimmer's pace is how I should approach all this. Racking up the laps over time puts me in that meditative state. Hopefully, I can coast in this zone for the next couple of weeks until I face my next challenge, which is the callback.

The big open shower room off the pool seems particularly active today. Some guys are paying more attention to lathering up certain areas than others. I have to admit I've just gotten used to it. That's been typical for a Sunday afternoon lately. With all the gay bathhouses closed, there seems to be a considerable uptick in the membership here. Of course, you'll get kicked out if you're caught fooling around, and I'll definitely avoid the steam room regardless.

Back on Central Park West, I look uptown at the classical and graceful line of historic apartment buildings on my left. The view has a certain romance to it. If all those building facades could talk, what tales of glamour they might spin. They have a sophisticated urbanity, evoking a bygone era. Too rich for my blood. But I can only imagine the incredible views of the park some of them have, watching the seasons come and go.

The stretch of trees on the east side of the street extend along the stone wall border of the park for as far as my eye can see. Finally, the trees are popping with little green buds, and some are even opening into tiny blossoms, rewarding me with the whispers of spring being born once again.

I take advantage of the 69th Street opening in the border wall. As far as I'm concerned, Central Park is my backyard, considering I live on this lovely tree-lined street that leads into it. I can't even imagine my life in this city without this vast patch of green, especially as the temperatures start to feel more livable and the park literally springs to life.

My walking trail takes me east as I cross over the bridle path. I rarely see anyone actually riding horses on it, but it's still pretty sweet to know that they do occasionally trot along this wide dirt path.

West Drive is closed to cars today, but I still take my life in my hands as I try to maneuver across all the runners, bikers, skateboarders, and roller skaters. It's such a magnificent spring day; the park is packed. So much for having my backyard to myself.

I spot the mineral springs just north of the path, where nineteenth-century New Yorkers used to "take to the waters," thinking it would cure them of all manner of ailments.

My cure, is my favorite view in all of New York City. I have arrived at Sheep's Meadow. Looking south, I never tire of seeing this fifteen-acre expanse of lawn, the perfect hangout for picnics and sunbathing in the summer. But it's the backdrop of Central Park South that feels almost surreal to my gaze.

My eyes start with the serene green of the grass which gives way to the rounded shapes in the trees that line its southern border. The high-rise towers seem to grow up out of the trees, all vying for the aerial space above This view always puts me in a reflective state. The contrasting buildings are like a futuristic alien colony of concrete and steel. Towering accomplishments of humanity, juxtaposed between earth's natural beauty below and the expanse of heavenly sky above.

After making it to the park's southeast corner, I head east on 58th and arrive at a set of dark polished wood doors with two large oval windows. The first thing I notice is the Townhouse logo on the doors and the rounded awning above. It sends a message of class and breeding, like one would find on a gentleman's monogrammed clothing and linens.

I enter through the doors, and a sense of calm immediately envelops me as I take in the well-appointed décor inside. It's like an old and established gentleman's club with plenty of lush burgundy and gold damask wallpaper, the backdrop for various antique-inspired paintings of polo riders. More damask designs are on the draperies framing the windows and entryways, heavily trimmed with plenty of tassels and fringe. The grand piano is without a player at the moment, as I scan the subtly lit room for Gabriel.

It's pretty quiet on this Sunday afternoon. Still too early for cocktail hour. Just a smattering of elderly gentlemen who, shall we say, are nursing their beverage of choice, swilling the afternoon away. I hate to say it, but there you have it.

This crowd looks to be sugar daddy heaven for any young impressionable thing that might need a little helping hand with whatever he desires. I hope these guys read loud and clear that I'm not in the market for whatever American Express can offer. I make my way to the bar and order a drink.

Not a moment later, I hear, "Matthew, my dearest!" Gabriel is making his entrance into the bar with his usual flourish. "I was hoping to be the first to arrive so you would find me accessorized in all this interior finery."

"Hi, Gabriel. I must admit, this atmosphere does set off your luminous tones. How's that for a comeback?"

"You're learning my man-child," Gabriel says as he adjusts my shirt collar. "So, honey, how have you been?"

"I'm doing pretty well, actually." I scan his starched, white button-down shirt and break free of him, grabbing my drink. "I could use a job, but no real complaints otherwise. How about you? Have you recovered from getting arrested?"

"Oh yes, and I plan to place this fine behind in harm's way whenever the next protest gets organized."

"Good for you."

"And don't worry baby, you're forgiven for not sittin' your ass down with me. I was so caught up in the moment, I just went off on you. And I hope you'll forgive me, too."

"Of course."

"Sometimes this fierce bitch queen takes over, and boyfriend, you better steer clear, 'cause sparks will fly when this dark angel gets on her high horse."

"Absolutely. I want to be supportive, but I'm not into bondage."

"Aren't you the clever one? So, have you ever darkened these polished and preppy doors before?"

"No, never. I hardly ever find myself on the East Side, but maybe I'll come back sometime and belt out a few show tunes when they have the entertainment going."

"Oh, I'm sure you'd be a hit." Gabriel signals the bartender for a drink. "You're just the type of white bread boy that this place caters to and their clientele fawns all over."

"Yeah, this place is like sugar daddy heaven."

"I'll often come in and strike a tune myself. The patrons think they're witnessing Bobby Short at the Café Carlyle. You know we colored queens manage to worm our way in one way or another."

I'm not sure how to take that, as we grab our cocktails and head over to a table. Our community may have broken a considerable amount of barriers, but we still have a lot of work to do when it comes to the disparity of class and color. I'm wondering where he fits into all this. "So, you really come here often?"

"More often than you would think. My apartment is close by, so this is my neighborhood bar."

"Do you have friends who come here too?"

"I know what you're thinking. This doesn't really seem to be my demographic. I should be high tailin' my black ass to the Trilogy downtown, or maybe the Starlight Lounge in Brooklyn with all the other 'bloods.'"

"I didn't mean to assume."

"Then if I want to go out dancing, I join my people of color to sashay the night away on the dance floor of the Paradise Garage."

"Come on, Gabriel. You're taking this the wrong way."

"Oh, am I? And what *did* you mean, Matthew? Is it that my Oreo-colored exterior doesn't match my creamy white interior? That's been the *story of my life*, honey."

"Wow, I had no idea."

"When you grow up in Ivy League land, and Mummy and Daddy provide you with all the privileges that give you a false sense of entitlement, it's like a slap in the face when it comes to how this town can keep you down."

"I'm sorry. I've always thought of you fitting in anywhere. You know, you're funny as hell. You keep everyone entertained."

"That's just it, Matt. It's all an act. It's all for show. I play this game, but I'm always on the outside lookin' in. That's what I have to do to survive in the white world."

"I think the majority of gay people have that sense of otherness," I say, "but this adds another layer I quite frankly never gave a lot of thought to."

"That's because you're white, Matt. And lily white at that, with your sandy hair and blue eyes. I'm sure you have some sense about how it's opened doors for you."

"Yes, and this town and show business amplifies it even more."

"Show business is the main reason I wanted to see you today. I have some news. I got a callback for *Our New Normal*."

"That's fantastic Gabriel! I got a callback too!"

"Oh, Matt, I'm thrilled for you. I was thinking you didn't get one since I hadn't heard from you. This puts an interesting spin on everything."

"Yeah, I called them back for the specifics, and they said they want me to dress like a Wall Street executive. Wear a three-piece suit if I have one."

Gabriel doesn't respond and looks down at his drink, sticking his finger in and just swirling and swirling.

"What's wrong?" I ask, having no clue why he's shut down all of a sudden. He looks up at me, and downs the rest of his glass.

"Can you take a guess at how they want me to dress?"

I know better than to answer.

"Something that leaves my gender 'in question' is what they said. I'm supposed to be a drug-addicted transsexual prostitute. Can you fucking believe it? You know, one of those chicks with dicks that pick up quick tricks down by the pier."

I follow his lead and guzzle my drink as well. Coming up for air, I signal the waiter for another round. This afternoon hasn't gone quite the way I expected it to.

"I'm a highly educated college graduate living in an affluent neighborhood. Never mind that my folks are footing the bill. I shop in the best stores so I always look impeccable. And how does this casting director see me? At the bottom of the barrel. As a low-class pitiful tranny. I know it's not politically correct to say that, but this black-assed bitch is pissed!"

The bartender brings us our drinks as we both stew in these revelations. "I don't know what to say, Gabriel. There's such injustice in how our culture creates these double standards."

"You know me, Matt. I'm a fighter, and I need to stand up to this prejudice and make my voice be heard."

"All the more reason for you to embrace this role, Gabriel. Remember at the audition we were talking about minorities getting the short end of the stick when it comes to healthcare? You know what a real issue that is. If you get hired for this show, maybe you'll be the voice of the underprivileged. It may not be your personal dilemma, but it's a very real one."

"Since when did you become such a wise white boy? I know I'm letting my enormous ego get in the way here, but I'm not sure I can identify with what they're looking for me to portray."

"You can do anything you put your mind to."

"Child, I've honed my flamboyant bitch queen persona to a tee, but I'm still a guy and intend to stay that way. And by the way, my ego isn't the only thing that's enormous."

"Lord give me strength! You're going to have to hold me up if you intend to go on like that," I say, with both my hands flapping and pretending to collapse on the table.

That gives both of us the giggles and thankfully releases the tension of this conversation. "Seriously, Gabriel. You have such a strong spirit. Make it work to your advantage. Just think of the depths you could go, digging into a character like that even if you don't speak any lines. I think you need to just go for it."

"I can only imagine how my parents would respond if I get this. I might be losing my lease."

"I know you're joking. They're highly intelligent people. They'll get the underlying message."

"You're probably right," he says. "I didn't mean to take away from the good news that you're still in the running too."

"Thanks. Not sure what kind of character backstory I can come up with for Mr. Three-piece suit, but I'll give it my best shot."

Once we had exhausted all our theories of how our characters might be involved in this new show, we moved on to a topic constantly swimming circles around my mind these days, namely Christopher. I gave him my update on our new connection, even divulging our first kiss. Just getting out there at all in the dating scene is a big step for me, and it's nice to share it with a supportive friend. It certainly wasn't my place to discuss Christopher's health issues. Gabriel doesn't even know him.

I ignored the part of me that's got my gut all twisted up. It's hard to imagine that the only one I can talk to about this situation is a feline apparition of something I don't even know really exists. Best not to think about it too much. I have no idea who Christopher has shared his status with. Maybe he's told Helen.

The rest of the afternoon continued on a decidedly more pleasant note, with numerous regulars stopping over to make small talk with us. Gabriel is obviously a fixture here, even though he begs to differ about whether he fits in. He is in his element in a way that I never really could be, nor would want to be. I might look like I should be the poster boy for this place, but regardless of what he refers to as his "Oreo exterior," this is his crowd, not mine.

Twelve

Today is callback day. Hearing the prerequisite "Break a Leg" from Charlie and Helen yesterday was much appreciated. It's good to know I have friends who really care about me. Christopher called too. I got a "Merde" from him. It means shit in French, but that's the term dancers use since breaking a leg seems a little too close to home. I'll take whatever encouragement I can get.

Hobo is another story. She insisted that I get here at the crack of dawn. How did I ever let that wacky cat talk me into this? It's way too early in the morning to get any sense of the usual noisy clamor of Times Square. Soon there will be chaotic masses of people and taxi cabs, all weaving through each other like multiple schools of fish, crowded into the same giant bowl. The lights of Broadway aren't of much use in these slanting angles of the morning's hue. The sidewalks are mostly deserted except for a few homeless people, and the vendors are beginning to prepare for another day on "The Great White Way."

This truly is a big one for me. Will I remember April 24th, 1987, as the day that changed my professional destiny? Or will I just allow it to vanish—another ray of hope dashed and destroyed by the inevitable rejection that may result inside this theater today.

"Daddy Boy, you do know how to lay it on thick! Would you prefer I accompany your breathtaking inner monologue with the tragic tones of a lone violin? Unfortunately, 'Hey diddle diddle, the cat and the fiddle' was never my strong suit."

I spot Hobo draped over a ledge above the box office window. "Okay, Little Miss Mischievous. You talked me into showing up here, hours before this callback starts, for your big surprise, so what is it?"

"Patience, my thirsty thespian. You shall soon drink from the pool of sacred waters that this 'Temple of Drama' will offer you in abundance."

"What's that supposed to mean?"

I've been wide awake for more hours than I would care to admit, so instead of staring at the four walls of my apartment, I've opted to take the bait and show up in front of this stately brick and limestone trimmed structure. The Belasco Theater is truly a classic. If I wasn't so anxious about what this day could bring, I'd probably be enjoying it more.

"Take a gander at the grandeur of this Neo-Georgian façade, with its dental cornice and fluted pilasters," she says. "Doesn't it evoke the image of a Holy Shrine to the Theater Gods?"

"What's gotten into you today? Who have you been talking to? Timothy?"

"Well, that would be my big surprise, Daddy Boy. I've made special arrangements for you to meet a new acquaintance of mine, whom I'm certain you'll find of interest. We just have to enter the building and..."

"Wait, what? We can't go in here. That's trespassing! I'm not darkening these doors until they let us in for this audition."

"Funny you should mention the term 'darkening,'" she says as she hops down and strolls over to another door off to the side. "In times long gone, it was generally the people of darker complexions and the less advantaged classes that entered through this *particular* door, for a more distant view of the stage from the upper galleries. That way, the upper classes didn't have to rub elbows with them, and they were completely out of their privileged sight lines."

"You mean this door leads up to the nose-bleed section?"

"Yes, and the only way to enter or exit the upper balcony seating is through this singular portal. My, my... It just happens to be left ajar."

"I'm not going in there, Hobo. I don't want to get in trouble."

"Oh, come now. What about all those lectures you've been spewing about how gays are second-class citizens? This entryway has your name written all over it."

"Yeah, right. Discrimination rears its ugly head in infinite ways, but that doesn't mean I have to accept it."

"Think about it. Have I ever steered you wrong?" she says, with that all-knowing smirk.

She's got me there. I gaze at the crack of open space between the door and its frame and get the distinct feeling that I'm about to crack open a new reality. "Okay, just for a minute. I don't know why we have to go inside to meet your new pal. Still, if they communicate with you like I can, maybe they can give me some advice on how to corral you a little better into a kitty corner. I still wish you would just stay an indoor cat."

"Fat chance," she says as she saunters through the opening.

I reluctantly follow her lead and enter the dark interior space. There's just enough light from the dimmed sconces that continue up the long stairwell to guide me up the steps.

All of a sudden, the temperature drops, and it's freezing cold. I feel a distinct chill go up the back of my spine but continue up a second flight as the aroma of cigar smoke becomes apparent. When I reach the top, I find the entire theater almost completely black, as my eyes try to adjust to the one source of light on the stage below. This "Ghost Light" is a single incandescent bulb on a stand, placed center stage, barely illuminating the cavernous interior space, but ensuring that the theater never goes dark. It's almost as if it has its own spirit.

What the hell happened to Hobo? I don't see her anywhere as my eyes try to adjust to the murky interior. And then, from behind me...

"Do I have the pleasure of meeting a certain dashing young actor that I've heard so much about?"

I spin around with a start and see an older gentleman puffing on a cigar, with the smoke seeming to dance around him like it has a life of its own. He's standing three feet away from me in a clerical collar and wearing some version of a cassock. How did he even get there? "Hello, Sir. I'm Matthew McKinney," I say as I extend my hand.

"Of course you are, my dear boy. Your little feline friend described you to a tee. It's so very nice to make your acquaintance," he says, taking another puff. "I do hope that you'll not be too frightfully offended that I'm unable to shake your hand, but I'm afraid when you pass through the sacred veil of afterlife, physicality no longer becomes an option. But mark my words, the hereafter does have quite a few other perks."

Holy shit, another one! I can't fucking believe this... I thought maybe Hobo had decided to appear to another unsuspecting human. But no! This is another damn ghost! This is who she was talking about earlier. Stay calm Matt; he seems friendly. Hopefully, he's not reading my mind right now, or he'd realize that I'm about to lose it. *Really, Hobo? You*

dragged me into this theater to meet this antique priest or whatever he is...
"It's very nice to meet you too Reverend, uh..."

"Oh no, my dear boy. I haven't taken any vows, except for the covenant of excellence that I demand of all the theatrical endeavors that grace this grand stage. You may call me Mister B... I was often referred to as the Bishop of Broadway back in the day. Perhaps it was because of my reverential relationship to what I consider my true place of worship. My very own Belasco Theater. Named after yours truly, of course."

And with a grand sweeping gesture that would rival the likes of Isadora Duncan, he waves his arms, and suddenly, the entirety of this beautifully eccentric theater lights up in a lavish display.

I'm absolutely speechless. It's like some kind of ornate fantasy world of deep reds, accented with rich golds and greens. A purified microcosm of the Gaslight era, reflected in the rich jewel tone colors of stained-glass lights, each in an octagonal design and set in the beautifully carved coffered dark wood ceiling.

"Tiffany, my dear boy. I insisted on nothing less than Tiffany glass for all 22 of these ceiling fixtures," he says. "It's almost as if you're gazing up at a brilliant night sky. Seeing my Tiffany lights floating in space is like observing multi-colored planets. Be sure and take note of the Tiffany stained-glass capitals on the columns as well. I even had them add a bit of whimsy with those hanging bunches of glass grapes. Isn't it a bit of fun to have them dripping off of them?"

"Honestly, it's all a bit overwhelming, Sir. I've actually read up on some of your lighting innovations, like the changing light gels on the mechanical color wheels you introduced."

"My boy, I'm impressed. It's a comfort to know a fine young lad like yourself would understand that the discoveries of yesterday, indeed have a direct impact on today."

"Absolutely. You really pushed the envelope when it came to technical wizardry."

"When we opened *The Girl in the Golden West* on Broadway in 1905, the curtain rose to a spectacular sunset, which continued to change hues and lasted 5 minutes before the dialogue even started. That would be the advantage of writing, directing, and producing your own play. I could go on and on, but there were just too many to name."

"I guess I'm a little embarrassed to say I'm just here to get a spot in the chorus of a new show that's being developed."

"Now, now, my lad, you know the old saying…there are no small parts…well, you know the rest… just think big. I made quite a number of young actors into stars in my day. I believed in them and insisted that they believe in themselves."

"Yes, that's what our feline friend keeps telling me. Believe in yourself. I do know that I'm here for a reason today, and I have every intention of doing my absolute best."

"And I have no doubt that you will. As far as I'm concerned, there is no other theater on Broadway better designed to show off what I'm sure are your considerable talents."

He moves down to the edge of the balcony, leaving a trail of cigar smoke. "This theatrical space has a very shallow depth, designed to my specifications, for a more intimate effect on the audience. Back in the day, it was called the 'Little Theater Movement,' and it's obviously still in use today."

I find my sense of time beginning to shift as my ethereal mentor continues to hold me in his spell, regaling me with numerous stories spanning decades of past productions. Plenty of technical information is thrown in as he goes into great detail, describing the enormous fly space, how a particular set might move, the mechanics of the hydraulic systems he had installed, and the workings in the basement. He's particularly proud of the trap door on the stage, where a hydraulic lift can rise up on command. I had no idea of the level of sophisticated machinery. He clearly ran this entire theater like a complex but beautifully designed timepiece, constantly fine-tuning and polishing it to perfection.

"I'm not sure if this new production is actually slated to play in your theater, but I sincerely hope so," I say.

"Well, if it does, I must insist that you address me with a pleasant greeting every night when you enter this hallowed ground. I would find that particularly delightful, since we've now become acquainted. I detest rude actors who lack the manners of respect for past visionaries of the New York Stage."

"I have to get in the show first."

"Let's leave that to the Theater Gods, my fine young friend. And now I must depart, I'm afraid. I'd love to give you a more extensive tour, including my penthouse apartment in this very building, but regrettably, it has succumbed to considerable disrepair. In the meanwhile, look for me in the myriad of shifting reflections that I occupy amongst the shadows, in this, my true theatrical abode."

The theater goes to blackout, and he's gone. Only the smell of his cigar smoke and the ghost light remains on, as I once again give my eyes a chance to adjust to the darkness. This guy certainly has a taste for the dramatic. What an exit speech. Now I need to get out of here before anyone is the wiser. I carefully make my way back to the stairs and quickly descend. Hobo's still nowhere to be seen as I head out onto West 44th Street and look for a decent diner for some breakfast. Besides a meal, I need a little time to digest all this before I have to be back for the callback.

My return to the theater feels like I've entered an entirely different world compared to this morning. Young men of multiple ethnicities and shapes and sizes are hanging around chatting with each other, and I arrive just as the assistant opens the doors to the lobby and instructs everyone to wait in that area.

I scan this diverse group of about forty or so guys and try to get some idea of what I'm up against. Other than me, there are probably eight or nine yuppie types, so I'm thinking that's got to be my competitive demographic on display. There are about the same number of black guys too, mostly lithe and showing off varying degrees of skin. Some have even gone for a full-drag look. Everyone else seems to be sporting some suggestion of a variation on a gay clone—from the lumberjack, to the leather queen, to the club kid. I'm guessing 'the specifics' from casting were heard and obeyed.

"Y'all can just go on home now children," Gabriel announces as he dramatically pushes his way through the lobby doors, "because Miss Manish has arrived!"

Even though we're all pretty nervous and uncertain about each other, his surprisingly impressive entrance elicits quite a few generous chuckles, as he makes a beeline over to me.

"What do you think of my outfit, Mr. Button-down?"

I scan his sheer, gauzy blouse open to the navel and tied seductively at the waist. Add to that a pair of skin-tight leather pedal pushers. " I think it's brilliant, Gabriel."

"Isn't it just perfect how it shows off my tiny midriff and slender hips? I'm going for Judy in her skinny years."

"And those four-inch black stilettos look positively dangerous."

"How insightful of you Matthew, honey! I've already developed a backstory where I was forced to maim one of my johns after he beat me, by stomping right through his crotch with these high-heeled bitches."

"I'm glad to see that you've decided to embrace the character they're looking for."

"That would be partly thanks to you," Gabriel says, as he starts running his hands all over my shoulders and arms. "Don't you look to be the very hunky personification of a three-piece suit. Damn, you dress up just fine!"

"Thanks, it's my best suit."

"Matt, I have a brilliant idea. Maybe we could do an improv where you've snuck out from your Wall Street office and have come to sample my goods."

"Why don't we leave the instructions to the director? At least we know they're going to let us sing our entire song."

"Well, I should hope so. I've honed my considerable talents with a new song selection to show off my unique gender-bending persona."

"Don't keep me in suspense. What is it?"

"How does 'A Little More Mascara' from *La Cage* strike you? I think the lyrics are just too, too, fabu!"

"That sounds just about as perfect as you can get. You've really tweaked the idea that your gender is an open question."

"Yeah, baby, and I hope that director's eye starts with my spikey heels and wanders up these smooth leather lines of my yams leading to this big personality," he says as he displays his crotch with a thrust of his hips.

"Oh my Lord, Gabriel, could you keep that thing a little more tightly under wraps? You're going to frighten someone."

"Child, I just want to let them know that this queen has got it all. I can shake whatever version of a money-maker suits your fancy. I've decided I'm a high-dollar harlot."

"I have to hand it to you. You've certainly put a lot of thought into this. They didn't say anything about changing my song, so I'm doing 'Corner of the Sky' again."

"That's perfect! It's like you're a Wall Street exec, lookin' for that corner office in a high rise."

"That never even occurred to me. But it is a song about wanting to have it all. That will be my yuppie take on it."

They've started calling the guys in one by one. At least today, they're using our names. We're not just a number like the last time. One of the Black guys is the first to be led into the house as everyone else hangs around on folding chairs. Some of the guys who obviously know each other stay engaged in chatter, while quite a few others position their chairs on their own.

They call in a second Black guy, and it becomes apparent they're lumping specific types together for comparison. Gabriel seems unperturbed by this revelation and continues to rattle on about his character development. No one is in there too long, and suddenly we hear, "Gabriel LeBlanc."

"That's my name, and nailing this bad-ass bitch-of-a-part is my game."

"I know you're going to rock their world, Gabriel. Go get'em."

And off he goes, into that jewel box of a house. All of a sudden, I have no one to entertain me, so I find a place in the lobby and continue to stew in the anticipation we're all feeling. I try not to pay too much attention to what I know is my competition, but I just can't help myself in sizing them up. Do they look more like they work in an office downtown? Do they have some special quality in their voice that will make them the winning choice? I could go crazy with these questions.

Gabriel emerges from the lobby doors as the assistant announces the next name. I see a noticeable shift in his energy and hope his audition wasn't a disaster. "So, how did it go?"

"Well, it goes without saying that I was flawless," he says. "But let me tell you, child, this show ain't no comedy. Them bitches are serious as a heart attack in there, so just be ready to get grilled."

"What does that mean?"

"They practically wanted my whole life story. All these questions about what the plague meant to me, shit like that. So I fed them my story about getting arrested at the ACT UP protest. I think I scored big with that one."

"I'm sure you did," I say, wondering now if I might have had a better shot if I had gotten arrested myself. "How did your song go?"

"Honestly, I was very pleased with it. And I want to thank you again for encouraging me to go balls to the wall with all this. And let me just tell you, my sack is..."

"Please! Enough with the crotch talk, Gabriel. How do you expect me to concentrate for my audition with visions of your porn-worthy parts circulating in my head?"

"All right handsome. Guilty as charged. You know all this trash talk is just an act. Give me a slap when I get out of hand; otherwise, I don't know when to stop. But I do appreciate you. And now I gotta change out of these instruments of torture before my dogs start to yelp any louder."

Gabriel and I continue our banter while I wait out the rest of the morning. Soon they begin calling in the urban professional types. "Gabriel, I think I need some chill-out time before I go in."

"Absolutely, honey. Just close those baby blues for a minute or two," he says as he heads off toward the bathrooms.

Trying to keep a clear head is quite a challenge in this environment, but I manage. I take a deep breath when I hear my name being called out.

Back inside the theater, I pause as I look up at the Tiffany lights illuminating the space. I count ten men and women sitting in the front section of the orchestra as I'm led up onto the stage.

As I walk out, the theatrical phrase 'treading the boards' comes into my mind. All my senses seem to be magnified as each foot finds this hallowed ground, one step after the next. I'm actually standing on a Broadway stage. I'm actually about to sing an entire song on a Broadway stage.

Now facing out to the audience, I'm almost shocked at how close the raked orchestra seating section is to the stage. I remember the spirit of Belasco talking about it. No wonder they wanted to hold the audition here. It's like you're right in their faces. There's nowhere to hide.

"Hello, Matthew. I'm Laurence Cameron. I'll be directing *Our New Normal*. What are you singing for us today?"

"Corner in the Sky." I'm so overwhelmed by all this that I forget to give the pianist on stage my music. "Oh, I guess the accompanist could use this," I say, nervously laughing as I walk over and hand it to her.

"Why don't you tell us a little bit about yourself before you sing," Mr. Cameron says. "I'm particularly interested in your response to how the gay community is dealing with the AIDS epidemic."

After Gabriel's warning, I'm not surprised by this question. I hear the voice of Hobo in my head. "Open your heart. Your story of loss is worthy of being shared on this stage."

"Well, I guess I can start with telling you that the love of my life died of AIDS almost two years ago."

"I'm sorry to hear that."

"You ask about the community? He was my community. He was my family. The happiness and contentment that we shared together, something that we'd thought would last for a lifetime, was struck down by this deadly virus. We're all in the trenches of this now. So, I've come to think of the whole gay community as my family. We all need somebody, and we all need to feel like we're together in this, looking out for each other. Which also means standing up for each other."

"I couldn't agree with you more, Matthew," he says. "Thank you for sharing such a personal story. This play we're producing will be about a lot of personal stories. We want it to have a unique sensitivity that comes across even without any words or music, just by the actor's mere presence on stage. And that goes for the chorus, too. Now why don't you go ahead with your song?"

Speaking with the director actually calmed me down a little. I think I came across well. After feeling like I spoke from the heart, it was an easy segue into singing from the heart, too. It's anyone's guess now. After the standard thank you and a few more questions about my past roles, I'm told to wait in the lobby again.

Another hour goes by before everyone else has been seen. My stomach is in knots with even more waiting after that. Finally, the assistant comes out and calls out the names of the people they'd like to see inside again. I almost lose my bowels when I hear my name and Gabriel's called.

I look around the lobby now at all the guys gathering their things to leave. They are the names that were not called, more than half of our original group. It's a heartbreaking moment to watch. I don't know what walking back inside will bring, but they'll never know because it's over for them. All the preparation, all the hopes, gone.

The rest of us file in and are told to line up on the stage. Jesus, I feel like I'm in *A Chorus Line*, and I can't even dance. They separate us into three groups of four; each group includes the diverse looks they're going for. Then they start switching people around. Each new group of four gets scrutinized. We're all just standing there like pieces of meat, hoping not to be sliced.

After more huddling with the production team, a spent-looking Mr. Cameron says, "I want to thank each and every one of you for all that you offered of yourselves today. You're all extremely talented, and I'm sure any one of you would be a worthy addition to this production. Whether you're invited to join the cast of *Our New Normal* or not, you'll all be notified within the next two or three weeks after we finish with the casting of the principal characters. Thank you all once again."

Christ, more waiting. How am I going to get through these next few weeks? But I'm still in the game! I'm thrilled and freaked out and anxious and ecstatic all at the same time. It's like my life is no different from what it was yesterday, but the results of today could make a world of difference in the future tomorrows. Or maybe not.

Thirteen

How do people in Brooklyn even survive this miserable subway commute? And I'm only going as far as Park Slope. Honestly, I suppose I should be more grateful that Christopher got me this catering gig. He reverentially referred to it as a "ceremony of commitment," whatever that's supposed to mean. Maybe it's a lesbian thing. They seem to be in the vanguard these days when it comes to making a statement about tying some kind of real knot. I can't say I'm feeling the love at the moment. The only knot I'm feeling is in my stomach. I guess I'm just restless with all that's going on.

I'll be happy when I get above ground again and can enjoy the sunshine. And making some cash on this first Saturday in May won't be a bad thing either. Hear ye, hear ye—today, a pair of love-struck sapphic singles will be joined as two become one, speaking vows of their undying love, witnessed by friends and perhaps even some family. After which, all in attendance will feast on the finest of vegetarian cuisine catered by none other than Whole Wheat 'n Wild Berrys.

Christopher mentioned something about it being Ayurvedic. I only remember the word because I made him repeat it about five times. He said it had something to do with eating in a specified way to promote a more balanced body and serene consciousness. That's as far as I got with it. Luckily he couldn't see over the phone how I rolled my eyes at that one. Am I being a judgemental bitch? Yes. I'm just not sure I'm in the mood for all this mystical mumbo-jumbo today.

It's probably no surprise that the source of my crankiness is—drum roll—no word from the casting people yet. I wonder if Gabriel has heard anything. I made him swear to call me if he heard either way. One week and counting as I continue treading in the choppy waters of this ocean of emotion. Now I'm sounding like some kind of songwriter. But I have to keep up with my frantic dog paddling, waiting to see if I suddenly sink into my depths, or if a helping hand pulls me back to the dry land of theatrical employment.

Having my life stalled in this limbo hasn't helped much in the paying the bills department either, so I am grateful for the greenbacks. Maybe I'll even get some leftovers from this blessed feast to help "spiritually" balance out these mood swings. I was riding so high after the callback, but the doubts are beginning to creep in as the days drag on.

I wish they had at least told us how many people they're hiring for this Greek chorus, but it's possible that hasn't even been decided yet. It's a new show, so things can change. I keep having flashbacks of standing in those groups of four. They kept switching them. Will there be only four singers cast? Was I in the chosen group? I've got to let this go, at least for the weekend. No one will be calling now. Hopefully, next week we'll get some answers.

The subway car suddenly grinds to a halt. Now what? My fellow underground travelers and I find ourselves in a state of forced inertia. Feels like my life right now. All my physical senses tell me to move forward with Christopher, but I have to admit this HIV-positive thing is holding me back. This internal struggle I'm having is really working my nerves. The train seems to have given up after another attempt at some slow grinding and squeaking on the tracks. It's probably in desperate need of some lubrication.

I'm beginning to feel my own needs in that department, including some long-awaited friction to go with it. Those urges that were dormant for so long are back, and I'm wondering if acting on them is the right call. Damn it, I'm ready for something. I'm just not sure about going down that road with Christopher. Timing is everything. If we wait too long, the spark could fizzle out. If I go for it, the unknown is looming so large.

Miracle of miracles, the screeching and whining is back. At least we're moving again, and the train finally begins to rumble back to its standard speed. Hopefully, Christopher survived this ride today, since he seems to have issues with being stuck under these surrounding rivers. This time it's the East River, acting as a fluid barrier of separation between the two boroughs. I'm so rarely in Brooklyn, I actually have to pay attention to all these street locations until we land at my stop. Grand Army Plaza.

Finally, we've made it. The sunshine still reigns supreme as I head into this picturesque collection of nineteenth and early-twentieth-century buildings. Park Slope is a beautifully restored historic neighborhood of brownstones, especially as you get closer to Prospect Park. I'm heading to the Center Slope section, making my way to 4th Street, just a couple of blocks off the park. These inviting tree-lined streets, with plenty of wrought iron fences in front of the residences, add a distinct sense of sophistication to what is considered an open-minded community of families.

They'd better be, with all the lesbians cohabiting here, too. Christopher was all gaga with the idea that one of the women exchanging vows today is a yoga instructor, so I should be expecting a mind-expanding ceremony, whatever that means. I've got to pull myself out of this funk. What happened to that open mind I'm trying to develop? I don't know, but I think I left it back in Manhattan.

What I want to know is, who has the expanding bank account? These brownstones aren't exactly cheap. I can't even imagine what it would be like to own the entire thing. All that space with a little garden in the back would be an urban fantasy come true. Gay domestic heaven, even if the commute back to Manhattan is a pain.

I arrive at my destination and immediately notice little square flags in an assortment of bright colors hung on numerous lines and strung along the wrought iron railings and above the tastefully carved wooden door. Is that a sitar I hear playing inside as I ring the bell?

"Welcome, pilgrim," I hear as the door opens wide, revealing a tall, rather gaunt-looking middle-aged man with stringy long grey hair and dressed entirely in orange. His bright blue eyes are like saucers, beaming into me like he's canvassing my interior spaces. I'm a little thrown, but I hold my own as he continues. "You must be Matthew. Christopher's description matches my visualization of you perfectly. I'm Devarshee. Thank you for offering your services on this momentous day."

"Nice to meet you, Devarshee," I say as I enter a tastefully appointed living room of assorted antiques and a grand piano. The high-end traditional décor paints quite a juxtaposition with the groovy vibe of the guests mingling about. The party seems to have gotten started as I take in what mostly looks like a cast of characters from the musical *Hair*.

Speaking of which, there's quite a bit of it on display in both sexes, long and adorned with spring flowers to match their decidedly colorful outfits.

"Just deposit your shoes in this hall closet, and I'll show you where the kitchen is." He seems to glide across the room.

My shoes? I hope I don't have any holes in my socks, keeping that thought to myself.

"Matthew has arrived!" Devarshee announces, as I find Christopher's familiar face among what looks to be the rest of the catering crew. "I am certain he will be a beautiful addition to our celebration on this auspicious day." His hands come together like he's praying, as he makes his way back to the guests.

"Hi Matthew," Christopher says, "Welcome to Brooklyn. Did you ever guess it could be so bohemian?"

"Words escape me." He introduces me to a couple of other people in the crew, looking very cute in his striped drawstring pants—if only I could untie them. What is it with me? I'm just in pounce mode. His unaffected physicality has such a sexiness about it. I've got to get it together and focus on the job at hand, but I'm really not sure I can handle all this New Age stuff today. "You said to wear bright colors for this gig, but you forgot to mention to add a headband."

"Your hair's not long enough, or I would have. Here, make yourself useful and help me chop all these vegetables."

I satisfy myself by stealing a quick kiss as he hands me a bunch of carrots. "What's with that Devarshee guy? He's a real trip. And that orange ensemble, what's that about?"

"He's Tara's guru; she's the yoga instructor I told you about. He'll be officiating the ceremony. Orange is the most sacred color in the Hindu religion and is generally worn by its holy men. Wearing it symbolizes the quest for light."

"I doubt that he's gay, but light in the loafers sure does apply. Have you seen how he floats across the room like his bare feet are walking on water?"

"Yes, it almost looks like a dance."

"Speaking of which, you didn't tell me about no shoes. I might have worn some nicer socks."

"Oh, you'll probably want to take your socks off anyway. Most of us are just going barefoot. See?" He elegantly extends his leg up to his nose.

"Christopher, lifting your legs is a nice distraction, but you really should have prepared me a little for this. I didn't realize I was going to be working in an ashram."

"Oh, c'mon, you know that's not what this place is. This is Pat and Tara's home."

"Not a bad pad for a yoga instructor. Don't tell me Pat is one too."

"No, she's a corporate lawyer for a big firm downtown. She's not really into yoga, but she's very much into Tara."

Bingo. That explains the fancy digs. I did notice a few of the people in the living room that weren't as exotically dressed. They're probably in Pat's court. "So, which ones are the happy couple?"

"Here," he says, "take this tray of crudités out to the living room, and I'll show you."

He leads me out, and we position the tray, busying ourselves with rearranging the table as he gestures to a tall, willowy young woman all aglow with her sweet smile. She wins the prize for the most flowers woven into her hair, cascading halfway down her white peasant blouse. A lacy white skirt completes her ensemble. I'm guessing that must be the yoga instructor giving off a chic, hippie chick vibe, as her arms and hands elegantly animate the conversation she's having with a couple of other guests.

"She really is lovely, Christopher. That's got to be Tara. My goodness, she's really working that flower child fashion, isn't she?"

"I think she looks wonderful. I'd even say radiant."

"So, do we call her the bride or what? It's not like they're actually getting married."

"What difference does it make? They're creating a spiritual union. They even have Devarshee presiding over their joining. His name means 'a god-like saint.'"

"Whatever. I just question the whole notion of gay people imitating the straight culture's idea of marriage. For me, that's where the whole idea of freedom comes in—being free to choose who you love and free to define that—any way you want, and not be constricted by straight people's value systems."

"But that's what Tara and Pat are doing. Today they're celebrating their unique definition of a commitment. Just because this gathering has a yoga vibe doesn't make it any less serious or relevant."

"It just feels like we're at a wedding to me. Why is that necessary? Timothy and I were happily sharing our lives together without anything like this." Maybe I'm just missing Timothy today. That's why I'm in such a pissy mood.

"There's nothing legal about what's taking place today," he says. "But what if that becomes an option for us? All those protections and benefits would then be legal for us too. Wouldn't that be incredible?"

"I don't see that ever happening. Most straight people don't want to have anything to do with us. Especially now, with AIDS. Do you think they'd ever want to include us in their 'sanctity of marriage' tribe? I know my parents never would."

"Well, I'm sure mine would. I'm surprised at you. I'd been thinking you were more of a romantic."

"As far as I'm concerned, romance and marriage are two very different things, and I prefer the former." God, what is wrong with me? Maybe I'm just angry that Timothy and I never got to have all this. Would I want this with Christopher? "So where is Pat?"

"She's the short one on the other side of the room with the salt and pepper buzz cut and white blazer and slacks."

"I'm guessing we won't be calling her the bride," I say with a chuckle.

"Stop it. I got to chat with her earlier, and she was really very nice. Very business-like but obviously going with the flow of whatever Tara's vision of the celebration would be."

"Sounds like a match made in this mystical heaven, except their pearly gates out front are made of wrought iron. Say, what are all those colored little flags hanging all over the railings for?"

"Oh, those are Tibetan prayer flags. They increase the spiritual energy of the home. Come on, we'd better get back in the kitchen and finish up the food prep for after the ceremony."

I follow Christopher back into the kitchen and hold back the urge to swat his tush on the way in, no matter how sweet it looks. I've got to figure out a way of making more physical contact. Romance. I want some romance now, damn it. This whole thing is really pushing my buttons.

"Why don't you go see if anyone wants any refills on the champagne or sparkling water," Christopher says. "We're going to wait until after the ceremony to put the main food items out."

I grab a couple of bottles and start making the rounds. It's really not a very large gathering. Just about twenty-five or so people. Must be mostly friends since I don't see any old folks or children. I wonder if their families even know about it. Would they even want to witness something like this? Or is it just not discussed? My family couldn't relate to it at all. It's almost laughable to think about them being here, like they would have just landed in some strange alien culture, where the people and customs were some weird imitation of their own.

There are so many stories of gay people escaping their small-town lives to find more acceptance and freedom in the city. Nobody seems to care in this anonymous anomaly. You're just another one of the colorful threads that warp and weft themselves through this town. Many of us have issues with our relations, so we're forced to look for a life elsewhere. Our community becomes our family. I guess that's what they're trying to accomplish here.

I know my tribe, and this clearly isn't it, but it seems like it *is* Christopher's. He fits right in, in a way I never will. If I finally get together with him, will I end up like Pat? Just going along with it? One thing they say about weddings. It makes your emotions run high. Mine are all over the place right now. I'm cranky, I'm horny, I'm frustrated with my life. I've got to pull it together and get with the program.

I step out to the back garden and take in the groupings of chairs set up around a lovely white wooden arbor decorated with more prayer flags and flowers.

"Could we have asked the source of divinity itself for a more beautiful day?" Devarshee asks as he makes his way over to me for a refill and raises his empty glass.

"What would you like?"

"Matthew, was it? This jubilant day calls for a constant flow of the nectar of the gods. I'm never one to turn down a bit of sweet bubbly to float the afternoon away."

"Great. I'm not very versed in all this yoga stuff, so I wasn't sure."

"One of the attributes of yoga is to live in balance. If you go too far in any extreme, your energy systems are thrown off. Yoga works with balancing the mind and body—that's why the proper sources of food are as important as the asanas and meditation."

"And what about all these Tibetan prayer flags? What do they mean?"

"I'm getting the impression that you are a seeker, Matthew, despite your inexperience with these philosophies. Traditionally, prayer flags are here to promote peace, compassion, strength, and wisdom. The prayers are within them, and it is believed that they are blown by the wind to spread goodwill to the pervading space."

"Thanks for the lesson. I'd better keep making the rounds," I say. He bows and puts his hands together on each side of his glass. I guess it's a nice sentiment, but my Midwestern roots seem to pull me deeper into my tendency of just staying down to earth.

After another hour of pass-around service of hors d'oeuvres and drinks, the culmination of the afternoon—the blessed event—draws the colorful crowd out to the gardens. The happy couple takes their place, facing each other under the arbor, with Devarshee in the central position farther back.

Something Christopher tells me are brass "singing bowls," are all in a line on what looks like an altar, also under the arbor. Devarshee offers a Sanskrit prayer and then ceremoniously works a wooden instrument around the edges of the bowls of various sizes, stirring up the sound waves. I guess it's working for everyone else except me. I just find the ringing annoying. Add another emotion to my mood swings today.

Christopher and I hang in the back with the rest of the help while Devarshee continues his downward dog and pony show, guiding his limber long-haired disciple and her sturdy-but-willing companion through their vows. I guess you could say wedding bowls instead of wedding bells are ringing. Everyone seems really into it, especially Christopher. He even grabs my hand, and I'm thinking to myself: is this what it takes to get a physical connection out of him?

Once the ceremony is over, everyone seems happy with this version of nuptials. What do I know? I'm just a hired hand. The spread of food is a hit as well, not to mention a great carrot cake cut in the traditional marriage fashion by the newly joined couple.

I guess I've just participated in some version of my first gay wedding. Maybe these forward-thinking women are setting a trend. What's next? Announcing it in *The New York Times*?

Once the party is over and the clean-up is done, Christopher proceeds to teach me the proper yogic way to say goodbye: bowing my head with my palms together at my heart. "Nama-something-or-other" is supposed to be uttered. I just stick with goodbye. I couldn't be happier to make our way back to Grand Army Plaza as the sun is making its descent on—what did Devarshee call it? This auspicious day.

The underground Manhattan-bound platform is totally deserted when we get there. I don't know what comes over me, but I suddenly grab Christopher from the back and wrap my arms around him, locking him tight in an embrace. I can't hold myself back, so I playfully grind into his behind, fulfilling some version of my fantasies of the afternoon.

"Stop! Matthew, what are you doing?" he says, quickly pulling free of me.

"I thought I was being affectionate."

"Well, that didn't feel like affection to me. It felt like you were forcing yourself on me. Please don't do that."

"I'm sorry. I didn't realize touching you was so offensive."

"That wasn't touching, that was groping, and behavior like that actually makes me very defensive."

"So, what kind of behavior are you comfortable with? Just sweet kisses and holding hands? We're not in junior high anymore, Christopher."

"I'm well aware of that, but as far as I'm concerned, that was crossing into territory I haven't offered to you."

"What are you waiting for? A blessing from Devarshee? Because I have needs, too, and they're pretty simple. I don't want a lot of pretense. How much longer is it going to be? I know you said you wanted to go slowly, but this is getting ridiculous."

"I just can't be attacked like that."

"I didn't attack you," I answer back with all the calmness I can muster. "It's not like I'm some anonymous trick you don't know. Don't you trust me?"

"That's just it. I do have trust issues. I had a bad experience, and behavior like that just freaks me out. I can't deal with those kinds of surprises."

"What's so surprising about it? You must realize I'm attracted to you, and I'm just trying to express that in a playful way."

"And you have to realize that my reaction to being forced into you does not feel the least bit playful. It feels more like a violation of my space. I won't let that happen to me again."

I've never seen him look so tense. Where is his usual carefree and relaxed persona? "Do you want to talk about it?"

"Actually, no. I don't. The last thing I want to do is get into all this down in this cement hole."

"How do you think that makes me feel? I've been wanting to touch you all day. I start having these feelings for you, and you shut me down and won't even give me a decent answer as to why."

"I did give you a reason. I just can't go into detail right now. It's too painful. You're going to have to trust me now on that one."

"Don't you think you could trust *me* a little more? Because I have to tell you, I'm feeling pretty lost right now. I feel like I've broken some kind of rule, and I don't even know what the rules are anymore."

The train arrives and puts an abrupt end to our conversation as we just stand there, looking at each other. There is nothing left for me to say anyway. Until he's ready to really talk about this, there is no point in continuing. We both just surrender to the bench inside the train, bodies side by side and facing out, putting up with the rocking and shaking, stopping and starting, from one subway stop to the next as the train seems to grind time itself into a black hole. Could this train ride be any longer?

It feels like we're two anonymous passengers, strangers with no connection to each other, but our thoughts are in some kind of mutual entropy with no sense of how to resolve it. Maybe I should get off with him when we get to his downtown stop, but something keeps me in my seat. He needs to make the next move. Not me. We say very cool but cordial goodbyes from a distance, as the yogic protocols of bowing with palms together flash through my mind. Nama... whatever. I'm over it.

Fourteen

I can't even remember the last time I took a disco nap. But here I am, lying in this lonely bed, looking up at the blank ceiling I've grown so accustomed to, wondering how the present keeps getting hit with the past. Maybe that's a good thing after last Saturday's subway exchange. I'm so full of mixed emotions from that day that I feel like a human blender. Maybe that confrontation is telling me to put my energies elsewhere. I've already got enough drama.

After these past two years of sinking into a quagmire of my emotions, a dam has burst and is pushing me beyond it. I'm ready to get more out of my life again. Maybe I'll meet someone tonight without all this baggage. Charlie is at the helm, and he's got it all planned out. I plan to hop aboard the disco buggy and go for a joy ride.

I spot Hobo coming into focus across the room. "Look who's finally making an appearance," I say. "You know, it's been a while, Hobo." I take in her familiar black-and-white image on the dresser with a bit of relief. I'd been so used to seeing her pop in and out, that I now admit to feeling a bit forlorn, even forsaken here without her. "I haven't seen you all week. After that disaster with Christopher last Saturday, I was hoping you might be open to lending a furry ear."

"Oh, you know me, I've been out cattin' about town. What do you want to talk about, the fact that you acted like a total idiot last Saturday?"

"Give me some slack, Pussyface. I was just trying to get a little more physical, and he freaked on me."

"You can't always let your impulses rule your actions. Next time you need to read his body language better and slow it down, which is what he keeps asking of you. Remember how much time and space you gave me?"

"I'm not sure there's even going to be a next time. I haven't heard from him all week, and I'm sure as hell not calling him first."

"You know," Hobo continues, as she curves and arches her back, looking like a classic Halloween cat, "it wasn't so much what you did, but how you reacted to what he said afterward."

"How would you know? You weren't even there."

"Oh please, how many times do I have to tell you, I'm always hovering around for the juicy stuff. You're like a soap opera I can't help but tune in to daily. Just because you're not aware of me doesn't mean I'm not prowling about."

"I just got so frustrated. I have feelings too, you know. And they were being completely ignored because of his issues. And then he didn't even want to talk about it."

"You can't blame him for not wanting to open up in the subway. It's not exactly a conducive environment for discussion. He's obviously being triggered by a painful experience in his past. If he doesn't feel like he's in a safe place, he's not going to talk about it."

"Why does it feel like pulling teeth to get us together? It shouldn't be this hard. And after thinking about it all week, I'm just going to take a break from his demons and have some fun tonight."

"Just don't get too impulsive. Mama Puss knows all, and The Saint can rock your world, or you can end up on the rocks if you're not careful."

"Okay, I'm not even going to ask how you know that's the club we're going to, but I'm meeting Charlie at his apartment at midnight, so I have to start getting ready. I'm just going to have some fun for a change, no drama."

"Are you insinuating that I'm a drama mama?"

"Go catch a show somewhere else. Find a new leading man. Why don't you flip on the TV and watch *Dynasty* or something? Oh, I forgot, you don't have opposable thumbs. I'm hopping in the shower."

Why am I not surprised that this subway car is full of what looks like a bunch of creatures of the dark hours? It's not exactly a freak show, but the fluorescent overhead light adds an eerie pallor to their faces, like they've been corrupted in some way, even before their wild night of adventures begins. We're approaching midnight, and the body language of this edgy crowd has a rakish feel to it. The club kids are out in force, daring the night to satisfy the twitchy energy that I'm seeing in this subway car. The evening is just beginning, and the prospect of what it will bring is palpable as the train rumbles down the tracks.

The anticipation adds even more to the frustration when the L train becomes sluggish for no reason. After more grinding and shaking, it finally lets me off at 3rd Avenue and 14th Street. Just a few more blocks of walking, and I arrive at Charlie's fifth-floor walk-up. The building looks like it's never seen better days. Just your standard ugly. But he says it's rent controlled, so that's livin' large regardless.

I try to ignore the place's peeling paint and overall grunginess as I ascend all five floors. At each level, the air seems to grow more and more stale, like the building has its own signature decaying scent.

"Charlie, I can't believe I'm so out of breath," I say, after he opens the three deadbolt locks plus the chain. "I need to push my swimming laps harder."

"I don't care how good of shape you're in," he says, "by the fifth floor, everybody is suckin' air. It's all for the good. Suction is the ideal warm-up for my special guests..."

"No comment," I say as I take in the distinctly '70s vibe of the apartment. I'm surprised he doesn't have a bunch of black lights on some vintage posters to go with the rest of the outdated décor, not to mention the musty smell of what has to be a decades-old carpet. Maybe I should get him to open a window. "Nice pad, man. Did Private Detective John Shaft live in this apartment before you took over the lease? They must have filmed some of the scenes here."

"What? You're not a fan of brown shag carpets? It hides the dirt. That's all I care about. I inherited a lot of this stuff when I took over the apartment twelve years ago."

"Well, I didn't think you would buy any of it."

"I spend so much time on the road, I never got around to doin' much with it. Besides, all my tricks say it has a manly vibe they think is hot."

"You can spare me those details. How's the show going?"

"Just a coupla weeks, and we can lay it to rest. Thankfully, I haven't had to go on. Which is a good thing, because I'm not feeling very perky these days."

"Sorry to hear that."

"But all that's changin' tonight. Better living through chemistry. I just got in from the show a few minutes before you got here, so this is good timing."

"You know, all these years in the city, and I've never gone out to The Saint. Timothy said he used to go at least once a month before he met me."

"I know. I used to see him there. It was *theee* primo club in the early '80s. I haven't been in a few years, since it's lost some of its luster, but I can still guarantee you a mind-blowing time. Dr. Charles is here to prescribe your evening of delights."

"What's that supposed to mean?"

"Drugs, my man. We're gonna be flyin' high into the outer stratosphere tonight."

After these last two weeks, with still not hearing about the show and getting nowhere with Christopher, I'm ready to blast off. "Give me anything that gets me out of this head space. Christopher and I are kind of on the outs right now."

"I don't even want to hear about it. Tonight's just about havin' fun."

"Okay, I won't bring it up the rest of the night."

"Great. We start with a hit of speed and hang out here for a while until it kicks in. I'm guessin' this little pill will be a new experience for you?"

"Yeah, smoking pot is about as far as I've traversed into drug land."

"No worries. Charlie MD will take good care of you. When the drug starts working its magic, you'll be hittin' the can a couple of times. That's why we're sticking around here until the evacuation is done. Then we can just walk over to the club."

He hands me the innocent-looking pill, and I think of Alice going down the rabbit hole as I pop it in my mouth. "Tim said he was at the club the night it opened, and I think I remember him saying you were there, too."

"September 20th, 1980. That's closin' in on almost seven years ago now. No matter how much time goes by, I'll never forget that date. It will go down in history as one of the most amazing nights of my life." He gestures to the beat-up black leather sofa, and we take a seat. "That night, I felt like I'd been delivered into a fuckin' dreamland of disco ecstasy. Man, there is nothin' that could ever replace it."

"I hear you were a charter member."

"That's right. All summer long, the gay boys in all the clubs were buzzing about the opening. I got word you had to go up to a designated office and be interviewed for the membership. My connections made it a shoo-in for me, along with all the hottest club kids in town.

"They sold 2,500 annual memberships before the club even opened."

"That is amazing. Was it very expensive?"

"It was a hundred and fifty bucks to the first seven hundred and two fifty to the rest. After that, you were put on a waiting list. I was one of the first hundred to get my very cool black membership card with rays of colored lights shooting out. That card was like an entree into an alternate universe, man."

"My, weren't you special."

"Damn right. Once you checked in at the front desk and paid the nightly fee, the commoners had to queue up at this huge coat check that was like goin' to the damn dry cleaners. I bypassed that line since I had my own locker up the spiral stairs in the back. I even kept a pair of Capezio Jazz shoes for my smooth moves in it, plus whatever drug paraphernalia I was into. But I let all that go years ago, and now the membership is only fifty bucks. But the light show is still sensational, and I guarantee you an amazing time."

"Sounds great. I'm in."

"I don't expect much of a line to get in tonight, but when it opened back in 1980, there was a huge line of people goin' all the way around the block waitin' to get in. The energy in the crowd was electric. You could just feel the anticipation, and everyone knew they were about to take a trip to gay heaven."

"Didn't the space used to be an old theater they gutted?"

"Yeah, it was originally an old Yiddish theater, which makes sense considering all the Jews that live in this neighborhood. But more recently, it had been the Fillmore East, showcasing classic rockers such as Janis Joplin and the like.

"I was trippin' out of my mind on that opening night. Then the lights came way down. The first chord of Donna Summer's 'Could it be Magic' reverberated through the sound system and simultaneously kick-started the star machine. In that split second, the fucking heavens opened up. There was like this complete stillness, followed by thousands of disco devotees gasping out loud at the endless miles of stars that were movin' all around us all of a sudden. You literally felt like you were flyin' through space! The entire dance floor cheered as the drum beat took over. The whole fucking room just kicked into overdrive, man."

"This place sounds like it's going to be a blast!"

"You got that right. On the night it opened, we were all dancin' together in our own private cosmos. It was all for us, man, this special tribe blasting off on that dance floor. We were all connected. It was like total freedom. I'll never forget it."

Charlie spent the next half hour regaling me with more stories of his glory days as a club kid. On the one hand, it seemed a bit pathetic to me since his many years of trashing around had obviously worn him down. He'd taken on a tired look lately. On the other hand, I was getting amped up about what the night could bring. The speed was definitely kicking in. Everything in his apartment seemed sharper, like a bad '70s 3D movie. I was getting antsy to get out of there and get this party started. He was right about this stuff cleaning you out. Once that was out of the way, my energy really took off. I was totally wired.

"Christ, Charlie. This stuff is awesome! I don't know why I let myself miss out on all the fun all these years."

"What did I tell you? The doctor is in the house, and I prescribe liftoff. Let's get the hell out of here and go find some hotties."

Fifteen

If I didn't have Charlie leading the way, I never would have guessed the nondescript black matte doors with no signage would grant us entry into what Timothy used to call "The Vatican of Disco," aka—The Saint. No big lines, but plenty of boys all sporting the same uniform of black leather jacket, 501s, white tee, and running shoes.

Once we fork over our cash and check our coats, we begin to take it all in. The throbbing sounds emanating from the floor above feels like my heartbeat, pounding with an excited intensity as I scan this industrial space of black matte walls and charcoal grey carpeting, accented with steel columns and ramps that seem to float up toward the back. The cavernous downstairs area gives off a modern, technical look to the overall streamlined urban design of the club.

Steel and concrete abounds, the consummate backdrop for the sculpted bodies on display. Some gay boys are getting their drinks at the giant circular juice bar and taking them to the banquettes along the outer walls. Others are making their way up the two ramps and continuing up the steps that lead to the dance floor above.

"Let's get some juice," Charlie says, "so we won't get dried out. We're gonna be losin' a lot of moisture when we get upstairs."

"Works for me," I say, wondering if I can stand still even for a drink. I see groups of guys hanging out in the banquettes, chatting and drinking. How can they even be sitting down? They must not be feeling what I am. The pulsating music is calling me. I want to move. Charlie seems to be more in predator mode. I can see his edgy eyes snaking around the room, looking for some potential attraction.

I'm too impatient right now to wait for him to sift through the herd. "You've held me in suspense long enough, Doc. Let's get upstairs. I need to shake off some of this energy."

We make our way up one of the ramps and then up the switchback stairs leading to the main event. "Christ, Charlie. This is fucking fantastic!" I shout, trying to be heard over the ear-splitting disco beat.

"I told you it would blow your mind. And they haven't even turned on the star machine yet."

"What are they waiting for? It's already one o'clock in the morning."

"That's right. The night is young when you're talkin' about dancing into infinity."

We scan the huge circular dance floor packed with hundreds of hot shirtless guys. Multi-colored lights flash in every direction on a sea of naked muscular torsos, reflecting on the white tank tops that tribal rule demands they thread through the side belt loop of their tight jeans.

The lyrics of the Weather Girls carry us both out into the midst of sweaty bodies, all gyrating to the scintillating sounds of these Black Divas. That's all we need to rip off our shirts and explode into a rhythmic momentum that erases all our inhibitions as we cut loose to the driving beat. All this stimulation continues escalating in a throbbing force blasting through our bodies. I've never felt this kind of energy pulsating through me. I can't even conceive of slowing down. I want it to go on and on as one song leads into the next.

After a couple of hours of getting down with some non-stop stomping and shaking, Charlie finally drags me off the dance floor and we head back down to the lower level for some much-needed liquids. You can actually have a conversation down here, although the pounding beat from above never lets up.

"Doctor Charlie is back in the house," he says as we settle into one of the banquettes. "Time for more medicine." He hands me another pill.

"I'm not sure I need anything else, Charlie. I still feel fantastic and plenty energized. I could dance all night."

"Trust me, you need this."

"What is it, more speed?"

"No, it's MDMA. You thought you were having a good time? Well, this shit is going to make your head explode, and your entire body will be in ecstasy. It's a hallucinogen cut with more speed. You're gonna be blastin' off in a fucking rapture that catapults you out into the stars, man."

"Why not. When in Rome…right?" I chase my latest prescription with an entire bottle of water. I've never been so thirsty.

"This shit should kick in just about when the star machine hits the dome above the dance floor. You won't even fucking believe what you're experiencing when that happens."

"Hey, don't we know that guy?" I say, pointing to a redhead with a rockin' little fireplug of a body over at the juice bar.

"Yeah, well, ain't that a blast from the past. That's Phillip Henley. He played Barnaby in our production of *Hello Dolly!* back in '82. Man, the years have done nothin' but improve him."

"Damn, you're right. That kid's grown up and filled out in all the right places. He's hot."

I stand up and yell his name, which gets his attention. Not to mention a big toothy grin and a wave back. Could that be the same guy who played my little sidekick over four years ago? The innocent adolescent-looking actor that inhabited the character of Barnaby is long gone. And he makes that very clear in his swagger over to us.

"Hey guys!" Phillip says when he gets over to us. "We all must have gotten lost, 'cause this place doesn't look anything like The Harmonia Gardens."

"Yeah, but Dolly would approve regardless," Charlie answers. "You know how she loved the boys. Besides, it's below 14th Street, just like in the show."

"It's been too long since I've seen you guys. And Matt, I never would have expected to see you here. I didn't think you went in for this kind of place."

"Well, I'm into it now. And I'm having a blast. With Charlie as my chaperone, how could I go wrong?"

"I don't doubt it," he says as he runs his eyes up and down my frame, finally settling on my crotch.

"You know me. I'm always willing to offer my services when the opportunity arises," Charlie says.

"Yeah, I seem to remember quite a few offers that certain summer."

"You can't blame a guy for bein' persistent. Why don't you sit down and join us?" Charlie asks.

"Thanks, but I'm going to head back upstairs and meet some friends. But I'll look for you guys out on the dance floor. Great seeing you."

I'm thinking his backside looks as good as his front as he struts up the ramp back to the dance floor. "Man, that guy has got what I call universal appeal."

"Yeah, and I wouldn't mind traveling all over that expanse." Charlie's eyes continue to devour his potential prey.

"We'll have to maneuver our way around the dance floor and check out some more of his moves once we find him," I say.

"That's what I'm talkin' about, man. I like seein' the predator come out in you. This shit we just took will start kickin' in soon, and I can promise you all these boys will start looking even better. It's like all of a sudden, your connection to everyone and everything is gonna start pulsing through your body."

"What are we waiting for? I'm feeling that way right now!" I pull Charlie off his seat, and we head back upstairs.

And just like the good doctor predicts, the thrill of the driving beat gets us flying. The hydraulic lift ascends, and the star machine kicks on. It triggers the entire mass of shirtless devotees into an even more ecstatic frenzy as we all flip into a new dimension, each of us catapulting into a heavenly cosmos as our tingling bodies soar across the sky like shooting stars.

I'm so high I can barely contain myself inside my own body. I feel fucking amazing! And what is even more cool, I know every one of these hot guys is feeling it too.

It's like some kind of elated tribal connection. It's beautiful, it's total freedom, and so full of passion, even love. Whatever this euphoric version of love is, we're all feeling it together on this drug-fueled dance floor. The celestial night flies on and on. We find Phillip and his friends going at it full tilt. Man, he's even hotter when he's moving that well-formed physique of his. And much to my surprise and pleasure, he starts making the moves on me. We have a blast dancing our asses off, just tripping the night away.

I lose track of Charlie for a few more hours, but he finds me again when the music starts to mellow out. I'm still hanging with Phillip, literally hanging all over his sweaty torso. Yes! I'm finally getting to touch some skin again. I didn't even need his permission to run my hands over his shoulders and smooth chest and grab his ass as we grind our crotches together. Unlike someone else I know. We both get into it like it's part of the ritualistic rite of being here.

We'd just taken a break and were refueling with more liquid when Charlie shows up. "Looks like you guys have been makin' good use of this Pleasure Palace."

"What a night! I can't remember when I've had a better time. Phillip and I have been hooked into this music for I don't know how long now, and all his friends seem really cool too."

"I always make sure I'm in good company," Phillip says.

"I bet," Charlie says.

"How about joining us back out on the dance floor?" I ask, wanting to keep moving.

"No thanks. I have a date with a certain hunky someone up in the balcony section. If you don't know what goes on up there, I'm sure Phillip can fill you in. But before I go, Charlie MD is back for your final dose, now that we're getting close to dawn. It's six a.m. and time for a downer, my man. These little babies are called Tuinals." He hands me another capsule. "It will slow you down for the next few hours. I got extra if you want one too, Phillip."

"Sure," he says. All three of us chase the pill with our water.

"I'll catch up with you in a while. We call this early morning time the sleaze hours. See? They're lowering the disco ball now from the ceiling, and it's time to settle into whatever delightful dish you've chosen to finish off the night with."

Phillip and I continue to have fun with the retro songs that carry us and his friends through the next few hours as the latest drug winds us down. The disco ball and more toned-down warm lighting sync perfectly with the oldies the DJ is spinning.

At a certain point, he makes an obvious play to take things further, trying to get me to go up to the balcony. Strangely enough, that's just not what my body wants in this present condition. Full-on sex right now seems like way too much effort. This has been fun, but I still can't push back the feeling that Christopher should be first in line for the real thing. Regardless, I take a pass.

He gets it, but that seems to break the spell for now. Before he heads up to the balcony to find someone more willing, we find some paper and a pen at the juice bar to exchange numbers. It's clear we've made a connection. I've been around the block enough to figure out he's a party boy, and if he wants to continue that party up in the balcony, I'll just catch him another time.

I wander back downstairs to the wall of banquettes and find a nice corner spot to continue replenishing my body with liquids. What a night. I see Charlie coming down the ramp.

"I figured I'd find you down here," Charlie says. "All good things must come to an end. And man, I don't mean to be graphic, but coming is always a nice way to end it."

"I don't even want to hear about it, but I'm ready to go too. I can't believe it's already the middle of the morning."

"Matthew, my man, you've just experienced Saturday night at The Saint the way it was meant to happen."

"I'll say, and then some. I'm pretty spaced out right now, but I guess I'll just splurge for a cab ride to get me uptown to bed."

"Good call. You'll be fully recovered by Monday afternoon."

The bright sunlight is almost blinding as we step back through the entry doors, leaving our Wonderland behind. Talk about an alternate universe. It's like we've flipped the channel, and our entire world has shifted back to something that had completely vanished while we were tripping the night away inside those doors. Why does standing here on Second Avenue feel more surreal than the environment we just left?

It's like I've turned into some kind of two-dimensional cartoon character of myself, moving through a three-dimensional street scene I don't quite fit into. I see a typical Sunday morning happening in front of my eyes with New Yorkers strolling by, getting started on their errands. And I'm in total disconnect.

Time to flag down that cab. I turn around to search for one down the street, and I can't believe I see Christopher walking toward us. Fuck no, this can't be happening.

"Is that Christopher?" Charlie asks, with the same limited assurance of reality that I possess right now.

"I'm afraid so. There's no avoiding him now. I'm just going to have to own this."

We both walk toward him, and I can see his yoga mat strapped on his back. "Hi Christopher, are you on your way to yoga class?"

He answers me with his calm demeanor that experience tells me could crack any minute.

"Yes, actually I am. You remember Tara, she's teaching today."

We haven't talked since our fight in the subway, so I have no idea where this is going.

"What are you guys doing in this neighborhood?"

"I'm sure you've heard of The Saint," Charlie says. "Well, this is the place, and we've just had an awesome night."

Christopher's usual casual stance transforms before our eyes as he looks from us to the entry doors of the club. All of a sudden, he goes rigid and takes a step back. I know my sense of reality is still pretty tweaked at this moment. Still, I sense a sort of hard armor he's now creating around his periphery for protection.

"Last night?" he asks in a subdued tone, like he's caught in some time warp of confusion. "I'm not a big fan of this club, so I usually avoid this street in the evening. Even during the day, it's not a place I... I hadn't really counted on bumping into someone I know coming out of it during the day."

What's wrong with him? He looks so scared and uncomfortable. I'm the one who's not supposed to be thinking straight in this druggy haze I'm trying to shake myself out of. How am I supposed to answer that? What difference does it make to him that we've spent all night in this club?

"Matt, I'm glad I ran into you, because I did want to tell you in person how sorry I am for how I reacted last week. I've been working up the courage to call you…I'm dealing with… no, I'm sorry, but I can't talk about it here of all places… I honestly can't believe I'm seeing you here."

"What's the big deal? It's just a club," I say, now totally confused and exasperated.

"This place…I shouldn't have come down this street. I can't be around it or people who go here. I guess we'll just leave it that."

I can't believe everything is so black and white with him. "What do you have against this place? What's so terrible?"

"This kind of place is just not a world I can be a part of. You remember our conversations about how my surroundings and my inner being are interconnected for me. That's something I feel very deeply."

"I know, but…"

"I don't want anything to do with places like this and what goes on here. That's not who I want to be. I guess I need to apologize once more for maybe making the assumption that this isn't who you are, either. I thought you were different. But I guess I was wrong. I'm sorry. I've got to go now, or I'll be late for class."

All I can do is stand there like some kind of zombie as he rushes past both of us like he's about to be attacked by some wild animal. I can't deal with this right now. I'm starting to really crash, big time.

"Don't let Mr. Goody Two Shoes get to you," Charlie says. "We had one hell of a night, and there's nothin' he can take away from that."

"Yeah, I know. Thanks, Charlie. It really was terrific. You're a great friend, but now I've got to get home before I crash right here on the sidewalk."

Luckily, a cab appears, and I wave to Charlie as I climb in. That sinking feeling in the pit of my stomach is back as I make my escape uptown to my own much-needed bed.

The taxi moves north swiftly because of the light traffic on Sunday morning. Once again, reality is shifting. What just happened back there? I guess Christopher and I are over, even before we really got anywhere. Maybe it's the fallout from the drugs, but I feel like the weight of the world is pummeling me even further downward. Is this who I am? Is it fair of him to base his decision not to see me again on one night? I'm not sure I can handle his intensity, regardless. Certainly not at the moment. I sink into my own private oblivion as the cab continues uptown.

Sixteen

I look straight up into the disco mirror ball as Charlie and I sway in contented friendship on the dance floor, allowing the countless sparkling lights to shower all around us. The Saint is so awesome. I love being back here. My body tingles as the lights land all over me, tickling every pore as I move and shake. This more laidback disco beat seduces me with a sensual throbbing.

"What did you call this again, Charlie?" I grab his neck with both hands, and he does the same with my waist, rocking together in a satisfying rhythm.

"These are the sleaze hours. Time to relax, man, and think about who you're gonna make the moves on."

We let our bodies sense a slow simmering arousal for possible future carnal delights. "I'm glad you talked me into coming back. This time I'm definitely heading up to the balcony for some action."

"Now is as good a time as any," he says, "I'm goin' up. Happy hunting, you hound dog. This time make sure you get the bone." He breaks free of me and heads up the stairs.

I go for another water break, then take the stairs myself. It's so dark I can barely see the various groupings of people. Now that I'm above the circular dance floor, I pause to look down through the dome scrim at the disco ball and the bare-chested bodies dancing down below. I get the distinct feeling I'm about to have some real fun in what feels like a gay amusement park. Time to find my new ride.

I head deeper into the forbidden zone. "What the fuck! What the hell are you doing here, Christopher? And *with Phillip*? I can't believe it, after all the things you said."

"Why don't you go find your own piece of ass," Phillip says, without missing a beat to their grinding rhythm.

The room seems to be growing darker, filling with smoke. "Why don't you mind your own fucking business. I wasn't talking to you," I yell, trying to make out their images, now almost completely obscured by the smoke. At the same time, my voice gets interrupted by a harsh ringing sound. Is it a smoke alarm? It just keeps ringing and ringing.

Shit! That's my phone ringing, waking me up. My consciousness grudgingly shifts, and the scene disappears into what I realize is my own bedroom. I quickly glance at my clock, which reads seven p.m., as I lunge for the phone.

"Hello?"

"Matt, it's Helen. I hope I'm not disturbing you."

"No, not at all. I was just taking a little nap." Like since ten this morning. I'm hoping it's still Sunday.

"I'm calling you because I'm worried about Charlie. He didn't show up for the matinee today. I've been calling and calling. I'm so worried something is really wrong. I'm back from the show now and planning to go over to his apartment."

I guess I don't have any choice but to tell her what we've been up to. "Charlie and I pulled an all-nighter at The Saint last night. He seemed fine when I left him around nine thirty this morning. I thought he'd get a few hours of sleep and then go to work."

"That's a long time to have overslept."

"Well, I have to tell you there were drugs involved. Lots of them all night long. The last round being downers. Maybe he had a bad reaction." I'm still trying to pull myself together as I look around my bedroom. I'm relieved I'm not dreaming anymore, but wondering if being awake is a reality I can handle any better. "I'm a bit woozy myself, but I'm fine. I'll meet you there as soon as I throw something on."

"Thanks, Matt. I'll see you there."

I spring for another cab ride. This could be serious; no time for the subway. Early Sunday evening doesn't remind me in the least of what

Saturday night looked like. New Yorkers are always on the move, but it's just the usual hum of the city going on as the cab carries me south. I can't believe I'm going back to the scene of the crime, so to speak. I was hoping to be done with that.

The taxi pulls up to his address, and I see Helen looking frustrated on the landing.

"He's not answering his buzzer," she says.

"Well, let's see who else is home." I proceed to push multiple buzzers. Bingo! Someone buzzes us in, and we tear up the five flights.

"Charlie! Charlie, are you there?" I yell, trying to catch my breath as I pound on the door.

"Charlie, are you in there?" Helen joins in the yelling.

I continue to pound on the brown metal door with both of us yelling, wondering if the neighbors are going to call the police with all this noise we're making.

Finally, we hear, "Who is it?" very faintly from behind the door.

"Who the hell does it sound like, Charlie?" I say with a mixture of relief and exasperation. "It's Matt and Helen! Are you okay? Open the damn door."

The door opens to a frail-looking, stooped over, and haggard version of what only hours ago was my disco buddy. He barely resembles the Candy Man who was handing out treats throughout the evening.

"Charlie, I'm worried about you," Helen says. "You haven't answered your phone. You look terrible."

"Thanks. What a pleasant surprise to see you, too."

"I mean it, Charlie. I don't know if it's occurred to you or not, but you missed the matinee today. What if you were supposed to cover for somebody?"

"Holy shit! Okay, I fucked up. I'm sorry Mommy Dearest, are you going to beat me with a wire hanger now?"

"You've been in this business long enough to know that a no-show is a very serious offense," she says.

"I guess all those drugs took a bigger toll on me than I expected. That's what happens when you get old." He slowly goes over to one of his slashed-up old black leather easy chairs. He's even walking like an old man.

"I would have hung out with you," I say, "if I thought you were going to have a problem getting up."

"I'll call management," Helen says, "and let them know you're all right. I doubt that you'll get fired, but it won't be forgotten. You probably won't ever work for these people again though."

"The way I'm feelin', I may never work again anyway. My body still feels like a ton of lead. I need to sleep this off."

"Are you sure you're okay otherwise?" Helen asks with obvious concern.

"Compared to how lousy my bag of bones usually feels these days, it's just the same ol', only worse. I have all of Monday to recover, and I should be fine by Tuesday. Hopefully, my luck will hold out, and I won't have to cover for anyone."

"Can I make you something to eat?" Helen asks, becoming the Holy Mother once again.

"I don't think my stomach wants any company right now. I just need to move through all this shit I put into my system, and I'll be fine." He gets up again, making a few old man noises. "I'm goin' back in my bedroom now. Feel free to stay as long as you like. And I guess I need to thank you both for making sure I'm still alive. You guys really are great friends. I mean that." He trudges back to his bedroom and closes the door.

We both just sit there on his crappy black leather couch, wondering what to do next. "Do you think we should stay a while just to make sure he's okay?" I ask, wondering what difference it would make at this point.

"I do think it might be a good idea," Helen says, "but he's probably fine and just needs more rest. That seems to be the story of his life lately. It's like he's dragging through everything. I'm worried about his health in general, but he won't talk about it."

"I know. Charlie lives in a world of denial when it comes to most things." I look around at his unkempt apartment. Besides the beat-up, dated furniture and the little messes he's left everywhere, the dingy walls could seriously use a paint job. It's like he's just ignoring the responsibilities of life in general. "I think he may be trying to escape a more serious reality of what's going on with his body. He was flying high last night, but that was the drugs. If his immune system is already compromised, no wonder he's having this reaction."

"Neither of us has said what I think is on both our minds," Helen reluctantly states, sitting on the edge of the sofa seat, ready for the elephant in the room to make itself known.

I guess I'll be the one to start. "I know, maybe he's HIV positive, and that's why he's so weak. He might even have full-blown AIDS, for all we know. He's certainly never talked about being tested. That old denial thing again."

"I'm such a logical person," Helen says, standing up and moving around the room, picking up magazines off the floor and stacking them on the scratched wood coffee table. "It's hard for me to fathom that anyone wouldn't want to get tested at this point, when they actually have an approved drug that's supposed to help."

"AZT helps in some cases, but it's far from a perfect drug. The doses people are getting are extreme, and in some situations, it's actually making them worse with all the side effects. People are still dying every day."

"I know this must be particularly hard for you, knowing what you went through with Timothy."

"Helen, would you come sit with me on the sofa again? I need to tell you something." Her whole demeanor changes, as she calmly sits back down, facing me. "I've never been tested either."

"Oh, Matt. How is that even possible?"

"This disease is such a death sentence. If I test positive, I honestly can't bear the fact that the downward spiral is next for me. Does that make any sense? I know myself. I'd make myself sick if I had that news."

"But what about support groups? What about the Gay Men's Health Crisis? What about your family?"

I take a deep breath and prepare to open a stubborn wound that continues to fester in me. "Do you want to know how supportive my family would be? I went back to Chicago for Christmas last year, all excited about seeing my newborn baby niece. I get there and come to find out my brother and sister-in-law don't want her in the same room with me. Remember, I'm not sick in the least, and they still feel that way. And everyone else thought it was a good idea too, including my parents. Talk about feeling like a leper. I was so hurt and humiliated. I changed my plane ticket and left early. It's just fear and ignorance. But it really hurts when your own family shuns you. I can't even imagine how they'd react if I was sick with symptoms. I'm not sure I could face that kind of abandonment. If they refused to see me at all, it would break my heart."

"I'm so sorry, Matt. I had no idea you were dealing with this. No wonder feeling like we're family here is so important to you."

"I already have that sense of being 'other than' with my relatives and with society in general. If I found out I was positive, that would cement it. New York City can feel like a pretty lonely town sometimes, no matter how many people you're surrounded by. I think the illness would make that even worse. Maybe Charlie just can't face that."

"I see what you mean. All the more reason to be there for him right now. If he needs a nursemaid, I intend to sign up."

"You were really great when Timothy was going through it. He's a part of the reason I can't bring myself to be tested. What if I'm positive? What if I'm the reason he's dead? Maybe I gave it to him. I don't know how I could live with that."

"This disease is no one's fault, Matt. It was spreading before any of us knew anything about it. And now it's spreading to the straight community, too."

"Yeah, I've been seeing that more and more."

"I'm scared now, too. That's why I insist on safe sex. It can be a death sentence for anybody. I could tell you stories about how people on tour got lonely and developed close relationships that usually led to sex. Girls with girls, boys with boys, boys with girls, take your pick."

"I know. I've had the same experience."

"Being on the road is intense. Having someone to share it with is like a salve to smooth over the isolation you can feel. I hope everyone is taking precautions now, but in those early years, no one knew."

"Yes, but now we do. I can practice safe sex, but being scared to get tested is also tied to my not being ready for a serious relationship."

"What do you mean?"

"I think I would owe that person an answer to my status. Since I don't know it, it's holding me back. It's been that way since I even considered moving forward after Timothy."

"Before you continue, I want you to know Christopher shared with me both his status and the fact that he disclosed it to you."

"Honestly, knowing he's positive has really done a number on me, considering what I went through with Timothy."

"I'm sure."

"I'm glad you told me, even though he's basically called off any hope of a future together. But I was still willing to see where it would go."

"What do you mean he called it off? You were just getting to know each other."

"Charlie and I bumped into him when we came out of The Saint this morning. He had such a visceral reaction to seeing us there, combined with what he thought were previous inappropriate actions on my part. He basically walked away."

"I'm sorry to hear that, Matt. I thought you might be a good balance for each other."

"I haven't really had a lot of lucid hours since then to figure it all out. He's such an intense guy and obviously feels things very deeply."

"Yes, he does. I'm glad you shared this with me, so maybe he and I can talk about it."

"What would we do without you, Helen?" I take in an even deeper awareness of this beautiful, caring woman. "You're like a devoted army nurse on the front lines of this war we're fighting. Because that's what it feels like. Christopher is fighting there right now. I fought this battle so hard with Timothy too. Just like any war, getting killed is part of the luck of the draw."

"You're right, Matt. It is like a war."

"Right now, I'm still in what I assume is Charlie's camp. We can build a fortress of denial, but the enemy is still all around us. It's a horrible feeling to have hanging over our heads. If I end up being negative, then I've won a battle. But the war is far from over."

"I really can't see any end in sight," she says as she takes another look around this depressing room.

"Isn't it ironic that the act of safe sex is like our shield in this conflict?" I say. "Covering our 'swords' is what will help some of us survive. No wonder condoms are sometimes referred to as shields. Just like in: 'Shields up!'"

Helen smiles but still has an intense look in her eyes. She leans forward and takes both my hands in hers. "I'm so touched you shared all this with me, Matt. I think it will help me down the road with whoever I encounter who's dealing with this. You've been a wonderful friend, and I want to be the same for you."

She lets go and stands back up, striking a pose with her hands on her hips. "If I'm too pushy with Charlie, he'll shut down altogether, but I absolutely want to be there for him. If I have to become more of a smothering mother, I'm happy to play that part, too. On that note, he's got that extra bedroom he hasn't rented out, and it still has a bed in it. I think I'm going to spend the night."

"I'm sure Charlie would appreciate a familiar face in the morning. Especially one as beautiful as yours." I stand as well. This time, I grab her hands. "He's so lucky to have such a loving friend like you."

"Oh, aren't you sweet. I just want to make sure he wakes up at a decent hour tomorrow and is ready to come back to work on Tuesday night."

"Thanks for being the family I think we all need right now. You're the best." We embrace in an extra-long goodbye.

Back on the street again, I've lost all sense of even which day this is, from the all-nighter to passing out all day to that bizarre dream, and back to ground zero where it all began almost twenty-four hours ago now. It's all run together into one crazy scene. I do feel like a small cloud has lifted by confessing to Helen my inability to face the test. At least I know someone has got my back no matter what. Though seeing Charlie's condition just adds to my fears. It's the unknown. Any of us can be struck down at any time, no matter how young and beautiful and talented we are. I think of Christopher talking about how precious and ephemeral his life has become, knowing his status. Our lives may be even more brief than we ever would have dreamed. It makes me even more determined to embrace whatever time we have left.

Seventeen

I can smell the chlorinated water, still trapped inside my ears. My hair retains a cool dampness as I run my hands through my scalp, and I scrutinize my modestly toweled physique in front of the locker room mirror. Not bad, I think to myself. I may not be a total Adonis, but at least I make the grade for what would be considered the all-important gay standard. Is flawless too strong a word? Our people do set the bar rather high in so many ways.

Another day, another hour of power in the YMCA pool, now complete. Thank God for this place. I guess I should keep counting my blessings. The catering jobs are still coming in, so at least I know I can pay the rent.

I can't stop thinking about the show. I'm sure the director said two to three weeks. Well, it's been exactly three weeks today since the callback, and the phone call still hasn't happened. My apartment is spotless. Maybe that's inspired by Charlie's wreck of a place. The grocery shopping at The Fairway is done. I decided to take my mind off things and cook up a storm. So now the freezer is stocked too. Why not? What else do I have going on? It's the middle of the day, and I have the dressing room to myself as I head back to my locker... Or so I thought.

"That's quite a mental checklist you've crossed off," I hear Hobo say. I open the locker door to find her making herself entirely too comfortable on my pile of clothes. "My, my. I'm pleased to see you're being such a good Catholic Daddy Boy again—fine-tuning that buffed body of yours. Especially after your wicked ways last Saturday night."

"Seriously, Hobo? Now you're showing up at the gym? The treadmill doesn't exactly seem like a lifestyle choice you'd be making. Don't expect me to talk to you if someone comes in here."

"I'm just glad to see you've recovered from all those sinful goings-on. How could they even think of calling that place The Saint? I think Lucifer's Lounge would be much more appropriate. I chose the interior of this locker to make my appearance because it reminds me of a confessional booth. Wouldn't you agree? Anything more you'd like to divulge?"

"I think I pretty much spilled my guts out to Helen. I know, I know, I'm sure you heard it all. You were probably hiding behind that hideous black velvet cityscape Charlie has on the wall. So, you got the whole scoop, right?"

"Yes, and if a friend in need feels called upon to unload on someone who is genuinely compassionate, they should choose Helen. She's quite a gal. I'm actually very proud of the confession you made to her. That predicament has been buried deep inside you for years.

"Tell me about it."

"Speaking about AIDS as some kind of war, it was half the battle just opening up to her like that. You'll know when you're really ready for that test. Just take it a day at a time. You're feeling good and healthy today, right? You should be counting your blessings for that, too."

"Thanks, Pussyface. It's been weighing me down even more lately. It's the unknown. I'm looking through a dim filter at everything about my day-to-day life because of it. I can't say I'm ready to get the test yet, but at least I have someone to talk about it with, who I know really cares."

"You mean besides me?"

"All right, yes. Besides you. I've given up on trying to figure out what our little tête-à-têtes are all about. But it's good to know you're still around too."

"Why, thank you, Matthew. It's always nice to be appreciated. And your friend Charlie?"

"I haven't heard from either him or Helen, so I'm thinking he can at least get out of bed and is still in the show. But I am worried about him. What does his future as a dancer look like if he's struggling to keep up? He just doesn't seem to have any energy for it anymore."

"Time to start reinventing himself. It's lucky for you that you're not a dancer, so your career can last a lot longer if you keep at it."

"Thanks for the pep talk. I'll take that to heart. But in the meanwhile, I'm going to take this buffed bod over to Sheep's Meadow for some sunshine and to check out the boys. I'm sure you'll agree it's a much healthier environment for socializing than The Saint."

"L'amour, l'amour. Oh, the lessons of love we need to learn. You in particular. I'm sorry to hear Christopher has decided to call it quits, but it's healthy to keep your options open, so I do approve. Life goes on—for you anyway." She disappears, leaving only my pile of clothes in her makeshift confessional booth.

It couldn't be a more beautiful day in Central Park. It's like I'm walking into a New York City feel-good movie—in Sensurround, with imaginary orchestrations playing in my head. Today, the park feels like a sparkling wonderland. All the trees and bushes are bursting with green. Now that it's the middle of May, the flowers are in bloom, and everyone is flourishing in the bright sunshine, taking full advantage of the seductive breezes in the fresh air.

Sheep's Meadow feels more like home to me than anywhere else in Manhattan. And this great weather has brought everyone out, playing Frisbee, tossing a football, walking, biking, or just soaking up the warm rays on a blanket.

Talk about buffed bodies—they are definitely in abundance today. One redheaded Frisbee thrower in particular, playing with some other guys, catches my eye. I make my way onto the expanse of lawn with the shining cityscape holding court as the backdrop above the tree line. Taking a cue from him and many others prancing about, I peel off my shirt.

You can take your pick. It's a youthful vibe of young men and women. Doesn't anyone work nine to five anymore? They must be a lot of out-of-work actors and models. The pretty factor is very high out here on this green grassy playpen.

Hey, wait a minute. Now that I'm getting a little closer, I realize that it's Phillip. Getting another look at all those flexing muscles I had so much fun feeling up last Saturday night is giving me some feisty flashbacks.

Well, I'm stone-cold sober now, and his physique is even more amazing in the daylight. He looks like some kind of bare-chested young golden boy, running and throwing the Frisbee with joyful abandon. His red hair is the perfect bouncing crown, setting off the fair skin below, that the sun is busy polishing to perfection.

I catch his eye now and wave as he becomes aware of who I am. In a moment of inspiration, he tosses me the Frisbee, which I leap for and catch, then toss it back. How cool is this? He throws it back to one of his friends and then starts into a full-on run towards me. What did I do to deserve this greeting?

"Matt, what a wonderful surprise!" He gives me a sweaty hug and then steps back. "It's so great to see you out here. Are you celebrating?"

"What do you mean?"

"That you got the show. In fact, we both got cast in *Our New Normal*!"

"What? What are you talking about? I haven't heard anything yet, and I didn't see you at the callback for the Greek chorus."

"I was called back for a principal role, so I wasn't at the chorus call. I got the part of Felix. I just found out from my agent this morning. I went over to her office to celebrate, and she had a copy of the cast list, including the chorus. Your name was on it unless there's another Matthew McKinney."

"I can't believe it! Maybe they called while I was at the gym. This is insane! I had no idea you were even auditioning. You didn't say anything about it last Saturday."

"Neither did you. I guess we had other things on our minds." We both break into a grin.

"I'm still a little in shock, Phillip. But congratulations. Felix should be an amazing role for you." I'm hoping he doesn't detect my decidedly mixed feelings, knowing he now got the role I couldn't get a submission for. But if he's right about the list, I still got in. I'm still going to be working. I'm going to be on Broadway! "This is fucking unbelievable!" I suddenly shout, so full of excitement that I grab him and we both start jumping up and down.

"I know!" He shouts too, and we both continue making fools of ourselves with a little victory dance.

Suddenly my rational mind gets the better of me and I calm down, thinking about the fact that it's just hearsay for me. "Phillip, I'm counting on you being right about this, but since I still haven't heard it officially, I've got to get home right away and see if I have a message. If I don't, then damn it, I'm calling them."

"That sounds like a good plan, Matt. Hopefully, you'll get the good news. Maybe we can celebrate tonight. How about getting a drink later?"

"That sounds great. I've still got your number. Oh, I have another friend who's waiting to hear. I've got to call him too. If he gets in, do you mind if he joins us?"

"Not at all. If he's going to be part of the cast, it would be fun to meet him."

"Congrats again. I'll call you either way," I say, walking briskly back to 69th Street.

My walk turns into a run as I quickly exit the park and trot down my street. My mind is on fire, and it's beginning to inflame my whole body as I take the stairs in my building two at a time. I fiddle with the lock and immediately see the flashing light on my phone machine. I have two messages.

My stomach is in my throat as I press the button and hear the beep. "This message is for Matthew McKinney. I'm calling to let you know you've been cast in the Greek chorus for the production of *Our New Normal.* Please call Casting Inc at 212-555-7181 to confirm you received this call and let us know if you'll be accepting this offer."

Accepting this offer! Are they fucking kidding me? Of course, I'm accepting this offer!

A second beep precedes the next call. "Matthew, honey, it's Gabriel. I got cast in the show. Call me the minute you get this message! I'm hopin' and prayin' it's good news for you too, baby."

Time to sit down and take a deep breath. This is really happening. I got it. I got the job. I look around at my apartment and think about these last few years. It's a bittersweet moment. I look over at some of the pictures of Timothy and me with Hobo; in our version of a happiness, that's just a memory now. I know Timmy would be so thrilled for me. I've finally turned the corner on what has felt like a never-ending gridlock.

I can have some hope now. And hope is at the heart of love. I can love my life again. I can anticipate a brighter future now that I'll be back on the boards. And not just any boards. The boards of a Broadway stage.

"Congratulations, Daddy Boy. You've done it." I turn to see what's become my constant companion kitty, perched on the armrest at the other end of the sofa. Whatever this bizarre manifestation of this black-and-white feline is, I love her dearly.

"Hobo. What can I say? I'm just so full of gratitude. I really don't know if I could have gotten to this place without you."

"Maybe people will start to understand just because we're cats, that doesn't mean it's truly all about us. We may be demanding, but as you have seen, it's always in your best interest. Besides, witnessing your life has turned out to be much more fun than sitting on the window sill, looking through the glass like some kind of kitty TV."

"You certainly fill the bill when it comes to lapping up the drama, Pussy Mama. Somehow, I have a feeling this show's just the beginning, with this new project going into production."

"Don't worry, you haven't seen the last of me just because you got a job. I have other fish to fry when it comes to orchestrating your life, and I'm not talking tuna fish either."

"Maybe I should start calling you the Conductor Cat." For once I barely got the last word in, as she dissolves into space again.

Okay, it's time to make some calls. Gabriel is first on my list.

"Hello, Gabriel. It's Matt."

"You don't need no introduction, honey. Did you get the job?"

"That would be a yes!"

"Oh, my Lord in Heaven, I can't believe we both got this! We're going to be on Broadway! I can't wait to delve into the depths of my character. I already have a million ideas about how you can become part of my backstory."

"Let's see what the director has to say about that first. Now we just have to count down what I assume will be weeks before we start."

"Didn't they tell you? First rehearsal is July 20th, and the first preview night is on September 1st."

"I actually haven't called them yet to confirm everything. I just got both messages, and I called you first."

"I'm so glad you did. I've been on pins and needles, wondering if you got the job too."

"How about celebrating tonight with a drink at your favorite neighborhood bar?"

"What a fabulous idea, sugar man! I don't suppose we should bother showing up in a costume appropriate for our characters."

"Definitely not."

"Those conservative queens wouldn't know what to make of it if I made an entrance in my new high dollar Whoreena persona. But a three-piece suit on you would fit right in."

"Let's save it for opening night. Hey, I found out a friend got the role of Felix, so I'm going to invite him to come along too. Do you know Phillip Henley?"

"I can't say that I do, but the more the merrier. Did I say Mary? That term was so 1970."

"Yeah, we're definitely *not* doing a revival of *The Boys in the Band*. How about nine o'clock?"

"Perfect, see you then, mister."

After we hang up, I continue with the phone calls, leaving messages for Helen and Charlie. It's a good feeling to relay this kind of news to people who are close to you, and have a visceral understanding of what it takes to get to this point in this unpredictable business. And yes, Casting Inc was on my list as well. It's now official. I've accepted the offer to be a member of the cast of a Broadway show. It still hasn't completely sunk in. I guess the ghost of Belasco was right. Leaving it to the Theater Gods has paid off for me.

Eighteen

I walk up the four steps to the concrete landing, protected from the elements by the rounded, burgundy-colored awning above, elegantly inscribed with "TH" front and center. I have a similar reaction to these beautiful, carved wood double doors that I had the last time I met Gabriel at The Townhouse. It's like I'm about to step back in time into an older private gentleman's club. The elongated oval windows entice me to enter, like some kind of portal into an exclusive world inhabited by a privileged class of gay men. Even if your bank account doesn't fit the bill, if you dress the part, look the part, and can pay for your drinks, you'll be happily admitted to join the fraternity of Upper East Side queens.

I see Gabriel is once again in his element in this swank little hideout, joining a chorus of guys standing at the grand piano belting out a decidedly uneven rendition of "Let Me Entertain You" from every gay man's favorite caterpillar-to-butterfly fantasy musical, *Gypsy*. The story of our lives? Probably wishful thinking for the most part.

I catch his eye, and he abandons the chorus, sashaying over to greet me. "Hey, loverman, care to sample my wares?" he says. He places my hands on his rear and proceeds to plant a big smacking kiss on my mouth.

"Hi, Gabriel. What did I say about us not getting too far ahead of ourselves with the script?" I untangle myself and take a step away from him, trying to recover some semblance of calm. I know I need to placate this crazy queen so he doesn't embarrass us. Still, there's something infectious about his outrageous energy regardless.

"Oh, I just can't help myself, handsome. I'm so tickled with the idea we'll be doing a show together. And, like you, it will be the first time I'll be gracing the Broadway stage. Speaking of which, since I'm bound to be showing so much skin for this gig, maybe you can give me some pointers at the YMCA."

"Sure, I can show you how to use all the equipment."

"Perfect. I expect to have a totally hot body in one week, and I've already mentioned that my other equipment already fills the bill."

I ignore that last remark. "You'd better give it more time than that, but we do have two months until rehearsals start."

We find a table and order a couple of drinks while we wait for Phillip to arrive. There's quite a sizable, lively, and mostly older crowd tonight, giving me a better feel for the place than the last time Gabriel and I were here in the afternoon. The piano player seems to know every Broadway show tune, and the patrons are loving it. I get the feeling that this privileged posse is right where they need to be, and since we're celebrating our future on the Great White Way, so are we.

"So, Mister Matthew Man, who is this Phillip child?" Gabriel asks, snuggling into the booth with cocktail in hand.

"He played the young Barnaby character in the *Hello, Dolly!* tour I did when I met Timothy five years ago. Man, that seems like such a long time ago now. So much has happened."

"If you're not careful, time is more of a sprint than a march, honey. I just keep my fine behind in gear for what's comin' next. My motto is: Keep up with what's goin' down, or you may end up empty at the lost and found."

"Yeah, and I guess Phillip was able to keep up better than me, because he obviously has an agent and got the part of Felix."

"Stop the presses. That's the part you couldn't get a submission for, right?"

"The very one. But I've been out of commission for so long, I'm certainly not going to hold any grudges. He got the part, and we should be happy for him. Oh, look, here he is," I say, waving him over to our table.

"Hey, Phillip." I take in his decidedly club kid outfit of the evening—tight tee shirt showing off that rockin' little bod with some bun-hugging jeans. His look doesn't exactly fit in with this bar's traditional décor. But when you inspire thoughts of a shiny, smooth red apple just waiting to exude its sweet juices, no gay bar will give you much trouble at the door. I give him a quick hug. "I'm so glad you made it. This is my friend Gabriel."

"Hey," he says, standing there, giving the impression that he's slightly thrown by Gabriel's presence. I'm not sure why he appears to be confused. He barely gives Gabriel a glance.

"It's so nice to make your acquaintance too," Gabriel says, realizing he's being snubbed and then slathering on the attitude. He immediately goes into bitch queen mode after Phillip's rather careless greeting.

What's going on? I sense a subtle tension between these two, but maybe it's just because they don't know each other. I'm not convincing myself of that one, but I push on. "Why don't you have a seat, and we'll order you a drink?"

"Thanks. This place is a real crackup, isn't it?" He signals the waiter over. "All these tired old queens reliving their youth with these old Broadway standards."

"That's why I suggested it when I called you back," I say, "since we're all going to be together on Broadway."

"Wait, you're in our show?" he asks Gabriel, looking even more uncomfortable and clueless.

"Why yes, dumpling. What'd you think I was doing here, wipin' down the tabletops?"

An uncomfortable silence ensues, as all of a sudden, the background sounds take center stage in the room, and we hear "Old Man River" being belted out by the crowd around the piano. "Uh, no, I just didn't know—I mean, I thought maybe you were... I guess I had a different idea about...um, so what part are you playing?"

"Didn't your agent tell you? I'm playing Lucifer, your hot black lover from Hell, and I get to pound the shit outta your pretty white ass on stage." Phillip's jaw drops in shock.

"Oh come on, Gabriel," I say, in another attempt to salvage this encounter. "He's just kidding, Phillip! Like me, he's playing one of the ghosts in the Greek chorus."

"Man, you had me going there," he says with a chuckle and an obvious look of relief on his face. But the tension doesn't let up. As the waiter takes his drink order, I can see Gabriel has no intention of that happening. This fierce queen is going into battle mode.

"Actually, my character is a transsexual prostitute. How does that grab you?"

"Sure, whatever," he says dismissively.

"Do you know any?"

"No, actually, I don't. Not exactly my demographic."

"Oh, I think I get it, lambchop. How about hustlers. I bet you've met a few of those."

"What is this, the third degree?"

"There's another bar in this neighborhood, and I seem to recall seeing you there. I'm talkin' about that elegant little establishment known as Rounds?"

"So? What if you did? What were you doing there?"

"Oh, I live in the neighborhood. When I get bored with the TV, I go over to Rounds to watch the hustlers work the room. It's very entertaining. You know, you're looking more and more familiar to me all the time."

"I actually have made a few acquaintances there."

"I bet you have." Gabriel downs the rest of his drink.

"You'd be surprised at some of the connections you can make," Phillip says. "I'm sure you could say the same for this place."

I try to put an objective spin on this conversation. "Power and status is a game a lot of New Yorkers like to play."

"Like I said, this is my neighborhood, and some of these guys have become buddies of mine too. I just make sure to pay for my own drinks," Gabriel says, signaling to the waiter to bring him another.

"I don't think there's anything wrong with letting a guy twice my age pick up the tab. It makes them feel important. Everybody likes that."

"And you get to feel important too."

"Nothing wrong with that either, as far as I'm concerned. Why do you think we're all in this business? We all want the spotlight, right?"

"That depends on the price tag you put on it," Gabriel says.

"I know what you're talking about," I say. "But it's so much more than that. I have this desire to express myself. But you don't get that opportunity unless you're really aggressive in this business. It feels like a double-edged sword to me."

"What's wrong with being famous?" Phillip says, relaxing a bit. "I like the idea of calling the shots and making great money. I know I've still got a ways to go, but I'm definitely going for it. I want a Tony. I want bigger parts and maybe even to get into movies."

"Are you willing to stay in the closet for that?" Gabriel asks, trying to get under his skin again. "Because the New York theater scene is one thing, but film and TV are still very homophobic."

"Nobody has to know my business. My career is more important. It's all about who you know. I can be as good at putting up a façade as the next guy."

"Yeah, look what happened to Rock Hudson," Gabriel says. "What a shock that was to the world."

"At least he had a very respected career for a long time," I say. "But it was sad to see how his illness all but forced him to come out."

"Yeah, but he was so old by then anyway. He was in his fifties, right? His career was long over by that point," Phillip pronounces, beginning to scan the room to see if it might hold any other potential playmates. It's obvious he's tiring of us very quickly. I can't say I blame him, since Gabriel has decided to be such a bitch.

The waiter brings our drinks, and I try to guide the conversation into more talk about the show. Unfortunately, since it's a new script, none of us knows much about it. We'd all seen *The Normal Heart*, which was such a sobering evening, so we end up hashing over that tragic outcome.

Since the character of Felix is the only one we know about from the last show, we actually go through another round of drinks, speculating on what might happen with him being a ghost in this one. Of course, that means a lot of this conversation revolves around Phillip. I get the feeling he's very used to being the center of attention.

At least the show's subject matter being about the virus brings a civilized calmness to the conversation. All three of us have no choice but to face this disease in one way or another. But we have decidedly different reactions to it.

"I'm not going to let AIDS rule my life," Phillip says with a cockiness that I'm seeing more and more of in him. "We all know how to be safe, but sex can still be hot and really fun. And I intend to continue having lots of it."

"But what about all the poor people that are suffering and dying right now?" Gabriel asks. "It's not just about you. We're trying to band together as a community and help each other out. Matt and I even participated in the first ACT UP protest."

"I just can't go there. My career is too important to put much time into anything else. This will be my first principal role on Broadway, and I intend to really make it count."

I can't fault him for wanting to get ahead in this business. We all want that. But Hobo's lectures about having a certain kind of balance, one that encompasses more than just my ego, is making the most sense to me. I even think back on discussions I had with Christopher—his manifesto about blending with everyone and everything you come in contact with. It makes me a little sad now about the way that ended.

"I think I'm going to head downtown to my usual watering hole, guys," says Phillip, obviously looking for a different outcome to this evening than what I had in mind. "Uncle Charlie's is really more my crowd. Let's keep in touch. You guys have fun tonight. We'll be seeing each other soon, regardless."

He avoids any physical contact. No hugs this time as he stands to make a quick exit. "Sure, Phillip," I say, "let's get together again."

"Bye, pumpkin," Gabriel flippantly chimes in, looking in the other direction. A final jab that Phillip chooses to ignore.

As soon as he is out the door, Gabriel wastes no time in getting down to how he really feels. "Can you believe that arrogant son-of-a-bitch? That white boy needs a good ass-whuppin' and maybe that cute little pug nose of his broken. Someone needs to knock him off that privileged Caucasian pedestal he's obviously placed himself on. He walked in and took one look at my coloration and couldn't even conceive of me being in the same show as him. Am I right?"

"Unfortunately, I think you are. It really threw me, too. I'm sorry it had to happen. Even though it was uncomfortable at first, you actually made your status very clear."

"Oh, please, how could I not? Just because he checks all the fantasy boy boxes on the outside, it's pretty obvious on the inside he's just a conceited, self-absorbed bigot. And I would even say a racist. That queen only cares about one thing. His own stinkin' white ass."

"A lot has changed in five years. He was only twenty-one when we worked together. I think it might have even been his first professional show. He was so fresh and unassuming. Just a likable kid. I know you're going to be pissed at me when I say this, Gabriel, but I do think he's really hot, even if he is a bit full of himself now."

"Oh, and I suppose you have just the thing to fill him up. Am I right?"

"Like I said, he's pretty damn cute. And he's definitely grown up in ways I wouldn't have expected, but this business can really change people."

"Oh, Matt. Don't blame it on the business. That kid is a real shit, and it just took a few years for him to grow into it. We've both been at this longer than him, and I don't see either of us acting like that."

"You're right, but maybe if we did, we wouldn't be stuck in the chorus," I say half-jokingly as I down the rest of my drink.

"Come on, we both know plenty of actors doing leads who are warm and even generous people. We'll get there someday, honey. I refuse to think the way to stardom is about steppin' on whoever you can, to get to the top."

The evening takes on a much more pleasant quality after Phillip's departure. Gabriel and I each show off our chops with a few Broadway standards, much to the applause and appreciation from the crowd. I can't help but wonder if this type of casual entertainment, with no paycheck or grand stage involved, really taps into the magic of what performing is all about. The emotion of a song can come from deep inside you, and sharing it freely is an act of love.

In show business, that love comes in a multitude of forms. Some may not get you rave reviews in *The New York Times*, but this impromptu concert tonight that Gabriel and I performed, feels like a genuine example of that.

Too bad sharing the love on stage is so much easier than my current love life. I'm still so frustrated about what happened with Christopher. How could I have stepped so far beyond his comfort zone without realizing it? My professional life is turning around now. I can't let the blowup with Christopher hold me back from other options. I've turned a corner now, and I'm just going to keep getting out there in every way I can. I've seen too many lives cut short not to.

Nineteen

Timothy and I were pretty close to the same height, but his much leaner frame was more suited to his dancing abilities. That didn't leave a lot of options in the way of sharing clothes, but bathing suits were always fair game.

Digging through the top drawer of my dresser, I'm transported back to our summer stock days of frolic and fun. It's a bittersweet journey as I pull out his collection of Speedos from that time long gone. He was more of a fashion plate than I was, so I have plenty to choose from, packing for what I hope will be a fun-filled Memorial Day weekend.

"You seem to have quite a collection of skimpy skin coverings there, Daddy Boy. Licentious loin cloths may be a more apt description."

I give Hobo my now familiar eye roll and continue sorting. After her last vanishing act a week ago, I wasn't sure when she'd make another appearance. But I have been rather busy this past week with a certain redhead, which I'm sure didn't get past her observations either.

"I can't say I recall this sort of revealing fashion statement being quite your style in the good old days. You were a bit more modest back then," she says, lounging on my bed atop all the other clothes I've set out to pack.

"Things change. And it's a good thing you're not real, or I'd be kicking you off that bed so fast you'd be crawling under it. One thing I could never stand is a bunch of cat hair all over my clothes."

"What do you mean I'm not real? I surmise at least two of your senses have been engaging in my presence. Both sight and sound. Not to mention when I'm channeling some rare jewel of insight into your consciousness. And might I remind you of one of my favorite activities? I could never resist jumping in a freshly laundered load of clothes, still warm from the dryer. Remember how that would make Timothy laugh?"

"Yes, I do, and I'm sure you remember how I'd toss you off, too."

"Indeed. It's a wonder I've even bothered continuing this kitty companionship. But you certainly have been otherwise occupied lately, so I thought I'd give you a bit of a break."

"I'm guessing you don't approve of me dating Phillip," I say, choosing four Speedo variations on the same theme, aka—as much skin as I can get away with. "I've decided casual dating is the healthiest way for me to go right now. He's definitely not relationship material, but man, is he hot."

"Cupid's arrow has a way of piercing unmentionable places, but may bypass the heart completely," Hobo says as she daintily makes her way over to my pillow and settles in.

"I actually couldn't agree with you more, Pussyface. He's self-centered and probably not that bright, but you can't argue with the rest of the package."

"I'm just surprised you wanted anything to do with him after that little encounter with Gabriel."

"Talk about a drama queen. Gabriel was borderline rude to Phillip. I think they both were really at fault. Phillip called me afterward to explain why he got defensive and wanted to make sure I didn't get any wrong ideas about him. Then he asked me out."

"Well, fancy that! The first guy to come on strong to you since you've emerged from your hibernation in this apartment, and you just jump on it."

"Why not? I need the practice. We had fun at The Saint, and we've been having even more fun this past week between the sheets. He's really a likable guy, if you keep everything on the surface."

"But what good does that do you except that you're getting to *do* him?"

"You know, I was starting to have some strong feelings for Christopher, but look what a disaster that turned into. I figure I'm not ready for anything like that right now. So, if I keep it casual with no strings, at least I'm trying out the equipment again. And so far, it's working just fine. I would think you'd be happy for me that I'm finally getting laid after all this time."

"You can't keep this sort of thing up without feelings eventually getting involved. Have you ever heard the expression, 'don't shit where you eat'? What are you thinking? You're going to be working with this guy. Do you really think you can separate the two? There's a reason why you didn't put my food dish next to my litterbox Daddy Boy."

"I'll cross that bridge when I get to it, but for now, I'll be taking an alternative route over the water. This fairy is taking the ferry boat to The Pines on Fire Island!"

"So, Daddy Boy is off to gay mecca, just a short hop by train out to Sayville, Long Island. All that's left is crossing the bay to the ultimate island playground of beautiful boys in tasteful cedar plank beach houses lining the water."

"And your point being?"

"I'm sure you'll be experiencing the Bacchanalian delights of tea dance amidst the outdoor breezes of the Blue Whale Bar. And let us not forget that the dancing continues at The Pavilion practically all night long. Oh, and did I mention the private gatherings at the swimming pools, with little red wagons being pulled down the boardwalks to carry all that's required for party central?"

"How do you know so much about it?"

"Don't you remember planning a trip there with Timothy? Then he got sick, and you never made it. You might have thought I was dozing in his lap when you both were discussing it all in great detail, but elephants aren't the only ones who never forget. I seem to recall that Timothy called it 'The Homosexual Sovereign State.'"

"Yes, I do remember that now. It's a shame that trip didn't happen. But I have to move on with my life now, and I'm determined to start being more of an active participant. I'm not getting any younger, and who knows, I could be the next one to get sick. So many of the guys I know are dropping all around me. The time is now. Tomorrow may be a lost cause for some of us." I gather the rest of my clothes and toss everything in my bag. This cat is not making it easy to focus on just getting out of here.

"I'm sorry this disease filters into how you live your life. After what you went through, I know you have a clearer understanding of how fragile it can be. So, I'm going to trust that you will act sensibly and not over-emotionally react to whatever comes your way. And trust me, you had better be ready to play with fire out there on that island."

"Yes, Mama Puss. That works just fine for me. I like it hot, and in Phillip's case, getting into his pants is red hot. Now I've got to get out of here if I'm going to make the 11:25 ferry from Sayville. I'm going solo on the trip out and meeting Phillip at the dock once I make it to The Pines. He went out with our host yesterday to help him set up the house."

"And who, pray tell, are you staying with?"

"You know, he never told me his name. I'll get the introductions when I get there. All these plans got thrown together really fast. He'd been planning to go out anyway, but got the go-ahead to let me come along, once we started playing around this week."

"How generous. Don't be surprised if there's some sort of price to pay."

"That's the great thing. This guy lets his friends come out for free. Do you know how much people pay just to rent a room and share a house for the season? It's a fortune. He's obviously loaded, owning this place, and it's one of the primo houses right on the beach. We'll have all of Friday afternoon to hang out at the pool or go in the ocean before the real party begins. What a way to start off the long weekend, huh?"

"Well, Daddy Boy, what more can I say except bon voyage?" I look up from my packing with her last words and watch as her image fades away, like a ship disappearing over the ocean's horizon.

The day is pretty overcast when I make it to the Sayville docks, but that doesn't seem to dampen the lighthearted vibe of this animated crowd. With this being a holiday weekend, I shouldn't be surprised to see so many excited passengers, some already sporting wide-brimmed hats with even a feather boa or two thrown in. Hopefully, I'll get a seat. I can smell the salty air, laced with a sense of adventure that awaits.

The ferry ride only takes a little under a half hour as we make our way across to the barrier island. Gay Disneyland here we come! Everyone is friendly and in high spirits, anticipating the many pleasures that this slender spit of sand is famous for.

I can already imagine it. Our vision will take in the expansive ocean and sky above, and sprinkled across the smooth sand, a bevy of beautiful boys will magically appear before us. We'll hear the crashing waves mixed with the sound of disco music, pounding out our tribal party rituals. We'll eat fabulous food and drink way too long into the night, dancing and revving up for that ultimate sense, the sense of touch. That, mixed with the fleshy aroma of sexual desire, is what this island is all about. I can't wait.

I can already see Phillip's redhead from a distance, popping through a small gathering of guys, coming to greet our boat. We pass by the open-air Blue Whale Bar on our right as we slide into the inlet. The harbor is filled with vessels of all shapes and sizes, but I'm more focused on the theme park feeling of stepping out onto the boardwalk once we dock. The infamous Pavilion is on the right, and to the left, all the little red wagons are lined up for easy transport of whatever we've brought for this weekend of delights.

"Hey, sailor, new in town?" Phillip says, as he gives me a hug and wet kiss, making sure to grind our crotches together for good measure.

"This place is awesome!" I say. "Talk about a gay paradise. And it only took me two hours to get here from the city. Now I've officially landed on Fantasy Island!"

"That's nothing. Laurence treated me to a seaplane ride out here, and that only took thirty minutes. Talk about *Lifestyles of the Rich and Famous*. I could get used to this."

"So, I'm assuming this Laurence is our host, right?" We walk down the main central boardwalk, known as Fire Island Boulevard.

"Yeah, I thought I'd surprise you. Our host is Laurence Cameron."

"Laurence Cameron? Our director? No fucking way!"

"I thought it would blow your mind."

"I can't believe it. How do you even know him?"

"Like I said at The Townhouse, this business is about connections. I actually met him out here at The Pavilion last season. He's a pretty cool guy, even if he is on the old side. He's probably pushing fifty. Of course, he'd never admit that. But who cares? He's got one of the most flawless houses out here, right next to Calvin Klein's. And the party never seems to end."

"I'm still a little in shock, Phillip. What am I going to say to him?"

"How about thanks for hiring me?"

"That's probably a good start."

"Oh, and one more thing I left out. Laurence has only one requirement for his guests. Everybody is nude when you're out on the deck around the pool."

"You're kidding."

"No, I'm totally serious. He prefers you stay naked the entire time but only demands it when your hanging around the pool."

"Christ, Phillip. You could have at least filled me in on that before I came out here."

"What's the problem? From what I've seen this past week, you certainly have nothing to be embarrassed about."

"That's not the point. You should have told me."

"Oh, get over it. Boys will be boys, right? That's what we're out here for."

As we continue down the boardwalk, looking at the weathered grey cedar cottages along the way, I try to get used to the idea that I'm now going to be on display all weekend. We take a left on Driftwood, the boardwalk heading toward the beach, and I immediately notice the bar has been raised considerably higher now that we're getting closer to the beachfront dwellings.

The Laurence Cameron spread is the picture of modern architectural elegance, with clean lines and slanting angles. Once we're through the gate, we see the entire back of the house is a wall of floor-to-ceiling windows facing out to the pool and the ocean beyond. The sleek and tasteful pool area is temporarily empty of lithe and muscled male bodies that I'm sure will soon complete the setting. A weekend of gaiety is about to commence.

I recognize the man walking toward us, who I'm assuming made the final decision to advance Phillip's and my career to its current standing. He's sporting a loose tank top and shorts, so I guess his requirement of hanging out in the buff doesn't include himself. Besides the obvious hours he's put in to keep his body fit and trim, he must spend some time in a tanning bed since his skin already has that summer-bronzing look.

He wears his middle age well, not like some of our older crowd who try to pull off the Peter Pan look. "Hello, Matthew. Welcome to my pleasure palace. I'm so glad Phillip suggested you come out this weekend."

"Thanks so much for having me," I say, barely able to form a complete sentence. "Your place is so beautiful."

"And I've come to the conclusion that beauty is the ultimate ideal out here. I always aspire to be right in the center of it. I'm so happy to have you boys around to help complete the picture." He reaches out to Phillip and runs his hand over his chest.

"Happy to oblige," says a smiling Phillip, grabbing his hand and guiding it down to his shorts. "How's that for a complete picture?" Phillip laughs it off as he steps away and now grabs my hand. "I'll give Matt the tour and then maybe throw together some lunch for us."

"That sounds perfect," Laurence says. "We can have it out here on the deck."

I immediately wonder what kind of boundaries will be invaded this weekend by that last little exchange. Hobo's warning that there's always a price to pay comes to mind. Do I need to strip for lunch just because it's outside? I decide to cross that bridge when I get to it.

It all takes a bit of getting used to, as Phillip shows me around the casual but chic décor, and we drop my bag in one of the four bedrooms we'll share.

"This is home for the weekend," Phillip says as he pulls me down onto the bed.

"My, aren't we feeling frisky today," I say, rolling around with him for a quick make-out session. I can't seem to get enough of his muscular little gymnast-like body. "You certainly are touchy-feely with Laurence."

"Yeah, he loves it. It's really just a silly game. Oh, we trick once in a while too. It's no big deal. He knows I'm not into him, but Fire Island has its own set of rules—like none at all." He growls and rolls on top of me, pinning my arms back and sticking his tongue down my throat. "That was just an appetizer, let's go get some lunch, tiger."

I'm not sure what to make of the ramifications of this current game we're about to play all weekend with our host. But I'm here, I'm queer, and I guess I better get used to it.

I manage to keep my shorts on for lunch and actually find Laurence easy to talk to. Phillip is constantly turning the conversation into some type of flirtation, which I find annoying. It's almost like he's playing some kind of role to secure more invitations for this summer season. I keep bringing the conversation back to our future production.

I get the feeling Laurence is more interested in leaving the business end of it back in Manhattan. Still, he's very excited with how it's all coming together.

"I will tell you boys, our producers have secured the Belasco Theater for our show," Laurence says, pouring himself a second glass of white wine. "So, you boys better behave, or I hear the ghost of Mr. Belasco can be pretty mischievous. He demands respect from all the actors that perform on his stage."

"Oh please," Phillip says, helping himself to another glass. "That's a lot of bunk. I, for one, don't believe in ghosts. I believe in great reviews and sold-out shows. You want mischievous? That's *my* middle name."

"Aren't you the bad boy. Matthew, it sounds like your pal Phillip here is going to need a spanking."

"That can be arranged," I say, trying to keep it vague and stay in the game. "As for the Belasco ghost, I say there's no harm in heeding your warning." The memory of his appearance at the callback comes flooding back to me, like a visitation from an old relative I'm particularly fond of. "He was quite the impresario, and performing in that theater will be a privilege to be a part of his legacy."

"I couldn't agree with you more. Phillip, you might heed the words of your understudy."

"Understudy?" I gasp, not knowing whether he's on the level.

"That's right, Matt," Laurence says. "The decision was made that you'd understudy the part of Felix. You both have that classic All-American Boy look we're going for, and you certainly have the vocal range for the songs. There wasn't any need to tell you until we got to work, but after seeing you two out here together, I just couldn't resist."

"That's wonderful, Matt! Now we'll be working more closely together than ever," Phillip says.

"Wow, that's amazing! Thank you so much."

"No thanks needed. I have every confidence in both of you."

My head is spinning now with this news. What an incredible opportunity this is to have landed in my lap. If the show runs long enough, I may even get to go on as Felix. That's always a big if, but it still puts me into a new position, and I'm thrilled with the anticipation of the challenge.

"I don't care if it *is* cloudy today," I say, "I think this understudy needs an ocean baptism! Who's game?"

"You boys go have fun. I'm going to putter around here and welcome the rest of my guests as they straggle in throughout the day."

The ocean is freezing and a little rough. It's still early in the season, so the water hasn't warmed up much. Phillip and I have fun regardless, getting tossed around in the waves for a while. Afterward, we walk the long stretch of beach that will eventually land us in Cherry Grove, the decidedly second-string gay enclave. Not nearly the attitude nor the price tag for real estate, Cherry Grove caters to a crowd that doesn't fit the Gay A-list requirements. Lots more lesbians and more multi-ethnic, with plenty of drag queens thrown into the mix. They leave the pretension to the buffed gym boys here at The Pines. We're experiencing plenty of that as we stroll along the shoreline. It feels more like a catwalk as muscle boys pass us by, strutting their stuff, always on the lookout for a "friendly" encounter.

"I'm sure you've heard stories about the Meat Rack," Phillip says, leaving the beachfront homes of The Pines behind. We look inland toward the line of scrubby brush, camouflaging the half-mile trail that's officially named "The Judy Garland Memorial Pathway."

"Oh yeah. It's party central for anonymous sex at all hours of the day, especially at night. Not exactly my scene," I say, grabbing his hand. "Besides, what do I need that for? I have you to occupy my carnal desires."

"Oh, come on. Don't knock it till you've tried it. Where's your sense of adventure? It can be a real turn-on."

"I guess that means you've tasted the hanging fruit out there," I say, swatting his behind. "Laurence is right. You've turned into a bad boy, and a good spanking is in order." We both get a laugh out of that as I get a few more smacks in, chasing each other around before taking another dip in the water.

When we return to the house, we're greeted with five naked bodies out at the pool, including Laurence. Of course, they're all attractive, adhering to Laurence's visual agenda. I can't help but feel a little awkward, but Phillip waves a hello to everyone and immediately slides his Speedo off and jumps in. Now I really feel like a total idiot just standing there, so what the hell? I do the same and follow him in.

The warm pool water turns out to be a convenient catalyst for easing into my virgin entry as a participant in this nudist weekend. I put my self-consciousness aside and actually relax into the flirtatious fun as I get to know my housemates. Before I arrived here, I certainly had no idea just how much they'd be revealing, in the literal sense, that is.

Considering the situation, I stick to my game plan for the next few days and focus all my physical attention on Phillip, regardless of how the party weekend progresses. I can't help it. I'm just a one-man guy. He obviously has other ideas. His flirtatiousness is just the way he communicates with practically everyone he encounters.

And so, we progress through the Fire Island rituals of beach walks and afternoon pool parties, tea dances, and fun dinners. The grand finale each night being the disco at The Pavilion. That party can easily go until sunrise. Everybody just sleeps in until noon, and then it all starts all over again.

By the third night, I'm actually a little over it. How much drinking and drugging can a gay boy handle? I've made sure to steer clear of the drugs this weekend, after that crazy night at The Saint. But Phillip seems particularly wired tonight and is bouncing off the walls. He must have scored something from one of his friends. He knew better than to offer whatever it was to me.

"Holy shit, Matt. This music is so awesome!" Phillip shouts over the ear-splitting beat, as he whips his body around the sweaty and shirtless dance floor. "I feel fantastic! Look at all these hot guys!"

I'm not really into it, so when the music changes, I signal to him that I'm ready for a break. He's too caught up in himself to care, which I'm beginning to realize is typical of him. So, I leave the dance floor and head to the sidelines, just letting him keep spinning.

Once I get into an area where I can hear myself think again, I notice Laurence chatting with another young guy. He spots me and waves me over.

"So, you're taking a break from that little fireball I see," Laurence says, grabbing a pile of cocktail napkins. "Here, let me take care of some of that sweat. You're just dripping."

"Oh, that's okay." I intercept his attempt to blot my chest by grabbing the napkins from him. "The paper would probably stick to me anyway."

"Well, that might be fun. We could take turns peeling it off."

"I think I'll just wait till I get back to the house and take another dip in the pool."

"Perfect! We were just leaving. Matt, meet my new best friend, Alex." Laurence grabs the guy's ass and nudges him slightly forward toward me. "Let's all go back for some more pool playtime. I can demonstrate some of my directorial skills...if you like to be told what to do. I'm a pushover, you know, for some good visuals."

"Nice to meet you Alex, but you guys go ahead. I'm going to see if I can corral Phillip into leaving. It's after three a.m., and I'll be turning into a pumpkin soon."

"If you strike out with Phillip, you know where to find us. Maybe we can rustle up some pumpkin pie," he says, as he gives his "new best friend's" ass another squeeze.

"Have fun you guys," I say, trying to keep it casual as I untangle myself from this encounter and head back over to the dance floor.

It's no surprise Phillip's still going strong out there. I decide to just get another beer and be an audience member for a while. As one song tethers into the next, I muse over what drives these guys to keep this up all summer long. After a few days, it all feels like a song with just one note... though the ocean and beach are truly magnificent. What a difference from all that concrete and steel in the city, only hours away.

I think about Christopher and his experience of becoming one with his environment, blending with everything around him. But this social scene is something entirely different. I'm not feeling the connection and don't want to meld with this party scene anymore.

I finally convince Phillip it's time to go, and we walk down the boardwalk toward the house. He's still pretty revved up, but I wouldn't be a red-blooded and robust card-carrying gay boy if I didn't have a solution for that. I launch into a string of teasing innuendos to keep him motivated, and, of course, he's happy to play.

When we get to our turn at Driftwood, that leads to the house, Phillip suddenly grabs my hand, trying to pull me farther along Fire Island Boulevard.

"What are you doing?" I say, stopping dead in my tracks. "This isn't the way to the house."

"You think I don't know that?" he says, not letting up on his forceful tugging. "I'm not that fucked up that I don't know where I want us to go. It's time to present your ticket for the premier ride at this oceanfront amusement park. I'm dragging your ass to the Meat Rack."

"Not interested, Phillip."

"Oh, come on. You won't believe it. Last time I got hooked into an orgy of, it had to be like ten guys. It was so fucking hot—I just about died and went to homo heaven."

"Yeah, dying would be the operative word," I say, shaking off his grip. "There's no way that kind of behavior can stay safe."

"Sure it can. I'm never without condoms." He pulls a handful out of his pocket. "See?"

"Why am I not enough for you, Phillip? You come on to every guy you meet. It's not like we're some old couple that are sick of each other. Christ, we only just started into this last week, and all you want to do is fuck around with everyone."

"Where the hell is this coming from?" he shouts. "So, we've had a fun week. You don't get to tell me what to do or, for that matter, who I fuck."

"I know you think sleeping with people will help you get everything you want. It sure has worked great for you so far. You've cornered the market on getting invited to fancy houses. Maybe that's even how you got the part in this show."

"Fuck you, Matt. You're just so fucking jealous you didn't get the part."

I start to take a few steps back to the house. "I'm not interested in fucking directors for parts. Live it up at the Meat Rack, Phillip, and give my regards to Judy. She sure is a long way from the yellow brick road."

I don't give him a chance to say any more as I head down the boardwalk. Now what do I do? I'm certainly not going to be in his bed when he gets back.

All is quiet when I arrive at the house. It's four thirty a.m. now, so it's not surprising everyone else has finally turned in. I can't be here anymore. I don't want to see Phillip, and I don't want to be a part of any of this.

I try taking a shower to wash away this combination of sweat and frustration. At least I feel clean again, even if cleansing myself from this weekend is a whole other story. I write a short thank you note and apology to Laurence, explaining that we had a fight which forced me to make other plans and slip it under his bedroom door. I'm sure it's not the first time he's been host to some gay drama out here.

The darkness of the beach is calling me now. I can't believe how many stars I see out here. Looking up into infinity helps diminish this ridiculous situation I've gotten myself into. I can't believe I actually accused Phillip of sleeping with the director to help him get this job. It just came out. But it's probably not far from the truth.

After walking the beach for a while, I finally give up and lay down on the sand with my head on my bag, dozing off until the light of dawn breaks through.

What a night. I leave the beach and head down the boardwalk by The Pavilion. The pounding beat tells me the serious party boys are still at it. The first boat back to Sayville on this Memorial Day Monday is almost empty. I'm just grateful it's here. How come I keep screwing up these attempts at dating again? I just wanted some casual fun, and look what it's turned into. Am I even capable of being with anyone? Hobo was so right about paradise coming with a price. It's left me as empty as this boat.

Twenty

After my tepid reaction to all the yoga rituals at Tara and Pat's ceremony of commitment in Park Slope, I'm more surprised than anyone to be giving this stuff a shot. I wonder what Christopher would think. Desperate times call for desperate measures. It's pretty obvious that I've hit a brick wall with my attempts at relationships. I'm hoping this yoga class Tara is teaching in my neighborhood will help me focus my attention better on what's going on with my life. Maybe even open me up in a way where I can find more of a balance.

I've actually grown accustomed to the sequencing in this series of yoga poses. The result settles into my newly invigorated body as I move into the familiar supine position of savasana. My new yoga mat has experienced quite a few downward dogs in the last month. Not that I'm a big fan of sticking my butt up in the air, but whatever works. Now comes the best part, where we get to lay back and relax into just letting it be.

I feel every part of my body that's connected to my mat begin to melt more deeply into a relaxed state. It's almost as if the floor beneath me is sinking and curving around me like a hammock. I drop my chin down, lengthen the back of my neck, and draw my shoulder blades together, lifting my chest, and simultaneously allowing the palms of my hands to face up, signaling my senses to be receptive to whatever comes. I could get used to this.

Surrendering into gravity's gentle pull, I take in Tara's words. "Yoga is a thought system," she says. "It gives you a way to look inside yourself, and investigating the body's vibrations is your portal."

Well, that's what I'm here for. June is now coming to an end, and after committing to taking a yoga class every other day this entire month, I think I'm starting to feel myself coming into a deeper place, one that's been seriously lacking over the past few months.

"It means to unite," she continues, "a blending and tying the strands of the mind together, which forms your intention. Bringing that desire into action can bring about movement and change."

I had to do something after that catastrophic Memorial Day weekend. I just lost it out there. Yes, something has definitely got to change. It's time now to embrace life's changes instead of being afraid of them. Taking these classes is signaling that. Maybe they'll help me redefine what my life can be. It's the same life, but looking at it differently seems more possible these days.

"We begin where we are and how we are," I hear Tara say. "The practice of yoga is to act, and be attentive to our actions. Allow yourself to feel the breath as a movement of your inner being."

I inhale deeply and contemplate the fact that I obviously wasn't paying enough attention to my actions with Phillip, or maybe it wouldn't have blown up in my face. I'm glad I walked away that night, but I do regret how I left things so unresolved. I think back on Hobo's warning that I was playing with fire. She was spot on as usual. She hasn't appeared for a while. I miss her, but I'm doing okay regardless. Maybe that's some kind of sign as well.

Tara's guidance continues. "Soften the groin and the lower back."

I can just hear Hobo's reaction to that. She'd tell me if my groin was in a more "softened" state, I wouldn't have gotten into such a mess with these new attempts at relationships. Translation: Stop leading with your dick Matt.

Once again, Tara's gentle voice breaks through my ruminations. "Spread the collar bones and soften the face. Let the eyes sink into the back of the head and allow a softening of the root of the tongue. Release the brain to the back of the head."

You hear that brain? You're officially released. But what does that mean? I guess it comes down to trust and surrender. I need to trust in a deeper sense of myself. I need to know that I will be fine and just surrender to whatever is supposed to be.

Tara ends the class with the suggestion to honor all the elements of our being, including people we're close to. It dawns on me that means reaching out to people I have unfinished business with. I've made some inroads in putting Timothy in the past, but I can't seem to stop hitting barriers with the new people in my life. I should clear the air with Philip, for no other reason than I have to work with him. And Christopher. I've left that unresolved for far too long.

The location of this class on 72nd Street between Amsterdam and Columbus Avenue is an easy trek from my apartment. On my walk home, I think about Tara's words. I do think I've taken a decisive action just by opening up to the possible advantages of yoga. Never in a million years would I have dreamed of doing this, even a few months ago.

I've put the intention out there to make some changes. I remember the instructor saying that learning creates change, and change actually becomes the yoga experience. I guess it's up to me to keep that going.

I see the phone machine light flashing when I step inside the apartment. I can't believe what I'm hearing after I press the play button. "Matt, it's Helen. Charlie is in St Vincent's Hospital. He has pneumonia. Please call me when you get this message."

Holy shit, not this. "Helen, it's Matt," I say as soon as she picks up.

"Oh Matt, I'm so relieved to hear from you. I'm terribly worried about Charlie. The doctor says he has pneumocystis pneumonia. It's very serious. They're pumping all sorts of drugs into him right now to combat it."

"How could this have happened?"

"You know Charlie. He never lets on about anything even remotely negative."

"But did he seem sick at the end of your show's run?"

"Well, he was very low energy and seemed to be losing weight again. But he refused to acknowledge any of it. I guess it got so bad he finally went to the doctor. The show's been over for weeks now, so we haven't been in touch."

"Then how did you find out?"

"The hospital called me. He was delirious and was talking about wanting his mama. When they offered to call her, he gave them my number. I broke down in tears when they told me that. It's just heartbreaking. So, I've spent the morning with him."

"I'm not sure he has any kind of relationship with his parents. You know how vague he can be. We were talking about coming out once, and he said something like being out got him tossed out."

"That's horrible. I wonder how they'd feel if they knew their son had AIDS. You know that's what's at the bottom of this."

"Yeah, I know only too well." I don't want to go into it with her about Timothy right now, but all that heartache and suffering is flooding back to me. A crushing and debilitating sense of despair is seeping in again. It's amazing how my progress over these last two years can instantly vanish. Memories of the intensity of Timothy's decline suddenly paralyze me.

"I'm going back to the hospital this afternoon. Are you free to come by as well? He is alert now."

I've got to pull myself together. "I'll be there in a little while. See you then."

"Okay. Bye."

I have to face this situation just like I've faced all the others. I remember the yoga instructor's words: "We begin where we are and how we are."

Charlie has been a great friend all these years. I take a deep breath and think about what kind of intention I should bring to this visit. Being that friend for him will help. Holding his hand. Love and support are what he needs right now, and if I focus on that, it'll diminish my personal fears.

I hate hospitals. St Vincent's is where Timothy took his last breath—on the infamous seventh floor of the Spellman building. That's where they started the AIDS ward in 1984. It's ground zero for the desperately sick and dying, and it keeps expanding as more and more of us fall prey to this horrific disease.

After a very solemn subway ride, I stand outside this hulking, massive brick building, an institution that exists for the care of our loved ones. I have to keep that in mind. This is where Charlie needs to be right now.

The noisy streets are filled with cars and pedestrians that fly around me like some kind of tornado, infused with the vitality of everyday life. And yet here I stand in the eye of it, feeling the intense quiet and stillness of the many lives trying to survive inside this building, each one struggling in their private battleground. I'm about to enter and witness this palpable fight of desperation emanating throughout the hallways and rooms of the seventh floor above.

I remember coming to visit Timothy, walking down the central hall and feeling as if it was almost like a church, with the only sounds being the humming of the machines and hushed voices of nurses, all doing whatever was needed to ease the suffering. A wave of grief washes over me as I remember one of the sisters that oversaw the ward saying, "Death isn't what they fear; it's the dying."

I can't think about that right now. After confirming at the information desk that the seventh floor is my destination, I make my way up. Time to suck it up and just be there for Charlie.

The elevator door opens and I step out. It's like I've walked into a recurring nightmare. Everything looks just as it did two long years ago, when I would push past the fatigue and the helplessness of having no solution for the horrors the man I loved was facing. Once again, I'm besieged by the institutional lighting and faded colors of the walls that always remind me of the fading lives inhabiting each room. The combination of strong medicinal smells and foul human odors tells me this atmosphere is permeated with a sickness no manner of chemicals can mask.

I pass by room after room and wonder what stage of the illness each patient is dealing with. Do they have much life left to enjoy? Or will it be cut short, like so many before them.

I try to hold it together. Empathy and a genuinely deep affection for this dear friend of mine guide my final steps as I reach for the door. My heart is racing like I'm in fight or flight mode. Which one is it? Am I going to stay paralyzed with fear? Or am I going to walk inside and join in Charlie's battle—Charlie's fight for his life. I choose to fight. I open the door and enter his room. He looks very thin and pale, but his eyes light up a little when he sees me.

"Matt. How's it going buddy?" His hushed tones tell me he's reserving as much energy as possible just to get through this.

"Hey Charlie." I keep my voice down as I look over at a concerned Helen sitting at his bedside and holding his hand.

He forces his face into his usual grin. "Fancy seein' you here."

"Yeah, well, I thought I'd stop by."

"How do you like my new digs? They go so well with this hospital gown." He lets go of Helen and pushes down his blankets for effect. "I feel like the Statue of Liberty in this green schmatta. All I need is a crown."

"Hey, what are you doing?" asks Helen. She immediately pulls his covers back up. "You need to stay warm, Your Highness."

I can't help but laugh a little. "Now you're the Queen of Green."

"There goes my reputation as a black leather daddy," he says.

"This place doesn't do much for my color palate either." I give Helen a kiss and sit at the edge of his bed. "But hopefully, the drugs you're on are making it easier to take."

"Speakin' of which, I think you need to make some chemical adjustments to all these IVs I'm hooked into." At least he still has that sparkle in his eyes.

"Oh yeah? Like what do you suggest?"

"How about you hook me up to some MDMA like we had at The Saint. Now *that* I could really use right now."

"Okay, Charlie," Helen says, "you know what happens to patients who misbehave?"

"Tell me about it, Sister Mary Helen." He tries to pinch her cheek and she lightly slaps his hand away. "She's spending so much time here, I think she's pondering the idea of takin' the veil."

"Matt, will you make him stop." Helen begins to fuss with his bed covers again as I grab a chair to let her finish.

"Well, my dear," I say, "it would frame your face beautifully, but I'm not sure the rest of the outfit would be too flattering."

"Yeah, but think of all those painkillers she could hide in them deep pockets," Charlie says, with a chuckle that turns into a coughing spell.

"You've got to lay off the jokes." Helen seems to need to keep her hands busy. She adjusts his nasal breathing device like she's putting a mustache on Mr. Potato Head. "Your lungs can't handle it."

"Just don't crack yourself up with your own jokes and you'll be fine," I say. "Leave the laughing to us."

"How else do you expect me to serve my sentence in here? There's no VCR with this television, so I can't watch any of my porn tapes."

"Charlie, how can you even be thinking of things like that?" Helen's next self-imposed chore is adjusting his pillows. "You need to concentrate on getting well, and that includes plenty of rest."

"I guess gettin' well and gettin' off are a little different," he says. "At least they both come with happy endings."

"Hey, speaking of happy endings, maybe we could book him a massage in here," knowing full well I'm out of line with this suggestion.

"That's a great idea. Go pick up one of those bar rags where they advertise, and I'll order one up."

"Don't you even think of it," Helen says. "You've got to get your lungs cleared up before you have anyone put their hands all over you. Besides, I'm sure it's not allowed."

"What would those nuns who run this place do?" I ask. "Slap the masseur's hands with a ruler? That's the treatment I got in Catholic school. How dare I touch anyone 'inappropriately!'"

"A good boy like you Matthew?" At least Helen is starting to lighten up a bit. "I can't imagine you putting your hands where they weren't supposed to be."

"I can," Charlie says. "Call it gay instinct."

"Speaking of human behavior, you both might be interested to know that I've started taking yoga classes."

"Matt, that's wonderful!" Helen says.

"I've decided it's time I opened myself up to a new way of looking at why I keep hitting these roadblocks."

"Does that mean you're learnin' how to do it doggie style?" Charlie has an acute sense of smell for sexual metaphors. "I thought you already had that position 'nailed' down," he adds with more laughter, unfortunately leading to more coughing.

"That would be downward dog," I say. "It actually feels good once you...get behind it."

"All right boys. Enough is enough," Helen says in exasperation.

More laughter and coughing ends with an apology to the newly named Sister Mary Helen. She's insistent on keeping Charlie calm. But I know him well enough to understand that while this type of banter may not be good for his lungs, it's good for his head. He's got a long road to recovery in his future, and the more upbeat he is, the better.

We try to heed Helen's warning and just settle into some visiting time for the next hour that won't deteriorate into another coughing fit. I end up spilling the whole sordid story of my disastrous weekend on Fire Island. All that hot gay boy drama with Phillip certainly makes for good entertainment. Especially since everyone in the room worked with him in *Hello Dolly!*. And, of course it's no surprise that Charlie wants every description to include whatever sexual detail I'm willing to expose.

But the big news is telling them that I've been offered the understudy to the Felix character in the show. I'm pretty confident I'll work out any lingering tensions I have with Phillip. He's so full of himself—I'm sure he's just moved on to some new person to satisfy his ego.

"So, you think practicing yoga is really helping you move through some of these issues?" asks Helen.

"It helps me to look at various aspects of my life in a different way. It's really a whole new perspective on things. I'm learning to give myself time to look inside, and the classes help with that."

I no sooner finish lecturing them on my newfound philosophies inspired by yoga, when I'm shocked to see Christopher stepping into the door frame. The silence is deafening, and I'm without words to fill it.

"I couldn't agree with you more about yoga providing a new perspective," he says, breaking the moment. "I hope you won't think it's too crowded in here if I join you."

I can hardly believe what I'm seeing. We exchange a brief look that makes everything around us disappear. Time seems to expand, almost like a deep inhale infiltrating the body. There's a heightened sense of stillness in the moment, before the exhale releases the breath back out. Is this shock I'm feeling, or maybe disbelief? I have no words, but I'm guessing they will come later. In my complete bafflement, all I can do is take in his all-too-familiar beauty.

"Not at all," Charlie says. "The more the merrier."

"Helen called and let me know you were here. So, since I was in the neighborhood, I thought I'd drop by."

"Much appreciated, Christopher." Charlie's eyebrows immediately go up as he looks over at me. "You probably won't be seeing me at any cater waiter jobs for a while. So, I'm glad you did. No more carrying heavy silver trays for me in the near future."

"You'll get back to it eventually, if you really want to."

"Absolutely. I mostly just go to be around all those hot tuxedoed guys anyway."

"Another New York season, another grand soiree," Christopher says. "Matt, I guess you're taking a break from it too. Helen told me you're going to be on Broadway. Congratulations."

"Thanks. We start rehearsals in just about two weeks now. I couldn't be more excited." In reality, the excitement of seeing him and actually having a conversation with him is about all the exhilaration I can handle right now. He must have known I would be here. Such a clever boy, and so damn cute! He must have figured this was a great way to break the ice without having to deal with what went wrong with us just yet. I can only take it as a sign he's ready to open up.

"It really is wonderful," Helen says. "And I fully expect you to arrange some great seats for Charlie and me to the first preview performance. We both have to be there to see you set foot on a Broadway stage for the very first time. If that isn't motivation for getting well, Charlie, I don't know what is."

"You've got a deal. You should come back for opening night too. We can all go to the cast party!"

"In the meanwhile, Charlie and I have an announcement of our own. Would you like to tell them, dear?"

Charlie can't hide the little glow that comes over him, even in his current condition. "It seems I'll be breaking in a new roommate come the end of July. By then, we'll all probably be callin' her Mother Abbess."

Christopher and I spontaneously let out a cheer and then look at each other and giggle. I go over to Helen and kneel in front of her with my hands in prayer. "I'm going to have to pray for your sorry soul, Sister Mary Helen. I know you've already seen and, not to mention, smelled that place."

"Arise, my son," she says with a laugh. "Have I ever! I plan to use this entire month of July for a complete makeover. Charlie will be recuperating here, so Mama will get it spic-and-span with new paint, and furnish it just how she wants it. Even if I have to hire someone, all that dated stuff will be out on the street for whoever wants it, including that horrible carpet."

"I'd be happy to help you," Christopher says.

"You can count me in for the first couple of weeks," I say, looking over at Christopher, knowing full well we'll be doing it together.

"That's wonderful guys!" Helen says with a broad smile. "My agent will call your agent."

"Just don't let her make it too frilly," Charlie chimes in. "I wouldn't want to scare away any tricks."

"Don't worry," I say. "We'll keep her corralled into the gay tasteful zone."

After some more chit-chat, with Christopher giving us his dance concert updates, we can all see Charlie is fading and needs to get some rest. I'm the first to make the announcement that I'm taking off, and much to my surprise and excited uneasiness, Christopher says he'll join me. I try to ignore the knowing looks from Charlie and Helen as we say goodbye, wondering what the next moment of just the two of us alone again will bring.

The silence of our walk down the long hallway screams volumes of all that has been left unsaid. Neither of us can bring ourselves to say a word. It ended so strangely with us, and I can't help but think he's finally ready to explain himself. I'm bursting with so much I want to share with him, too. Does he even want to hear it?

But we also can't ignore where we are. Each door we pass is another story of what may become a tragic ending. I'm sure Christopher's positive status is weighing on him with every step. It's almost like two dramas are being acted out simultaneously, the angst of what could be our attempt to communicate set against the backdrop of this plague that may claim his life.

The elevator opens, and it's empty. We step in. Just us. Just this feeling of us. It has a staggering intimacy to it. The doors close, and we find ourselves together and alone.

Twenty-One

Could pushing the elevator lobby button be like flicking a switch and finally shedding some light on what Christopher and I are even doing here together? I wish it was that easy. I look over at this beautiful guy with his tousled hair and those deeply sensitive eyes. They're wide open and look like they're beginning to allow me in once again. Is that what I'm seeing? I'm just not sure.

Someone needs to start this conversation. I guess it's going to be me. "Charlie really is quite the character, isn't he?"

Before Christopher has a chance to reply, my question is left unanswered because the elevator doors now open on the sixth floor, with three more people entering. So much for my lame attempt to break through this heightened silence. Both of us resign ourselves to keeping our focus forward on the doors while we make two more stops before finally reaching the lobby. What's the point of saying another word in front of an audience?

"Yes, Charlie is a great guy," Christopher manages to say when we finally exit the building.

"I don't know about you, but it's a relief to get out of that place and into some fresh air again. Regardless, I intend to keep sucking it up and doing a lot of time here. He's one of my best friends. I really think of him as family."

"He's lucky to have family like you and Helen. She's obviously completely committed to his recovery. I'm happy to help in any way I can too. Now the challenge will be to get their apartment set up in a way that will benefit both of them."

"Yeah, I'm all in, too." Our eyes lock once again, both wondering what's next.

"Matt, do you have some time to talk? I know I have a lot of explaining to do, but first, I need to know if you're even interested in hearing it after all this time."

Finally, he makes the first move. It's about fucking time. I've never stopped thinking about him, wondering why it ended so badly. Of course, I'm still interested!

"Yes, I'd be open to it. And if I'm being honest, I think we both need to let our feelings be known. I have some things to say too. I'm good with right now if you are."

"I don't live too far from here. Why don't we walk over to my studio?"

"Sounds like a plan."

"I live on West 12th Street between Greenwich and Washington, so it's just down the street."

We start heading toward the Hudson River on West 12th. It's got to be as strange for him as it is for me to be walking together, side by side. A little over a month and a half has passed since the blowup at The Saint. My drugged up head wasn't exactly clear that morning. But after he saw me come out of the club, he made it very clear that I wasn't worth talking to anymore.

"Isn't this a nice street? I've gotten very comfortable here in the West Village, not to mention the convenience to the Cunningham Studio," he says.

I can tell Christopher is nervous. Is he afraid that I'm going to bite his head off because he freaked out on me that morning outside The Saint? All I know is that I need to stay calm and grounded. He'll pick up on that and maybe relax enough to say everything that's on his mind.

"Yeah, it must be nice to be so close. You've got everything you need down here. Are you still working part-time at the restaurant?"

"Still there. It's been great, actually. Nice people, good food, and again, I can easily walk to work."

"That food really was great. I have to admit, though, I still like my animal protein. But everything in moderation, right? I've learned a little more about balance from my yoga instructor, so I alternate my meat meals with vegetarian."

"It's so wonderful that you're exploring yoga, Matt. Tara had told me you're taking class with her. That speaks volumes to me." He stops for a moment when we reach his block. "We're almost to my place. I wanted to wait and not get into all this until we got there, but I have to tell you right now how sorry I am about how I acted that morning outside The Saint. What you were doing in there was your own business, and I shouldn't have judged you the way I did. I hope you'll accept my apology."

"Sure. I think I mainly went there as a reaction to the frustration I was feeling about our blowup at the Park Slope subway. I just needed to cut loose."

We begin walking down his street again. There's a calmness to this neighborhood. Maybe because it's so far west, it feels more out of the way. I can see why he likes it down here.

"It's all part of the same issue," he says. "I guess the timing couldn't have been worse because it took me all that week just to get up the nerve to talk to you about it. Then I saw you walk out of that place, and it just sent me over the edge."

"I guess, for me, it's been this journey about trying to re-find myself after Timothy. You were the first person who made me feel I might be able to share a deeper part of myself with again. I know we were both just feeling our way into it, but when you reacted the way you did, it completely threw me, and I went in the opposite direction. Of course, that ended up being pretty much a disaster too."

We reach his pre-war brick building and head inside. Nothing fancy, but it's not a cheap area to live in. It's got an elevator, but we take the stairs to the second floor.

"You're probably wondering how I can afford to live alone," he says as he leads me down the hallway. "My folks are helping me with the rent. My mom came out to visit when I moved here and helped me make some adjustments to the interior to suit my needs. It's just a small studio, but it works great for me."

He opens the door, and I feel like I've walked into a Zen retreat. I immediately experience a sense of calm wash over me. All the walls are covered with a gently textured grass cloth, and each panel is trimmed with a thin strip of natural light wood. The entire room has an organic quality, with the beige and wheat-colored wall coverings threaded with hints of sage green, beautifully complementing the wood framing.

The entry floor, with a small kitchen and bathroom off to the side, has a simple creamy tile surface, but the majority of the space is raised up a step and completely covered in tatami mats. The only furniture on the mats is a low square table with flat square pillows stacked in various areas. Talk about living an ascetic life. Two long windows face the back of the building and border a simple altar set in between them. One of the side walls is made up entirely of floor-to-ceiling wood cabinets, so whatever stuff he has is obviously tucked away, leaving only this clean, spare quality to the space.

"Welcome to my little postage stamp of urban paradise. I hope you don't mind taking off your shoes before you step onto the mats."

"No, not at all. What a beautiful and serene space you've created for yourself. I can't say that I'm surprised with all our discussions about actually being and blending with your environment. This one suits you to a tee."

"Thank you. You're right. Everything about this space is a reflection of the kind of reality I'm most comfortable being in."

"But where's your bed?"

"I roll out a futon from the cabinet, and I have lots of extra pillows in there to prop myself up for reading and whatever. I don't deprive myself of comfort. It all works really well for me. The mats are also great for stretching."

He goes to a cabinet, pulls out some large pillows, and tosses them on the mats. "Make yourself comfortable; I'll get us some nice herbal tea that I made this morning."

"That sounds great." I almost feel like a little kid when I grab an oversized pillow and roll around with it a bit. "What about these flat square ones? Are they what you use when you're sitting at the table?"

"Yes, that's right. They're called zabuton cushions. You can also use them when you're sitting in meditation."

"I haven't gotten into that yet, but who knows? I never thought I'd actually enjoy taking a yoga class either."

Christopher returns with the tea. We pull up a couple of zabuton cushions and sit cross-legged across from each other at his exotically carved low table.

"This is actually called an opium table. My mom found it in an antique store in the village. But we'll just stick with iced tea."

I guess I'm a bit nervous because my mouth has gone dry. So, I take a long drink. "This is delicious. Is it a special blend?"

"Good choice of words. You already know my theories on blending. And yes, it's a combination of a bunch of herbs and citrus."

"Very refreshing."

"Thanks. So, Matt, I've been thinking a lot about how I want to approach this talk with you. At a certain point, it occurred to me that Hobo's journey of trusting your love and affection is a good way of explaining what I've been going through."

"She certainly was a special cat." I'm obviously not going into details about how special she's ended up being.

"When you first got her, you couldn't grab her from behind or make any sudden moves, right?"

"Yes, she was feral. Any move like that, and she would instinctively react as prey, running away or lashing out."

"Do you see how similar she and I are? I reacted the same way when you grabbed me by surprise. I lashed out initially because it felt like an attack, and then not wanting to talk about it was just like running away. We both know that behavior is based on fear. And that comes from not trusting the person or situation. I've been dealing with these reactions for some time now. But I've finally come to an understanding that life is too precious to waste in that mindset. Not just the fear of being hurt physically, but emotionally too."

"I would never intentionally hurt you in any way."

"Yes, my rational mind knows that. But I had a horrific experience a couple of years ago, and sometimes my fear instincts take over when I'm taken by surprise. I was sexually assaulted and penetrated against my will. And it happened at The Saint."

"Oh, my God. I'm so sorry."

"I hadn't been in New York very long and was completely naive about what can happen in this city. I went out to The Saint with a few new friends, and even though clubbing isn't usually my thing, I had a lot of fun dancing into the night. I eventually met a guy on the dance floor and really got into it with him too. After a while, he suggested we go up to the balcony and get more comfortable. Stupid me, I thought it would just be a make-out session. I was thinking it was sort of like my New York City rite of passage.

"It was so dark up there, and everyone had their private little spots. We were getting pretty heavy, and I let it go further than I had intended because it led to some mutual jerking off. He even pulled out a small container of lube. It felt good, but that was definitely as far as I thought it would go.

"Then he pulled out some amyl nitrate. I stupidly inhaled way too much of it and practically passed out. The drug flooded into me. My mind and body were spinning out of control. I suddenly had no willpower in that moment. I was so overwhelmed by a rushing sensation that I lost it completely, and before I knew it, he was inside me."

"I don't know what to say."

"The music was blasting, and I was barely understanding what was happening, with my head and body being overpowered by both him and the drug. It was like I was in the middle of some drug-fueled nightmare I didn't know how to wake up from. Then it was over before I knew it, and he just thought it was all in fun. I was so humiliated and in shock, I just pulled up my pants and left."

"Jesus, Christopher. You were raped. I can't even imagine it. I'm so sorry. It's no wonder the trauma is still with you, and that fear instinct kicks in."

"Now you see why sudden moves set me off. I still have some deep-seated trust issues. It all came back to me when I saw you come out of The Saint, and I just lost it all over again. I'm sorry it's taken so long for me to unload all this on you, but my fears aren't just on a physical level either."

"How do you mean?"

"Unfortunately, my HIV-positive status is the result of that sexual attack."

"Oh, my God. Are you sure?"

"Yes. There's been no one else. And if the positive diagnosis wasn't bad enough, it's *being* positive that makes me now fear anyone having to go through this with me. I'm afraid of someone getting close, because I'm not sure I can take watching how they'll suffer, dealing with me. You've been through that already. If I get sick, it will be overwhelming enough. But to have to share a lover's experience of witnessing it, that just feels like it would be too much."

"I think it comes down to trust, Christopher. You have to trust that the love of your relationship will override everything else. You have to trust in the process of growing into love. That it will see you through. And you know I can say that from experience."

"Yes, you can."

"Trusting that you can be loved opens up your entire world. Look what it did for Hobo. It was such a gift to witness how she came to accept more and more of our love. The trust was so hard-won, but it made the reward even greater."

"I guess it's sort of like the coming out process. We can all relate to that. The first time I explored the touch of another guy, I had to cross a bridge to get to that other side. I had to trust that the bridge would support me getting there. And I had to trust that I would be where I wanted to be once I made it to the other side... There was no going back."

"Hobo crossed that bridge with Timothy and me, too. It took her many months and really a series of bridges. Each one represented a new level of trusting in the physical love she was receiving. But enough about her," I say. "My feelings for you never left. Playing around last month was just a reaction to how frustrated I was about it not working out with you."

We stare into each other's eyes for a moment, suspended in this heightened connection we've re-established. I place my first two fingers on the table. "So, this is me. And let's say this table is our bridge. I'm going to start walking my fingers across now."

Christopher immediately puts his first two fingers down as well. We both slowly walk them out to the middle.

"I trust this bridge. Do you?"

"Yes, Matthew. I do." And we both grasp onto each other's hand.

I look into his luscious eyes and see them light up in a joyful smile. "I could get used to this hand-holding thing," I say.

"Me too."

"Now it's my turn," I say, not letting go of his hand. "I have something I need to share with you."

"Okay."

"I've never been tested for HIV."

"That occurred to me when I shared my status with you, and you didn't share yours. Matt, that's a decision everyone needs to make in their own time. I'm sure you practice safe sex."

"Of course. I don't want to get into all my issues with not testing right now, but I just thought you should know."

"Thank you." He places his other hand on the table and walks his two fingers out to the center as well, opening his hand. "Is this sort of like when Hobo started to make an actual move toward physical contact with you?"

"Something like it." I walk out with my other hand to be enfolded in his as well. "You know, she eventually began to hop up on my lap."

"Is that a request?" he asks with a smile, slowly standing up. "Have you ever heard of the adagio section of a ballet class? That's when the music slows way down..."

He begins walking toward me as if in a gentle, leisurely dance. His seamless and fluid movements almost look like they're riding on a tender wave-like vibration as he reaches my side of the table. I push back, and he effortlessly seems to float down and straddle my legs as he sits down facing me, crossing his ankles behind my lower back and placing his hands around my neck.

"This is more my version of lap time," he says, with beaming eyes. "Or maybe we can call it a yoga hug."

"You're much better at this than Hobo was." A gentle kiss initiates the delicate dance of two souls finding their way into bonding and blending as one.

I run my hands through his thick hair and massage his scalp and neck as we probe deeper into a more passionate kiss. His hands are all over my shoulders and arms and back. We press our torsos harder together, in a kind of desperation, to link us as close as possible to each other. There's a driving need to feel this new expanse of us, and yet it slowly evolves into a letting go, a mutual melting of our hearts. We find new meaning in what it is to become one.

"I've got an idea," Christopher says when we finally come up for air. "How about really making a clean slate of it and taking a shower?"

"Works for me."

Twenty-Two

The first day of rehearsal always feels like the first day of school to me. I have my sack lunch packed. I've carefully considered my choice of clothes that will make just the right impression on my fellow "students" of this theatrical production. No homework yet, because we're all making a fresh start. But scripts will definitely be passed out today. The anticipation of the beginning of this project has finally reached its peak. It's now time to step out into my new destiny.

I'll probably get there a little early, which is fine. I can start introducing myself to the rest of the cast before we begin. I lock up, race down the stairs, and step outside.

"And I'm sure you'll be the most popular boy in the show."

"Hobo! I haven't seen you in so long!"

"Well, you've made a lot of changes, and I thought it was time for you to figure things out on your own." She makes herself comfortable on a trash can very similar to the one where she made her first appearance to me on that bitterly cold winter day so many months ago now.

"How nice of you to show up for my send-off!"

"How could I not? After all we've been through to get you here. The last time you saw me on a trash can, you were heading inside to throw the covers over your head. And now, just the opposite is happening. You're heading out for the challenge of a new theatrical adventure. You really have come full circle in so many ways."

"Including my new beau. Christopher and I couldn't be happier. We both finally let our guards down in these past couple of weeks. Helping Helen with the apartment has been the perfect excuse for being with him almost every day, which has turned into quite a few nights, too."

"Shocking! My Daddy Boy has finally started putting all these notions into practice. And as you know, practice makes perfect."

"You're preaching to the choir on that one. I've got to run, but I thought you should know that I called Phillip, too."

"Let me guess. He was so caught up with himself that he had difficulty placing your name."

"Well, not quite. He basically told me to fuck off. But at least I got my apology out before he hung up on me. I still think sleeping with the director didn't exactly diminish his chances at getting the part."

"At least he knows where his true talents lie. Best we not be too 'catty,' and let others work out their own karma."

"Hobo, you're turning into a yoga kitty!"

"Maybe I've learned something from you, too."

She suddenly disappears into the ether, which is good, because now I've got to hustle to make it down to 890 Broadway on time. Luckily, the trains are working in my favor, and I find myself once again striding past the Flatiron Building. Just a couple of more blocks, and I'll be having another moment of reflection in front of the 890 building, the hub of so many theatrical projects.

I pick up my pace as I consider the countless auditions that I've done there. But somehow, it's the cattle call for this show that's still with me. Almost like a badge of honor, but in this case, it's a badge of effort, proclaiming what it took to push myself through it. And now as I stand here, looking at these entry doors, I finally get to be part of the "in" crowd again. At last, I'm a working actor. Hallelujah!

The rehearsal space is set up with a circle of twenty or so chairs and a piano off to the side. Given the relatively small cast, I'm sure that includes some of the production people. I scan the room and immediately spot the director, Laurence Cameron, chatting with Phillip. Why am I not surprised? Then Gabriel comes into my view, getting some coffee and checking out the spread of pastries and bagels. I make a beeline over to him.

"You better steer clear of all those carbs," I say. "No telling how revealing that costume of yours will be."

"Matthew, my manchild, you are so right. These ebony curves have been on a strict diet for I can't remember how many weeks. Best not to indulge now and let it all go to fat."

"You look pretty flawless to me. Even if you never did show up for any of those workouts at the YMCA."

"Yeah, sugar, sorry about that. I decided my character might be too distracting if I started developing bulges all over this fine frame from weightlifting. Besides, they might detract from a certain other bulging area."

"Gabriel, you never change. How are you?"

"Oh, absolutely flawless as always. Couldn't you just pinch yourself right now?"

Before I can answer, the stage manager gets everyone's attention. After introducing himself, he instructs us to take a seat. We all quiet down and look around at one another, taking in each person. We're probably all wondering how our relationships will evolve as we now all bring our shared awareness into this production. The intensely personal experience of bonding as a cast has arrived. It's anyone's guess what shape and form it will take, or how long we'll be an integral part of each other's lives, just because we're doing a show together. That's just the nature of what all this is.

Laurence takes over and begins a welcome speech. I'm sure everyone is listening, but the alternate reality of looking around at the faces in the room and imagining the intimacy of working together overpowers his words, at least in my case. There is so much emotion that goes into working in a play. What will I learn from these people? How will they influence me as a performing artist? I can't help but wonder what it will be like to blend our emotions and voices, working to sing and act out a singular creative statement.

Phillip and I share a moment of focus, sitting across the circle from each other. It's like looking at a zombie—no acknowledgment. I'm sure the closeness that's all but required in a play like this has crossed both our minds. It can only be in both our favor to be as professional and easy on each other as possible. Hopefully, the tensions will ease as we get into rehearsal. It doesn't always work out that way, but I'm certainly willing to give it a try since I'm going to be shadowing his every move to learn the blocking for his character.

The play is what's important. That thought catapults me out of my head and back to Laurence's persuasive words:

"The inspiration for this project began with the title of the groundbreaking play, *The Normal Heart*," he says. "A phrase that originated in a poem by W.H. Auden. That poem's title is 'September 1, 1939.' On that day, Hitler invaded Poland, and two days later, Britain and France declared war on Germany. The essence of Auden's poem is about being united as a form of fighting back. Taking on what might seem like an indomitable monster. Understanding that there is no surrender. Defeating it is our only option.

"Now, this is *our* message. This is our cause. When we, as a community, can come together in mutual love and support for each other, we can make a difference. Just like the words and music of this play can make a difference too. That's the power of theater. It's why we're here—to engage this power in a creative way that's both entertaining and enlightening.

"The title of our musical drama, *Our New Normal*, gives a voice to this struggle we're all facing and, more aptly, describes what this creative project is about. It deals with the fact that we're now engaging in real combat, ramping up this fight against AIDS and the appalling lack of action taken by our government. Unfortunately, this new normal is not going away anytime soon.

"We've all witnessed casualties of this war. That's where our Greek chorus comes in. These victims of this plague will rise up from the dust and be heard, with the character of Felix leading them. You guys are representing so many tragically lost souls. I know you will make them proud."

Thoughts of my lost love, Timothy, enter my mind as I begin to tear-up, listening to this. What an amazing soul. Like so many others I've known that are gone. Timothy was a relatively early casualty, before we even had anything to fight with. Now, my good friend Charlie is facing his own battle. I'm so glad to be there for him, and being involved with this play is a part of how I can fight for him, too.

The day continues with a read-through of the script that confirms even more how important this experience will be. Plenty more tears are shed as each of the actors plow into their characters and the conflicts inherent in this piece.

At the piano, the composer plays and sings the songs inserted throughout the two acts that will be sung by the ghost of Felix and the Greek chorus. I find it particularly poignant to hear him singing his own words. We all feel the sting and struggle of so many emotions as they come through him, reaching out to us from his heart to ours.

By the end of the day, we're all drained from this emotional rollercoaster that has apparently become "Our New Normal." And yet we're filled, too, with the anticipation of how it will all unfold.

In my semi-euphoric state, I try reaching out to Phillip again as a few of us step out onto the street and say goodbye to each other after calling it a day. "The songs written for your character are going to be so beautiful. You must be thrilled with the idea of bringing them to the stage for the first time."

He seems thrown that I'm even approaching him. "Oh yeah. They're going to be good."

"Good? They're absolutely fantastic!" I hear Gabriel say, walking up and joining in the conversation.

Phillip is even more taken aback by Gabriel chiming in. What was he thinking? That we'd never speak to him? He looks around to see if any of the rest of the cast is within earshot. When he sees that it's just us, the real Phillip emerges.

"Look, chorus boys. Keep your distance from me. I intend to have as little to say to the two of you as possible. I'm not interested in what you think of my songs or my part in this play. As far as I'm concerned, you're playing backup to me, and the farther to the back of the bus you get, the better."

Gabriel doesn't hold back. "You little motherfucker! How dare you make such a racist comment to me. It just goes to show how really low-class you are, Phillip. If you weren't fucking your way into this job, you'd be nobody. You don't even have the grace to act like a professional."

"I don't give a shit what you think of me. I'm in the spotlight, and you two are going to be moving furniture around in between songs. That says it all as far as I'm concerned."

"Phillip," I say, trying to salvage this conversation. "I am your understudy, and that's going to require some communication."

"All my blocking will be notated by the stage manager. You can get it from him. I can't be bothered with you. As far as I'm concerned, you both can fuck yourselves." He walks away as full of himself as ever.

"What a little jerk he's turned out to be," I say. "I have to wonder if some of his bluster isn't based on some kind of insecurity he feels about himself and his talent."

"Honey, some folks are just rotten to the core, and that would be the racist variety. It's all based on fear. From a racist's point of view, we colored folk are a threat to their superiority. And I think in terms of this play, he thinks we're both a threat to him as well. Maybe that's one thing he and I can agree on. I ain't gonna make that little shit's life easy from now until closing night."

"It's not worth it, Gabriel. He's not worth it. Let's just be professionals and do our jobs. You know the opposite of love isn't hate; it's indifference. That's going to be my strategy, and I advise you to do the same. We have an incredible opportunity with this experience, and neither of us is going to let him ruin it for us in any way."

"I guess you're right. After that little encounter, I need a drink. How about taking a cab up to The Townhouse so we can throw some chilled cocktails on this fire? My treat."

I take Gabriel up on his offer. I think we both could use some decompressing after this day. It's been a lot to take in. Our play has all the elements of a cutting-edge hit. Will it be amazing? That's yet to be seen. Will it be challenging and emotionally draining? I can pretty much guarantee that. Regardless of the negativity, I'll obviously be dealing with, I am so up for this.

Twenty-Three

This show is going to be awesome. Thinking back over the past few weeks, time seems to have been on fast-forward. I can only be humbled by the creative energy that has been pouring out of our cast and creative directors. It has far exceeded anything I could have imagined. So now it's time to really roll up our sleeves.

Today, we start the "ten out of twelves" in the theater: we work ten out of twelve hours every day through the first preview. And that can continue through opening night if more rehearsal is needed. It's the first day of tech, which is slow going, but I can't wipe the smile off my face as I stand outside the Belasco Theater and look up at our marquee. It seems like an eternity since they had us lined up, scrutinizing who would be chosen to be a part of this moment.

I'm standing in front of what will hopefully be my home away from home, at least for this Broadway season. "Good morning, Mr. B.," I say, remembering the protocol Mr. Belasco requested of me. "It's a fine morning for our first day in your theater."

Yes, I feel like an idiot saying those words out loud, and I can't help but chuckle to myself with the memory of our encounter. Either I have quite an imagination, or my sense of reality has a way of being altered from time to time. I'm sure Hobo has an opinion about that.

Arriving at this theater is like a homecoming as I walk down the alley to the stage door. Checking in gives me a feeling of belonging and security—like I've found my place. I've become attached to this project and everyone in it. We've created our own sense of family, and now we're about to test that out.

The cast is gathered in the house's first few rows, waiting to get some direction from Laurence. As I take a seat, the aroma of cigar smoke dances across my senses. So, this is Mr. Belasco's way of answering back. Now I know I've been welcomed.

"Is everyone ready for tech?" Laurence asks, getting some groans and laughter in response. "It will be over before you know it. Today, I want to give you all a special welcome to this beautiful Belasco Theater. Most of you did your callbacks here, so it's not unfamiliar. But we have a lot to work out technically on the stage, so I appreciate all your patience in advance for these long hours we'll be putting in. Constantly stopping and starting will get tedious, but I'm sure we'll work through the glitches and be running the show in no time."

As Laurence continues to outline how this will all work, I take another moment to do a panoramic scan of this jewel box of a theater. It almost feels like this ornate space is a *grande dame* about to get all dolled up for a leading role— like Norma Desmond getting ready for her close-up. Bringing all the elements of this production to life is like applying her makeup and dressing with care, putting on the final touches before she steps out on display for all her admirers.

Laurence takes a more dramatic approach in his speech now. "I'm sure that you've all heard the rumor that the ghost of Mr. Belasco is still in residence here." That elicits quite a bit of laughter, but he interrupts it. "Maybe rumor is too pale a comparison. Woe to the actor who doesn't heed my words now. Make sure you greet Mr. Belasco out loud every day when entering. Wouldn't you like some recognition if someone entered your home?"

"Oh, come on, Laurence," Phillip says. "You've got to be kidding. Don't we have enough ghosts in this production already?"

"What's the matter, Phillip?" Gabriel asks. "Afraid of the competition?"

That gets another laugh, but Phillip won't be undone. "As long as he doesn't get top billing over me. But I'm not about to make nice with thin air."

"Come now, Phillip," Laurence says. "Maybe if we all say it together, just for today. Hopefully, you'll be inspired to join in. All right now, everybody... one, two, three... "Good morning, Mr. Belasco!"

More laughter ensues as Laurence directs us back to the task at hand. "Okay, enough of the joking around. We have safety issues that need to be addressed. You all remember from rehearsing at 890 that the ghost character of Felix and the Greek chorus ghosts will appear on stage by entering through a trap door on the stage floor, with the assistance of a hydraulic lift from the basement.

"More kudos to Mr. Belasco, who had an earlier version of the machinery installed way back in the day. This new lift is up-to-date. Let's all go up and see how this mechanism is going to work. Everyone on stage needs to be aware of it, once the trap door is in the open position. At that point there will be a giant hole in the stage. So be careful. Especially since your vision will be obscured by the stage smoke."

For the next couple of hours, lighting cues are being called that don't require the lead actors. Laurence and the stage manager begin to instruct the Greek chorus on which set pieces and props will need to be moved on and off the stage. Now that we are actually working with the physical objects, it feels like a whole new production.

I remember Phillip's slurs to Gabriel and me on the first day of rehearsal, calling us furniture movers. But the seamless effect of the Greek chorus participating in that process is all part of why the staging has ended up being so brilliant in this production. Because we're playing ghosts most of the time, the other actors on stage play their parts as if they don't even see us. The haunting harmonies of our singing voices are an integral part of these transitions as well. We blend with the action and create the change that takes place. It will be quite a challenge to sing while we move props and parts of the set, but stunningly effective.

There are always a million things to remember when we get to this moment. It's a layering of all the details our characters are responsible for. I even have the extra job of needing to know where Phillip's character, Felix, will be at any given moment, not to mention already having his lines and songs down. There's only so much you can prepare for as an understudy, but repetition is key.

After lunch, we begin the plodding process of holding our staged positions for each lighting cue. Before we start, Laurence informs us the play will begin with the curtain up and the stage in total darkness. As the overture of songs is being played by a small ensemble orchestra, a prolonged sunrise effect will be accomplished by the stage lights evolving through various hues. This will be complete when the stage is fully lit as the overture ends.

"It's another nod to Belasco," he says, "who staged a five-minute sunset in the opening of the play *Girls of the Golden West* in 1905, with nothing else happening on stage but his technical wizardry."

That information is music to my ears, remembering I heard the same story from Belasco himself... The long day finally ends with that familiar feeling of being drained by information overload. But with each day of rehearsal, that much more is accomplished and refined, as the lighting and staging are finalized. Once we get it all stitched back together again, it actually feels like we're starting to reclaim what we achieved in the rehearsal space.

As the ten out of twelves pass, tech problems mostly get resolved, and we begin to move into full run-throughs. After each one, Laurence has many pages of notes for cast and crew. It still feels more like a work in progress and not quite a real polished show yet.

The next day is a full run-through with partial costumes. Then, another run-through with the costumes mostly complete and a full orchestra. Finally, we're pulling it all together.

We're so close now, coming into the home stretch. The final day before the first preview with a paying audience has arrived. I made good on my promise to arrange tomorrow night's tickets for Helen and the now-recovering Charlie. And, of course, my new sweetheart Christopher will be there as well. I couldn't be happier with what the two of us are becoming. I know Hobo has something to do with that.

This play is intense but also full of hope. Charlie will need that as he continues to face the ravages of what this disease can bring. He's out of the hospital for now, but his future is yet to be written. It's pretty obvious now that Helen will be there every step of the way. I couldn't be more grateful for her devotion.

We have two full dress rehearsals today and tonight, with costumes now complete, including a full orchestra. There's been so much to adjust to—I don't think anyone has really had the time to let it sink in. We run it all once with a minimum of issues. And after a break, we're all back for the final dress rehearsal.

Half hour is called as the four of us in the Greek chorus settle into our tiny dressing room, with just enough table and mirror space for us to be nearly shoulder-to-shoulder. Our costume rack is directly behind us and lined up with our designated spots. Of course, Gabriel has arranged to sit next to me.

"All right!" Gabriel says, fully made up and in character already. "Now hear this, now hear this! All you gay ghosts better do our people proud as the fearsome foursome in this fabulous fantasy production."

"Angel Gabriel," I say. "You, my dear, are certainly a fantasy come true. Can you believe this is the last time we're going to do this before the first preview tomorrow night?"

"It is hard to fathom what that will be like. I can only imagine how many stage door johnnies will be lining up after the show when they get a look at this fine behind of mine."

"Yeah, you win the prize for most revealing costume. And I have to admit, it's hard not to be distracted by it."

"Hard, being the operative word, my manchild."

Gabriel continues to entertain us as we get ready and joke around until places are called. The camaraderie has been wonderful. I'm relieved Phillip hasn't done anything to dampen it, since we have quite a few scenes with him. Not sharing a dressing room with him helps.

With places called, the four of us still have a little while before we head down to the basement to get ready for our first song. Making our entrance as ghosts doesn't happen until the third scene. It's Phillip's first entrance and song as well. We've all gotten used to his attitude, so it's not really surprising nobody is speaking to him when the five of us eventually gather and take our positions on the hydraulic lift.

The third scene opens in a dimly lit dining room with a table and four empty chairs. We are the spirits of what were once vital and living beings, who had places at this table of life, until we were all cut down at the peak of our lives.

The trap door opens upstage of the table as the five of us rise up from the basement on the hydraulic lift. There's plenty of smoke blowing in for a surreal effect, as the timing with the music and our appearance are in perfect sync.

Phillip jumps up on the table with ease when we all reach the stage floor level, and his song begins. The driving notes and rhythms have a repetitive military feel, as each of the four spirits in the ensemble march to a chair and lift it over our heads. It's time to reclaim our place at the table. We launch into a choreography of battle mode with our chairs—because this is war. It's a war of cultural acceptance. It's a war of visibility. It's a war of redemption. We sing, refusing to be victims, continuing to do battle through our spirits even though our bodies have expired.

Phillip's song and voice are reaching a crescendo, standing above us on the table, as the four other ghosts march directly down stage with our chairs positioned like machine guns, the chair legs pointing at the audience.

All of a sudden, his song becomes a scream, and we all turn around and see that the table is empty. I'm so shocked that I forget I'm in the middle of a show. I drop my chair and run back to the empty table, only to find the trap door behind it mysteriously open as I look down at a groaning and crying Phillip on the basement floor below. The other three guys have joined me and we're all looking down at Phillip in disbelief.

"Oh my God, Phillip! Are you okay?" I ask.

"No, God damn it! Do I look like I'm fucking okay? I think I might have broken my leg."

"Why am I smelling cigar smoke?" Gabriel asks.

I'm not about to answer him.

Needless to say, the Theater Gods have indeed spoken. With the very probable help of a certain theatrical impresario.

With his leg broken in two places, Phillip will be in recovery for quite some time. He certainly can't go on stage in a cast. No one has any idea how it was even possible that the trap door could have been open. Phillip also has no clue as to why he felt an invisible force push him backward off the table, causing him to fall through the trap door and end up on the basement floor below.

I can't think about any of that right now. I've spent the entire day fine-tuning all the staging and songs for the character of Felix. Our first preview performance with a packed house, and I'm going on in the principal role of Felix. I can barely believe it, but anything can happen in show biz.

I'm looking at a good six weeks of making my mark in this role before Phillip recovers and gets the cast off. I'll get reviewed. I'll make sure to get multiple agents to see it. But mostly, I'll get to fulfill my dream of performing on a Broadway stage and really owning it.

My sweet Christopher, Charlie, and Helen are already in their seats, very likely surrounded by others in our gay tribe. Word is, tonight's audience is made up mostly of women and men in our community. We do love being in the vanguard when it comes to cutting edge theater.

I have some time before I need to be in the basement when places are called, so I decide to go stand in the wings when the house lights go down.

I think of Christopher and all his yoga talk about body vibrations as I make my way over from my dressing room—my body feels like it's vibrating on overload. The intense connection I'm experiencing in this moment and everything that's led up to it is a revelation of what was meant to be.

The curtain rises, and the overture begins as I watch the darkened stage very slowly begin its gradual journey toward sunrise. What am I actually seeing? The stage should be empty, but I make out a dark figure of a young man sitting on the now infamous table, holding something in his lap.

"Daddy Boy, I would think after all this time you'd recognize me, even in the dark. And guess who's joining me tonight?"

I'm too shocked to speak, which I wouldn't do anyway since the show has now begun. The image of Timothy with his dazzling smile, holding Hobo in his lap, is now becoming brighter before my eyes.

"We wanted to let you know that we wouldn't miss your Broadway debut for anything," Hobo says. "Congratulations Daddy Boy! After all this time, you've really learned how important trust is. And here you are, proving it. By trusting in your ability to create a career again and trusting in your willingness to give and receive love, you've come to understand that it's all just a reflection of what's already within you."

The music of the overture continues to soar from one song to the next, with the sunrise on the stage slowly growing brighter. As the journey of this illuminated transition occurs, the image of Timothy and Hobo slowly begins to dissolve into the brilliance of the radiant hues. They both fade and blend into a glorious completion of music and light, but not before I hear Hobo's last words to me.

"You'll be happy to know that our next stop, after your final curtain comes down, is the Rainbow Bridge. Remember how you told me that was where I was supposed to be going? Well, Timothy has already been lecturing me in great detail about its architectural significance... 'Cat'-choo later Daddy Boy..."

Somehow, I understand that my feisty feline apparition has disappeared from my vision for the last time. I know she's in good hands now.

I take a deep breath and head back down to the basement, taking my place with the other guys.

"I'd tell you to break a leg, sugar," whispers Gabriel, "but I don't think we want to go there again." I just smile and give his hand a squeeze in response.

It takes just another moment before we feel the hydraulic lift ascend up toward the floor level of the stage, as the music for my song begins. My eyes now become level with it, and we continue to rise up. I see the stage smoke dancing around me as if an ephemeral energy has just been born, swirling and circulating with a life of its own.

We're almost standing at stage level now, and I see the table in front of me. The low lights reflected on it are filtered through the murky smoke. I jump up on the table to my music cue, and the white-hot spotlight hits me full-on, with a brightness that amplifies all my senses. I feel like I've been reborn. I'm on Broadway!

Epilogue

Christopher takes my hand once we get comfortable in two of the chairs placed around the perimeter of the lobby. I see other couples and singles waiting patiently in quiet anticipation as well. The fluorescent lighting in this clinic creates its usual unflattering harshness. Still, I'm holding firm, with my own warm inner strength, supported by Christopher at my side.

We've had an amazing two weeks of previews, and tonight, we finally officially open. Christopher insisted I unwrap my opening night gift from him this morning. A blender. Of course, we made breakfast smoothies.

My parents are in town for the big event, but I've put off shopping with them this morning and have arranged for us to meet for lunch instead.

"How are you doing?" Christopher asks, gripping my hand a little harder.

"Okay. I'm really glad you came with me today."

"Of course. Your decision to get tested, on today of all days, took me by surprise, but I really want to be here for you."

"Thanks. My boyfriend, I think I'll keep him," I say, cracking us both up. "Do you realize you're the first boyfriend of mine my parents will have ever met?"

"No, the thought hadn't even crossed my mind. I'm honored to be the one to break them in for you."

"It only took me thirty years to get to this point, but I'm glad it's finally arrived. They're good Midwestern folks, so I'm sure it will go fine."

"I was thinking about your decision to do this today, Matt. Remember our conversation about crossing bridges? I think you've stepped out into the middle of one right now."

I look at Christopher and smile. He's so very right. Getting tested has been a big one for me for the longest time. I think this show has helped me to understand even more how I have the power to take command of whatever circumstances come my way. I've learned to believe in myself and have faith that Christopher, my family, and all my chosen family of friends will be there for me, no matter what I encounter when I reach the other side."

Acknowledgments

The inspiration and prelude to *A Cat in the Act* began when a hungry feral cat showed up in our backyard one afternoon, and my husband and I decided to take on the daunting task of socializing her. We named this little vagabond "Hobo," and with the generous guidance of the Urban Cat League, we came to understand she was as much our teacher as we were hers. Hobo's lessons in establishing trust and allowing for the giving and receiving of love are at the heart of this tale—a writing journey that began as an idea and solution for expanding creatively while sheltering during Covid. My deepest gratitude goes out to all the people who were instrumental in helping transform that intention into a completed work, beginning with my husband, Skip, who is my rock and helped make corrections to the first few chapters and encouraged me to keep going as more chapters began to take shape. Special thanks also go to author and publisher Lou Cici, who was so generous with his time and expertise when I began this exploration, and, on his recommendation, Jerry L. Wheeler, who took on editing the first draft. Not only did Jerry do a stellar job (thank you!), but he recommended Rattling Good Yarns as a possible publisher. So much heartfelt thanks go out to Ian Henzel and Sukie de la Croix for giving *A Cat in the Act* a home. Ian's insights and expertise in the final editing process have been immeasurable. He's truly been the wind beneath my wings and made me a better writer. I couldn't be more grateful to both Ian and Sukie for giving me the opportunity to share this story with others.

About the Author

Brian Arsenault was born and raised in California, receiving a BA in Theater Arts from UC Santa Cruz. Following graduation, Brian headed to New York City, where he spent the next 10 years singing and dancing professionally. He appeared in *Fiddler on the Roof* on Broadway at the Gershwin Theater, *Up Against It* off-Broadway at The Public Theater, *Carousel* at The Kennedy Center in Washington D.C., and numerous road shows of National and International musical touring companies. Brian also danced with The Rockettes at Radio City Music Hall, and performed in regional and stock theaters around the county. His favorite role was performing Che in the musical *Evita* at the Diamond Head Theater in Honolulu, HI. Upon leaving show business, Brian found a rewarding second career helping others when he transitioned into Personal Fitness training. He also became an accomplished yoga instructor, leading retreats in Costa Rica, California, and Florida. *A Cat in the Act* is Brian's first novel. It has inspired him to continue writing, bringing characters to life through his storytelling. He lives in beautiful Pawleys Island, SC, with his husband, Skip, and their two cats—Pippy and Linus.